Don't Let Me Die!

Don't Let Me Die!

Lindsay Caldwell

SCHOLASTIC INC.
New York Toronto London Auckland Sydney

No part of this publication may be reproduced in whole or in part, or stored in a retrieval system, or transmitted in any form or by any means, electronic, mechanical, photocopying, recording, or otherwise, without written permission of the publisher. For information regarding permission, write to Scholastic Inc., Attention: Permissions Department, 555 Broadway, New York, NY 10012.

ISBN 0-590-56735-7

12 11 10 9 8 7 6 5 4   0 1 2 3/0

Printed in the U.S.A.
First Scholastic printing, July 1998

Part One

Chapter 1

Lucy St. Cloud arrived at the home of her friend, Kendra Lindley, on a cool, misty late May evening. She parked her mother's white van on the wide, tree-lined street. Jenny Cooper's red convertible was parked directly in front of her. Lucy jumped from the van, her heart skipping a beat as she spotted Dash's motorcycle at the curb. He'd made it, after all. She hadn't seen him since yesterday afternoon. Way too long. Any second now, she'd start feeling Dash-deprivation pangs. They were both so busy, he with sports, she with her part-time job as a library page, and the musical, and making sure the house didn't burn down around her younger brother while her mother was working. It was all too much, because it meant she didn't have enough time for Dash. There were too many other girls who'd gladly give up eating, sleeping, and breathing to make time for David "Dash" Cameron.

Tia Perez, a small dynamo dressed, as always, in a wonderful mixture of brilliant colors, burst out of Kendra's front door and ran down the steps to meet Lucy. Tia's short-sleeved sweater was tomato-red, the skirt hot-pink, the sandals banana-yellow. Though both girls had long, dark hair, Tia's was wildly curly, while Lucy's was straight, with thick bangs she was constantly sweeping aside. Tia's face was round, her eyes dark, in contrast to Lucy's oval, fair-skinned face and deep-blue eyes. And Lucy was taller than Tia's five feet by six inches. In spite of those differences, the two girls were so in tune with one another, people often mistook them for sisters. They walked with the same light step, laughed in the same unrestrained way, and were considered friendlier and more outgoing than the quieter Kendra and the more sophisticated Jenny.

A waterfall of words cascaded from Tia's mouth as she ran. "It's about time! I thought you'd never get here. Dash has been here for practically *hours*, and if you ask me, Jenny's flirting like mad with him. What gets into that girl? I love your hair, it looks neat pulled back in a bun like that. You look like a ballet dancer, especially in that tunic and tights. Which is cool, since everyone knows you're the best dancer in school. That blue is perfect on you. It matches your eyes exactly. You're so lucky, having those eyes. What I'd give . . . isn't it a great night. Can't you just feel summer coming on even though it's not June yet? We're going to have the best time ever. I can't wait!"

Lucy had often thought that if Tia were ever kept from talking for more than ten minutes, she would explode. All those words fighting to escape, and no way to set them free. The girl would definitely self-destruct.

Now Lucy laughed, partly in exasperation at Tia's nonstop patter, partly to ease her sudden uneasiness. Jenny was flirting with Dash? Did the girl never stop? The fact that she was not just pretty but, face it, drop-dead gorgeous, all silken blond hair and flawless satin skin, didn't give her license to wrap her tentacles around every male neck within reach. Especially when that neck belonged to David Cameron, better known as "Dash" because he was the track king at Seneca High School. He was the best miler in Dutchess, Putnam, and Westchester counties.

Dash is *mine*, Lucy thought vehemently and wondered, not for the first time, why she was still friends with a shameless flirt like Jenny Cooper. She had Tia, who thought flirting was stupid, and Kendra, who was always loyal. Lucy didn't really *need* Jenny.

But they'd been friends since first grade.

And when Lucy's father died so suddenly, Jenny had dropped everything in her very busy life to be at Lucy's side. For a while, anyway. That wasn't something you tossed out like yesterday's garbage. Besides, flirting came as naturally to Jenny Cooper as breathing. She didn't even know she was doing it most of the time.

"She never got over Dash going for you instead of her," Tia went on as they hurried up the front steps to the big, wide porch. "She can't figure out why he didn't pick *her*, and it makes her nuts." Then, realizing how that sounded, she added hastily, "I mean, you're every bit as pretty as she is, and a lot more popular because you don't make the other girls nervous, like Jen does. I just meant, Jen usually gets the guys. But Dash was the one she really wanted."

Lucy already knew that. She'd known it since the first day Dash strode into a favorite high school hangout in late December of their sophomore year. Jen, standing beside Lucy at the jukebox, had let out a deep sigh of joy and murmured under her breath, "Oh, my, look what Santa's brought us!"

But it had been Lucy Dash chose, not Jen.

There had been times in the year and a half since then when Lucy had wondered if Dash regretted his choice. Especially during that awful period following her father's death. The shock had left her dizzied, in a haze of grief and sorrow. Many days she'd come to school with her thick hair uncombed, her face red and puffy from crying, in the same clothes she'd worn for two days. Worse, she was moody and snappish and stormed through the halls with her head down. Meanwhile, Jen was the picture of perfection and as sunny as a smiley button.

Lucy knew that Jen had consoled Dash during those awful weeks. She just wasn't sure how far that consolation had gone. Even if her other best friends were aware that it had gone too far, they would never have told Lucy. Not then, when she was already hurting, and probably not after, when she was feeling a little better. Kendra, the most sensitive of Lucy's friends, would have insisted quietly, "Lucy doesn't need to know. It would only hurt her." Tia's reasoning would have been different, but with the same result. She would have said, "Lucy doesn't want to know. She hates that kind of reality. She wouldn't believe us. So why tell her?"

If Jen and Dash had betrayed her, even in some small way, Kendra and Tia were both right. It would hurt, and Lucy *didn't* want to know. That way, she didn't have to deal with it.

Besides, she'd had enough to deal with back then.

Dash and Jenny were dancing in the family room when Lucy and Tia entered. Tia made a sound of disgust, but Lucy was stricken by how perfect the two looked together. Both tall, both blond, both in perfect shape. Lucy was reminded of the pictures of gods and goddesses in her mythology book. She could easily envision the pair dressed in flowing white togas, sitting on golden chairs high up in the clouds, gazing down with amusement on the mere mortals far below.

If he thinks, she told herself as she pasted a fake smile on her face and plopped down on the couch between Kendra and Tia, that I'm going to sit here and watch him make a fool of me with my friend, he can think again. I'll close my eyes and pretend I'm taking a nap if I have to.

Her strongest emotion was disappointment. It didn't look like this was going to be as much fun as she'd thought. She had looked forward to spending the evening with her friends, in spite of the long drive to join them now that she was living on the opposite side of town. The apartment, though they'd been in it nearly a year now, was still basically undecorated, like a Christmas tree that had just been set up. Her mother had been too busy to do much with it.

If Lucy's older sister were home, the apartment would be cozy and welcoming by now. But Elizabeth was finishing her last year at college.

And when she did come home, she'd be so busy planning her wedding in December, she'd have no time or energy for decorating a home she'd soon be leaving.

Weird to think of the apartment as home. It still didn't feel like home, and leaving was a relief. Usually. But maybe not tonight. Right now, it looked like she'd have been better off staying home. Seated on the couch between Tia and Kendra, watching Dash scuff up the shiny hardwood floor with Jennifer Cooper, Lucy felt like part of an audience. "What are we doing here?" she muttered angrily. "I feel like we're watching MTV."

Not only was Dash dancing with Jenny, he had the nerve to look as if he were having a really great time. Whatever he was sharing with Jenny, it must have been amusing, because they were both laughing.

Dash glanced over and smiled, waving a hand at Lucy, but he didn't stop dancing and rush to her side.

I can dance rings around Jennifer Elaine Cooper, Lucy thought angrily, and everyone knows it. Especially Dash.

"Why," Tia asked crisply, "don't you just go over there and grab him? I would, if he was my boyfriend." She made no effort to keep her voice down, but the loud music kept it from carrying to the dancers.

"Oh, you would not." Lucy spoke firmly, but kept her own voice low. She would never let Dash or Jenny know she was rattled. "You just like to think you would. Not true. Public humiliation is awful, and you know it."

"We're not *in* a public place, Lucy. We're in Kendra's house, and we're the only ones here. Her parents aren't even home."

"The people who count are here. That's enough humiliation for *me*."

Lucy didn't go and "grab" Dash, and she fought to keep the expression on her face noncommittal. But it was hard. While Kendra and Tia talked about upcoming events at Seneca High — like the Azalea Ball held every May to celebrate spring, and the track meets they would all be attending, Lucy and Kendra to compete, Tia to cheer them on — Dash and Jenny went right on dancing. Lucy sat lost in dismal thought.

She could have stayed home and played on her computer. She wasn't quite the expert her eleven-year-old brother Tim was, but she'd met some interesting people in chat rooms on the Internet. It was fun, and it kept her mind off her father, whom she missed fiercely.

Everything had changed for all of them when Lucas St. Cloud, hale and hearty and just three weeks shy of his forty-sixth birthday, suddenly clutched at his chest during a board meeting at work. His heart had stopped. Forever. That was the first horrifying blow to his family. The second came when it was announced by their family lawyer that because Lucas was healthy and not yet forty-six, he had skimped on life insurance, probably intending to buy more of it later, when the dark hair at his temples began to turn white.

But he had died while his hair, like Lucy's, was still pitch-black.

Although Lucy's mother Sara kept saying, "We're not going to be poor, far from it. We just have to make a few adjustments, that's all," those adjustments were difficult. Sara was unwilling to move in with Lucas's parents, because they lived too far out in the country. She was forced to sell their own large, colonial home and move to an apartment in a different neighborhood.

Culture shock, big time. Lucy still attended the same high school, and had kept her most loyal friends in spite of her changed circumstances, though they all had to drive further now when they wanted to get together. Her grandparents had offered her the use of their large, comfortable home and grounds any time Lucy wanted to have a party. So far, she hadn't taken them up on their offer. She was saving that for her seventeenth birthday next January.

The music came to a stop. Lucy waited for Dash to stride over to the couch with those long legs of his and grab her hand, yank her upward, and dance with her.

That didn't happen.

A new CD fell into place, and the strains of a slow song filled the room. To Lucy's shock, Jenny walked straight into Dash's arms, lay her head on his gray-sweatered shoulder, and they began dancing again.

Kendra and Tia shifted uncomfortably on the couch, and fell silent.

Lucy's eyes moved to the long, wide windows at the rear of the room. Darkness had fallen outside, accompanied by a heavy mist that spotted the glass. The spots reminded Lucy of teardrops.

Dash had done things like this before. He was very popular. Outgoing. Charming. At dances and parties, even club meetings at school, he often found a pretty girl to talk to or dance with. If Lucy complained, he would grin, raise a hand in mock warning, and say, "We don't own each other, right?"

True. People didn't own people. But Dash had said "I love you," and to Lucy that meant "I love *only* you." That was certainly what she meant when she said it.

Now . . . here, in this room, right in front of

her, he was dancing and flirting outrageously with her friend. How could she overlook that? She couldn't.

Was he doing it on purpose, hoping she'd get mad enough to break up with him? Was it really Jenny he wanted now, as some of the girls at school had hinted? Why didn't he just say so? He could at least be honest, instead of humiliating her like this.

Lucy didn't want to give up Dash. She loved what she had with him. They were one of the most popular, best-looking couples at Seneca. No one had to tell her that. She knew it. And what would an evening in the lonely apartment be like if she didn't have her nightly phone call from Dash when they were too busy to see each other? She'd feel so lost without those long, fun conversations.

But this was too much. She couldn't sit here like a statue while he ignored her. Couldn't, wouldn't —

She jumped up, grabbing her purse and clutching it to her chest. "I'm out of here!" she announced, loudly, clearly, fury in her voice.

Kendra and Tia protested.

Dash and Jenny didn't even hear Lucy's angry statement over the music. They went right on dancing.

Lucy turned and ran out of the house. Down

the steps. Into the van. Ripped free the emergency brake, turned the ignition key, hit the lights, and slammed a foot down on the accelerator. The van tore away from the curb as if propelled by jet fuel.

Chapter 2

The windshield was so coated with mist, Lucy couldn't see. She switched on the wipers. "Damn, damn, damn!" she cried softly under her breath as she sped up Route Nine. "He's a jerk, and Jenny is a back-stabbing viper! I don't care about either of them, I don't! They deserve each other. And *I* deserve better!"

The wipers weren't working fast enough to keep the windshield clear. There was little traffic on the road in what had become a gloomy, chilly evening, but Lucy needed to see. She turned the wipers on high.

Determined not to cry, she concentrated instead on her driving, anxious now to get home and crawl into the safety and comfort of her bed. Her chest hurt, and she wondered if that was how her father had felt when he had his heart attack. She knew it wasn't. His pain had been physical. Hers was something else.

She was still twenty minutes away from home when the huge tractor-trailer came around the curve she was approaching, lost control, and began skidding sideways directly into her lane. It jackknifed as it did so, forcing the massive body of the truck to slide around from behind until it was moving sideways in the road, completely blocking the highway. It stayed that way, remaining perpendicular to the cab of the truck, as both sections continued sliding into Lucy's path.

To Lucy's horrified eyes, it all seemed to happen in slow motion.

Just before she was blinded by the truck's headlights heading straight for her, she saw the words COSTANZO MEATS PUNXATAWNEY, PA printed in huge black letters on the side of the trailer, which was now facing her like a giant billboard.

Then the truck's lights hit her eyes and she could see nothing but a misty haze of bright yellow. Instinct told her to wrench the van's steering wheel violently to one side or the other to avoid a head-on collision with the truck's cab. But she knew it wouldn't have helped. The long, fat body of the truck was a giant wall, blocking the entire highway.

There was nowhere to go.

There was nothing she could do.

Unwilling to admit defeat, Lucy pressed

down hard on the brake pedal with both feet. The muscles in her calves ached, but the brake was her only hope. The tires screamed in protest, wanting to obey the brake's command, but unable to on the wet, slick road. The smell of burning rubber was sickening, the headlights of the oncoming tractor-trailer blinding. It was bearing down on her faster now, sliding straight toward her, a giant red-and-white behemoth glistening with mist.

Three shrill screams filled the air. One came from the brakes on the truck, another from Lucy's brakes, as both drivers pumped the pedals frantically, hoping to bring their vehicles to a halt before it was too late. The third scream came from Lucy. When it finally sank in that nothing she did was going to make any difference, nor would anything the truck driver might do, her hands flew off the steering wheel and pawed at the air, as if grasping for an invisible lifeline. Only then did she scream out, "Oh, god, help me! Somebody help me!"

Then it hit. The huge tractor-trailer collided with Lucy's van head-on, crushing it into a wasted pile of twisted metal, pushing the pile backward down the highway with an ear-splitting shrieking of brakes and the crunching of metal, as if the truck were swallowing up the van bite by bite.

On impact, the upper half of Lucy's body was

thrown viciously forward, in spite of her seat belt. Her forehead slammed into the steering wheel. She felt no pain from the blow. She was too terrified. Fully conscious, she lay facedown on the steering wheel as the van continued to slide backward. It was now completely under the control of the tractor-trailer pushing it from the front, like a snowplow intent on clearing the road. The sight of both her legs still pressing down hard on the brake struck a dazed Lucy as ridiculous. What good would *that* do? But her feet were frozen to the pedal, and she hadn't the energy to try to move them.

She was still slumped over the wheel as the van was propelled backward into the thick, wide trunk of a gnarled old tree on the side of the highway. Compressed between the formidable tree and the tremendous driving force of the tractor-trailer, the van was squeezed between the two, accordionlike. As both vehicles came to a grinding halt, the weight of the truck pushed one last time against the heap of metal that had been the front of the van.

There was no place for that heap of metal to go.

No place except the front seat.

Lucy, her head still on the steering wheel, watched in stunned disbelief as bits and slices and chunks of twisted metal burst into the car's interior, slicing into the very seat beneath her and filling up the space between driver and dashboard. There was no time to get out of the way, and no place to go even if there had been time. She felt sharp stabs of pain here and there . . . on her right thigh, her left hip, on both hands dangling from the steering wheel, on her right arm. It all happened at once and melded into one hot, enormous pain that consumed her entire body.

Her legs had disappeared, buried now beneath the pile of metal nearly surrounding her. Lucy stared at where her legs had been only a moment earlier, and wondered why they seemed to be the only part of her that didn't hurt.

Then something sharp and piercing dug into her left side with so fierce a pain that she lost consciousness, fading away into a soft, welcoming darkness.

Chapter 3

Lucy awakened buried to the waist in crumpled metal, to a scene of utter chaos around her. With great difficulty, she lifted her head from the steering wheel, shook it twice to clear it, and gazed around her with wide, uncomprehending eyes. It took her many long, dazed minutes to take it all in. Part of the windshield on the driver's side was gone, giving her a jagged-edged view of the mist-bathed area.

A fire truck, long and red and bathed in the bright-yellow headlights of twin police cars parked nearby, sat on one side of the road. An ambulance, white and red, sat on the other side. Orange flares behind her on the highway were reflected in the rearview mirror, which was still intact. There seemed to be people everywhere, most of them in uniform. Firemen in yellow raincoats. Police officers in shiny blue slickers. Ambulance attendants in white jackets under clear plastic raincoats. A few people in street clothes stood along the side of the highway, craning to get a better view. It made Lucy angry that they were staring at her.

It was raining harder now. She could feel it on her face and hands as it blew in through the gaping hole in the windshield.

Lucy tried to think. Why was she still in the car? Why hadn't all of these official-looking people pulled her free of the wreck? Was she hurt? How could she not be? But she was conscious. So maybe she was okay.

A sharp rapping on the driver's window brought her head around.

A fireman in yellow bent to call to her. "Can you roll the window down?

Lucy shook her head. The window was automatic. She couldn't use the power button with the ignition key completely hidden behind a pile of crumpled metal.

He moved forward then, to talk to her through the hole in the windshield. "Are you hurt?"

She felt no pain except some mild stinging from various cuts. Her hands, particularly, hurt. When she looked at them, she saw blood. "I don't know," she answered honestly. "Could you please just get me out of here?" Her voice amazed her not only by its calmness, but by its politeness. She didn't *feel* calm, and she was certain there was no need to be polite under the circumstances. But that was the way the words had come out of her mouth.

That might not be so good. If she sounded too calm, they might not hurry to get her out of the wreck. "Please," she added, then, her words laced with urgency, "please get me out of here. I don't want to die. Don't let me die in here, please!"

The words astonished her. Die? *Die?* Why had she said that? She wasn't going to die. Look at her, all in one piece, perfectly conscious, not even bleeding very much, except for her hands, and the left side of her face felt sticky. Her left side hurt. But blood wasn't exactly gushing from her, as far as she could tell in the darkened interior. And she wasn't even dizzy, in spite of the blow to her head.

Still, something had compelled her to beg for her life. Maybe it was all those official-looking uniforms out there, or the sight of the ambulance standing by, or the ugly, still-terrifying sight of that enormous truck looming over her, reminding her of the devastating collision.

Or maybe it was because she knew people died when they least expected it. Like her father.

She could still smell burning rubber. And something else . . . gasoline? That seemed to make sense. The collision had been so brutal, one or both of the gas tanks had probably ruptured. Or a gas line. Must be spilling out underneath the vehicles. That was probably why the firemen were there, to hose any spilled gasoline off the highway. No need to worry, with the firemen there.

Lucy realized she was trembling. But her voice remained calm. "Could you just open the door and drag this stuff off me? she called to the fireman, still standing beside the van. "So I can get out? I can't even *see* my legs."

"Oh, sure, we'll get you out," he answered easily. "The door's stuck, that's the thing. But," he added quickly, "we've got a tool with us that'll slice it open like a can of tuna. Don't worry. Take just a few minutes, miss."

"Maybe you could just pull me out through the front, through the windshield hole. Wouldn't that be faster?"

The fireman shook his head. "Looks like you're kinda stuck just now. Gotta get that debris off you first." The smell of gas grew stronger. Lucy's stomach turned over, but from nausea, not fear. With firemen gathered all around what was left of her car, why should she worry about gasoline? They'd take care of it. That's what they were for.

She lay her head back against the seat,

closed her eyes again, and waited to be rescued. She was trembling violently. A sudden, agonizing pain in her side took her breath away, and she fainted.

When she came to again, the first thing she was aware of was a grating, slicing sound somewhere to her left. She turned her head. The fireman who had spoken to her was attacking her door. Lucy couldn't see what he was using. A saw? A giant pair of metal-cutting scissors? Something designed to set her free.

Oh, God, she wanted that more than anything. Except . . . to stay alive.

Whatever the tool was, it wasn't working very quickly. The smell of gasoline was stronger now, increasing her nausea. Her head was pounding, probably from being slammed into the steering wheel, and the rest of her body hurt, as well. Except for her invisible legs. She felt no pain there, none at all. Amazing, since she was buried up to her waist in a heap of crumpled, jagged metal.

Uneasy because of the close proximity of the cutting tool, Lucy turned her head away from the door. And thought she saw, through the partially shattered passenger's window, Dash and Jenny. She peered more closely through the falling mist. It *was* them, standing side by side on the edge of the highway, staring at the wreck. Staring at *her*. What were they doing together? And why were they just standing there? They had to recognize the van, or what was left of it. They had to know she was inside.

Why hadn't they rushed to the van to pull her free? Why wasn't Dash trying to get her out?

Lucy tried to call out to them, but no sound came from her mouth. Her throat was too dry. She turned her head again to see how much progress, if any, the fireman had made, and as she did so, she noticed something that caused her heart to stop. Smoke — in curving gray-white tendrils — was curling lazily from beneath the hood, as if exploring to see what was out there.

Lucy tried to tell herself it was only steam she was seeing, maybe caused by the cool rain hitting the warm hood of the car. But science had never been her best subject, and she wasn't sure her theory was accurate.

A moment later, she knew it wasn't, because the smallest of red-orange flames flicked its way out from beneath the hood, and then, almost simultaneously, another and another.

The van was on fire. And Lucy was trapped inside.

She opened her mouth again, and this time a sound emerged.

But for the second time that night, her cry was drowned out, at this moment by the sound of the ongoing effort to remove her door and set her free.

Chapter 4

Until that moment, Lucy had successfully fought panic. The area surrounding the wrecked vehicles teemed with uniformed people bent on rescuing her. Although it was taking far too long, she had clung steadfastly to the belief that sooner or later, they would succeed. The ambulance standing by would race her to the hospital, her various cuts and bruises would be treated, and she'd be on her way home to her own room, her own bed. Even if the doctors insisted on keeping her overnight, they'd release her in the morning. She struggled to remember what day tomorrow might be. Friday, it would be Friday. Now that football season was over, nothing very important happened at school on Fridays. There were no pep rallies before the track meets.

It wouldn't kill her to miss a few morning classes. But she had play rehearsal after school.

Didn't want to miss that. She had beat out Norah Pratt for the role of Rizzo in the junior class musical, *Grease*. Norah was just dying to take her place, probably hoping Lucy would break a leg or an ankle before opening night. The best part was, Dash was playing Rizzo's boyfriend, fitting rehearsals in between track practice.

But when Lucy saw flickering flames darting out from underneath the crumpled accordion that had been the van's hood, she forgot there were firemen on the scene, and she did panic.

Her head whipped around again. Her terrified eyes flew to the face of the men still doggedly working on her door. "Fire!" she screamed, pointing with one shaking finger. "The car's on fire! Get me out of here, hurry!" Her voice rose higher and higher in her panic. "I don't want to burn to death! Please don't let me die in here, not like this. You have to get me *out!*"

The fireman took only a second to nod an acknowledgment and pat the window glass reassuringly before returning to his work, head down, concentrating on the tool in his hands, while other firemen in shiny yellow calmly attacked the flames, smothering them with white foam.

Trembling again, tears streaking her cheeks, Lucy sagged back against the seat. She'd been silly to panic, with all those firemen right there.

She needed to get a grip. But it infuriated her that she could do nothing for herself. If she hadn't been so firmly pinned against the seat, she'd have kicked out a window or forced open a door, crawled out through the broken windshield. Something, anything.

Her anger served one useful purpose. It eased her fear. As she calmed down, she reminded herself there were firemen all around her car. If the rain didn't put out any new flames, they would.

But as she sank back against the seat, the crushed-metal blanket shrouding much of her body pressed painfully into her lap, creating a new worry. When they got the door open — and they *would* — how were they going to lift this metal tonnage off her to set her free? Did they have the proper tools, the necessary equipment?

She had just turned her head toward the highway again to look for Dash and Jenny when there was a loud, painful, wrenching sound, and a rush of cool, damp air as the door gave way.

Lucy sobbed in relief, crying out, "Oh, thank you, thank you! You got it off! Please get me out of here, right *now*!"

But just as she had feared, it wasn't that simple.

Two paramedics arrived first. Lucy did everything she was told. When asked, she extended her left arm to receive a blood pressure cuff. She obediently turned her head so that a paramedic could shine a light into her eyes, and she made no complaint when the soft cuff on her upper arm became painfully tight. She had already decided that she would do anything, anything they asked if they would just get her *out*. If they would save her life.

It took a while.

It took two firemen and two policemen, using hammers and metal-cutting shears and at times an acetylene torch, to remove the twisted mass of metal that enveloped Lucy. The firemen worked from the left side of her, the policemen from the right side. Space in which to work was limited, and they apologized profusely when they accidentally bumped Lucy or inadvertently pushed a sharp slice of metal against an arm or wrist, cutting into her skin or flesh.

She was so tired. Her head hurt. She couldn't think. More than once she felt as if she were slipping away. The temptation to slide into darkness became almost overwhelming. But the part of her mind that was working was afraid that they might need her cooperation, and forced her to stay awake.

"Please," she murmured in anguish at some point, "please don't let me die in here." She felt at that moment that she couldn't stand it for another second: the pushing, the prodding around her, the noise, the blue-white light of the torch, the rain, cold now, blowing in upon her and soaking her blue tunic, and worst of all, the people staring from the edge of the highway. Although Lucy told herself they couldn't go anywhere with the wreck blocking their path, she wished fiercely that they would just stop staring at her and disappear.

During another dismal moment, she wondered angrily where Dash was. Why hadn't he rushed to the car to talk to her with comforting words while the firemen and policemen worked around her? Why hadn't he saved her?

Maybe no one would let him.

Lucy had no way of knowing how well the work was going. Her head was resting against the back of the seat, and she no longer had the energy to lift it and check out their progress. Once, one of the men working at her feet said, "Oh, sorry, that must have hurt. I'll try to be more careful." Lucy didn't know what he was talking about. She hadn't felt anything, anything at all.

"Damn!" she heard a moment later at her feet. "I don't know how I'm going to get this piece off without hurting her."

But when Lucy said, "I don't care, just get me *out*!" the policeman returned to his work. Although he worked steadily for what seemed a long time, she decided he'd worried for nothing, because she never once felt any pain.

The left side of her face was wet . . . and chilled. When a paramedic reached in over the backs of the crouching firemen to wrap a thick, soft blanket around Lucy's upper body, she nearly wept in gratitude. The blanket had been heated. Its warmth embraced her like a hug. She almost stopped shivering.

The ripping and wrenching sounds at her feet stopped for a moment, and one of the policemen let out a sound. Lucy couldn't tell what the sound was. It wasn't quite a sigh, wasn't quite a gasp, more like a mixture of the two.

Before she could ask why he had made the sound, before she could ask if something was wrong, one of the firemen said heartily, "Well, we're almost done here, miss! Only one more chunk to remove, then we'll have you out of here."

There was something about his voice that didn't sound quite right to Lucy, but she couldn't put her finger on what was wrong with it, and she was too dazed to care very much. He had said what she wanted to hear — that they were about to set her free. That was all that mattered. She hoped he was right.

He was.

When at last they lifted her, they did it gently. Lucy felt as if she were floating. They were careful to keep her covered from her feet to her neck, wrapping warm blankets around her. The only part of her that got wet with raindrops was her hair. Her face was already wet. It seemed unimportant.

Dash and Jenny did appear then, as the gurney reached the open rear doors of the waiting ambulance. They stood beside Lucy, looking down at her. She couldn't read the expressions on their faces, which were as wet as hers. But it struck her that they looked much sadder than they needed to. Well, of course. They'd seen the wreck. They probably thought she was hurt much worse than she was.

"I'm fine," she said, her voice husky. "Tell Norah not to get her hopes up. I might not make rehearsal tomorrow, but I'll be there Monday. Remember, Dash, *I'm* your Rizzo."

"Right!" He smiled then, the smile she loved so, and reached out as if to take her hand. Realizing that he couldn't do that because she was swathed in blankets, he lowered the hand helplessly. "We'll follow the ambulance. See you at the hospital. You want me to call your mom?"

"A policeman already did that," one of the paramedics said. "Now stand back, please."

Then Lucy was being lifted into the warm, well-lit ambulance and the legs of the gurney collapsed and she was lying flat, safe at last. She closed her eyes. But she didn't let go immediately. And she thought, just before she finally sank down into a warm, dark place, that she heard someone whisper, "Did you see? What a mess! It's a shame. I mean, she's so young. . . ."

But since she knew they couldn't be talking about her, because she was fine, after all — not all bloody and broken like one might expect after such a terrible crash, not even unconscious, or worse, dead — since they couldn't be talking about her and must have been talking about the driver of the truck, Lucy gave up and gave in and disappeared into a cozy, dark little nest.

Chapter 5

Lucy awoke to the sound of a male voice talking far too fast for her dazed mind to grasp the meaning of his words. The words seemed weird, something about "arteries and tendons and muscles and blood loss." He might as well have spoken Greek for all that Lucy understood what he was saying. The only part she really grasped was the phrase, "Think we can pull her through . . ."

Pull *who* through? Pull them through what? And who was the voice talking to?

"I'm not one for sugarcoating things, Mrs. St. Cloud," the voice went on. Her mother's name was Mrs. St. Cloud. So he was talking to her mother. Her mother was here. Good. But . . . where was *here*? "You're a grown-up," the voice continued. "You can handle things better if you know the truth. She's lost a great deal of blood, and we're also dealing with the danger of embolisms. Blood clots. If, as we suspect, they're there, one could break free and shoot straight to her heart. We won't know what the problems really are until we get to surgery and take a look." The voice cleared its throat. "It's going to be a long night for all of us. Is your husband with you? We may need to ask family members to donate blood."

Lucy heard, "I'm a widow. But my son is here, and we can call her sister at college if we need to. She'll come, right away." Then Lucy's mother said, "My husband died. Fourteen months ago. So you can't let my daughter die, too. You can see, that, can't you? How I can't lose her, too?"

Without making any sound, Lucy gasped. So it was *her* they were talking about. Her mother only had two daughters, and one of them was away at college. That left Lucy as the only daughter they could be discussing. Her mother didn't want to lose her.

And I don't want to *be* lost, Lucy thought groggily. She struggled to listen for the doctor's reply.

"We'll do our best. You can come upstairs and wait in the surgical waiting room. There's coffee up there, maybe a doughnut or two. I'll come out and talk to you as soon as I know something."

A moment later, whatever it was that Lucy

was lying on was whisked away. She heard the faint whisper of wheels along a floor, and caught glimpses of a doctor, a pair of nurses, and a man in a green tunic running alongside her.

Where were they taking her? Why didn't she know what was happening? What was the matter with her brain?

It was all very terrifying. Too terrifying to deal with, so Lucy closed her eyes again.

The next time she awoke, her mind was a bit clearer. She knew she was in a hospital even before she opened her eyes. There was that unmistakable smell — medicinal, antiseptic, the cloying smell of dying flowers — reminding her of the day she and her mother, summoned by telephone, had rushed into the hospital, only to find out they were too late. Her father was already dead, and they hadn't even been there to hold his hand and tell him good-bye.

And then there was the pain, which explained why she was in a hospital. Because a hospital was where you went when you had pain. She had plenty of it. Her head ached, her left wrist hurt, her left side was throbbing. When she moved a hand and touched the sore spot in her abdomen with exploring fingers, she encountered a soft, thick wad . . . a bandage?

What had happened to her? She couldn't remember. The worst thing was, her legs felt as if they were being held over an open flame. Hurt was too insignificant a word for her pain. "Hurt" was a word you used when you banged your elbow on the kitchen counter or smacked your forehead on an open cupboard door. That kind of hurt, painful as it was, lasted for a few minutes and then faded. The pain in her legs, from her toes to her hips, wasn't fading. Far from it.

Lucy opened her eyes. She didn't want to, because groggy though she was, she knew she was facing something really nasty. Anything that put you in the hospital couldn't be good. She was sleepy enough to put off thinking about it as long as possible, drifting in and out of a comforting darkness. Finally, after what seemed a very long time, a need to know forced her eyelids open.

She was surrounded by white, in a small cubicle crowded with medical equipment. That was pretty much what she'd expected. A nurses' station, in an open area in the hall, stood directly in Lucy's line of vision. They'd have no trouble keeping an eye on her, if that was what they needed to do.

Did they *need* to do that? Was there something so wrong with her that they couldn't let her out of their sight? Scary thought.

Her mother was standing beside her bed. When she saw that Lucy's eyes were open, she cried, "Oh, thank God, you're awake!" Tears of relief shone in her eyes. "You're in the hospital, honey." Sara took Lucy's unbandaged right hand in her own. "But you're going to be fine, just fine. Don't worry."

Lucy wasn't alert enough yet to begin worrying. The grogginess that made her head feel as if it were packed full of cotton told her she'd been given some kind of painkiller. It wasn't working very well. There was a needle in her right arm, another in her left, and there seemed to be IV hookups everywhere, standing like sentinels around her bed.

"Do you hurt?" Sara asked anxiously. "I can call the nurse. And you have a call button right here, Lucy," holding up a white plastic rectangle. "See, you just push on this little button and a nurse will come right away."

Lucy, beginning to perspire as the pain in her legs intensified, stabbed at the button. "What happened?" she asked her mother, hoping at the same time that Sara's interpretation of "right away" was accurate. "What's wrong? Why am I here? What happened to me?"

Sara explained about the accident. She had just finished when a nurse in a white pantsuit hurried into the room. She was young and very pretty, a reddish ponytail swinging out behind her as she strode toward Lucy's bed. "Uncomfortable, honey?" she asked Lucy, who was trying desperately to digest everything her mother had told her. "We'll get you fixed right up. If you were a little bit older, you could dose yourself with medication. But you have to be eighteen for that. So we'll be doing that for you."

"Are you going to give me a shot?" Lucy hated needles.

"Nope. I'm going to give your IV a shot. You won't feel a thing, but in just a few minutes, your pain will go away. And I want you to call us any time you need us, okay? Don't be shy about it."

Lucy struggled to remember the accident. Her mother had said . . . a tractor-trailer? A huge truck had slammed into her? She'd been trapped in the car for a long time? Why couldn't she remember? It was maddening, not remembering. "How long have I been here?"

"Three days. The accident happened on Thursday night. This is Sunday afternoon."

Three days? She had missed most of a weekend? She *hated* missing out on a weekend. They were the most fun.

The nurse busied herself again, adjusting Lucy's pillows, checking her temperature and blood pressure. Then she lifted the blanket and sheet.

Glancing down, Lucy saw two thick pillars of white where her legs were supposed to be. She felt a stab of terror. "Are those bandages? What's wrong with my legs?" She remembered then, from somewhere, a strong smell of gasoline, and cried out, "Was there a fire? Were my legs burned? *Tell* me!"

Sara was able to answer honestly, "No, honey, there wasn't a fire. Your legs weren't burned. They're just . . . cut, that's all."

But Lucy saw the look her mother exchanged with the nurse as the blanket was quickly replaced. "Just cut? That's why they hurt? But they'll be okay in time for me to be in the musical, won't they? And why does my side hurt?"

Sara's eyes moved to the wall over Lucy's head. "You had surgery, Lucy. To fix the cuts. You lost a lot of blood. You'll be in intensive care just until they're sure you're okay. Your legs hurt because you've got a lot of stitches. But they'll heal quickly. You're so strong, and healthy. I've been telling everyone that, haven't I, Nurse O'Toole?"

"Yes, you have," the nurse answered quietly. She checked Lucy's chart again, told her one more time to be sure and press her call button any time she needed anything, and left the room.

Lucy digested her mother's information. Her legs were cut. Well, that didn't sound too bad. And they'd heal quickly, just like her mother said. She *was* strong and healthy, so why wouldn't they?

"But . . ." Sara hesitated, then forged on, "it's going to take a while, sweetheart. I mean, your legs, well, they received most of the serious damage. They'll take time healing. I'm afraid you're going to have to forget about being in the musical. I've already talked to Ms. Turner. She understands, and sends her best wishes. She wants you to get well really fast, and you will. I believe Norah Pratt is taking over the role, so you can relax, honey."

"Norah sucks," Lucy said bitterly. "She couldn't carry a tune in a grocery cart, and she dances like a hippo." She fell silent then. She wanted desperately to sort things out, figure out what was going on. But she couldn't think. When the medication flowing through her veins began to act as an eraser on the pain, it clouded her mind as well. She began feeling drowsy, and protested aloud, "I don't want to go back to sleep! Not yet. I want to know what's happened to me. If anyone else was hurt. How long I'm going to be here. Tell me, quick, before I fall asleep again!"

"No one else was hurt. The driver of the truck is being questioned by the police, though. Apparently, he dozed off at the wheel. Before he picked up that load in Punxatawney, he'd driven down from Canada, and apparently was exhausted. I don't know if he's going to be charged or not. I guess falling asleep at the wheel isn't a crime, unless he'd been taking pills of some kind . . ."

Lucy was already asleep again.

When she awoke a second time, her mother was gone. The room was empty, and its complete whiteness made it seem colder than it actually was.

The pain in her legs was back.

But if she asked for another shot, she'd go back to sleep again, and if she kept doing that she'd never find out what exactly had happened and how bad she was hurt.

Lucy held on as long as she could, trying to recall what had happened. She remembered going to Kendra's house Thursday night. Had she actually arrived there? Or had the accident happened on her way?

By the time she remembered arriving at Kendra's and entering the house and seeing Dash dancing with Jenny, who'd been wearing a new green outfit, Nurse O'Toole came in with a tray. When she saw the expression on Lucy's face she said, "Uh-oh, you waited too long! What did I tell you about that? This is not the time to be brave, Lucy. We can control that pain, and you have to let us." She hurried to the IV, prepared the medication, and delivered it with speed and efficiency. "Please, honey," she said earnestly, taking Lucy's right hand and holding it, "don't wait so long the next time. It's not good for you. Pain drains your strength, and you can't afford that."

"But I don't want to keep sleeping!" Lucy protested. Still, she went weak with relief as the pain medication began taking effect. "I need to know things. I don't understand what's going on. Could I please see a doctor? I have so many questions. Why haven't I seen a doctor? When can I go home?"

Nurse O'Toole said, "You get plenty of rest and build up your strength, and then you'll be able to handle things better."

Lucy was already drifting back into the warm arms of sleep. But with a last morsel of awareness, she wondered what "things" she would be expected to "handle better."

That phrase was the first thing she remembered when she next awoke. It had sounded so ominous. One thing she was certain of: her mother wasn't telling her the whole truth. No one was. She hadn't even *seen* a doctor yet. If one was coming in to check on her, he or she must be doing it while she was sleeping.

That seemed ominous, too. Was it because they were afraid to face her?

When her mother returned, Lucy asked, "Why isn't anyone coming to visit me?" She was alert enough to know she hadn't seen Dash in a long time. She missed him. Why wasn't he here? She needed him. Where was Tia?

"Not allowed," Sara answered. "This is ICU. Family only, and then just for a few minutes at a time. That's why I told Elizabeth not to come home. She wanted to, but she has finals right now, and I knew she wouldn't be able to spend much time with you in here. So it seemed silly for her to come now."

Lucy agreed. Elizabeth *would* have wanted to come, the minute she heard about the accident. "Can't I see my friends? It's lonely in here."

Sara nodded. "I know. When they move you out of ICU into your own room, your friends can come. I haven't been home much, but Tim says the phone has been ringing off the hook. Just about everyone at Seneca High has called, according to him."

Lucy sighed. "Why hasn't Tim been to see me? He's family."

Sara shook her head. "Not allowed. Too young for this unit. Some of the people in here are in a really bad way. It wouldn't be good for Tim to see that."

In a really bad way? But Lucy was "in here" too. Her heart did a swan dive. "Am I?" she asked abruptly. "In a bad way? I'm not ... I'm not going to die, am I?"

Sara hastened to reassure her. "Of course you're not dying! Don't even say that. The worst is over now. It was touch and go for a while, but I wasn't worried."

Liar.

"I knew you'd be fine. And now you're getting the very best of care. You'll still be prone to infection for a while, so they have to keep an eye on you. But the doctors have assured me that in time, you'll be good as new."

Lucy smiled. "Oh, right, the elusive doctors. What are they, nocturnal? They only come to my bedside in the dark of night, is that it? Because I have yet to see so much as a stethoscope in this room. And I know why," she added before her mother could say anything. "They're afraid I'll ask questions, which I *will*, and they're afraid I won't like the answers, which I probably won't."

Sara patted her hand. "Oh, the doctors have been here, all right. Constantly. You've just been asleep, that's all. You'll have plenty of time for questions later, sweetie. Just rest now, build your strength back up, that's the important thing."

Chapter 6

Lucy drifted in and out. She was aware at times of pain, at other times of voices around her, though she couldn't grasp what they were saying.

Her mother seemed to always be there, patting Lucy's hand, brushing her hair, which felt sticky and stringy, offering words of encouragement. "You're doing great, honey," she said, over and over again.

But just as Lucy was beginning to believe her, something new went wrong. Suddenly, her whole body felt as if it were on fire. She had nightmares in which she was tied to a pole, like Joan of Arc, a roaring blaze at her feet. Cool, wet sponges on her face, chest, and arms did nothing to assuage the heat. Now and again her mother's worried face drifted into her line of vision and Lucy wanted to cry out, "Why aren't you doing something to cool me off? What's a mother *for*?"

It was only May. Why was it so hot?

A painful pinprick in her arm ... movement ... being wheeled somewhere ... good, maybe they were taking her somewhere cooler ... Alaska ... Alaska would be good, all that snow and ice ...

She thought she heard, from somewhere far away, the words "infection" and "surgery."

No. No! She'd already *had* surgery. She didn't want more. If they had some operations left over, they could just give them to the other patients. No point in being selfish. "I don't want any more operations," Lucy muttered. But her brain was so overheated, she couldn't be sure she'd actually said anything, and no one stopped the wheeled cart and turned it around to take her back to her room.

When she next awoke, the terrible heat had left her.

"You had an infection," her mother, leaning over the bed, told her. "In your left leg. They had to operate again. But your fever's down, and the infection is gone. You're going to be fine, just like I told you."

"I want to go home," Lucy said clearly.

A doctor, the first she'd seen or remembered seeing, moved then to stand beside her mother at the bed. He began speaking. He explained to Lucy, slowly and carefully as if, she decided, the accident had caused some serious damage to her brain instead of her legs, that not only could she not go home right this very minute, it was possible that she wouldn't be going home for quite some time. He explained to her that there would probably be the need for plastic surgery on both legs, and that there would be, for a while, continued danger of infection.

It all sounded horrible, worse than Lucy had expected.

"You are a very lucky young lady," said the doctor, a short, round man. He had a mustache larger than his mouth, which made it look to Lucy like his words were being dispensed by a dark, hairy caterpillar. "No one on the medical staff can believe that you're still alive. I hope you appreciate that," he added almost sternly. "And the fact that we saved your limbs."

Lucy saw herself as a tree, limbs sprouting every which way, reaching up to the sky. They had saved her limbs. She supposed he wanted her to appreciate that, too. Well, she did. What was a tree without limbs? Or a girl without legs? Now, if he could just take the pain away. *That*, she would really appreciate.

"You've had the very best surgery available. Never seen anything finer." The mustache turned upward, as if it were pleased. Then it turned serious again. "The rest is up to you, young lady. You're not out of the woods yet. You can't afford another infection. And you've got a lot of hard work ahead of you if you're going to walk again."

Lucy gasped. *"If?"* *If* she was going to walk again? What was he talking about? Was there some question about that?

Her eyes, gone a deeper blue with shock, sought out her mother's face. Sara looked away, at the blank, white wall.

"It'll be rough, of course," the mustache went on, calmly, as if it were discussing what was on the hospital menu for dinner ... we're having meat loaf, of course, it being Sunday ... always have meatloaf on Sunday, no surprise there. "Going to be a long haul, might as well know that now. But you're young and healthy, and your mother here tells us you're strong. If we can keep the infections at bay, you should be out of here in a month or so."

Lucy fought to grasp what he was saying. No one had told her anything for so long, and now here was this mustached doctor throwing nasty pieces of information at her.

Unable to deal with any of it, Lucy did the only thing she could do. She went into total denial. Ignoring the doctor still standing at her bedside, she turned her head toward her mother to say, "My hair feels like glue. Can't someone wash it for me?"

Looking relieved that she, too, wouldn't have to deal with this new, dismal information immediately, Sara said, "Oh, sure, honey, I'll do it. I'll just go get a basin from one of the nurses. Be right back." She had the presence of mind to turn to the doctor and say, "Thank you, Dr. Altari. Lucy and I will discuss all of this later when she's had time to think about it."

He nodded grimly and left, scurrying out of the room on short, bow legs that gave his walk a slight bob-and-weave appearance.

Lucy had no intention of thinking about anything he had told her. None of it could be true. Thinking about it as if it *might* be true would only depress her. Why make things worse? She *was*, of course, going to walk again, no question there. And she was *not* staying in this awful place for another four or five weeks. If the doctors wouldn't discharge her, she'd discharge herself. Just get up and walk out and go home where she belonged.

No reason why she couldn't walk home. Couldn't be that far. She'd always loved long walks. Always.

But when her mother began awkwardly washing her hair over a basin and accidentally jostled the wheeled bed, a shaft of pain shot up Lucy's right leg. It scared her.

If a tiny, accidental jar to her bed could cause pain like that, how could she even think about actually leaving her bed to walk out of the room and down the hall to an elevator to go home? For that matter, how could she even think about *walking*?

Was that what the doctor had meant? That it wasn't that she *couldn't* walk, but simply that it might be too painful? If he had, that wasn't so bad. Because after a while, the pain would go away, just as it did with any wound. She'd had the surgeries, they'd sewed her legs back up, and of course they hurt now. But they wouldn't always. *Then* she could walk.

She was saved from dwelling on Dr. Altari's frightening remarks by a move from intensive care into a small, sunny room with pale-pink walls and flowered curtains at the one wide window set into the far wall. There was much more activity on this floor. Nurses, doctors, and orderlies hurried past the door of her room, music drifted in from other rooms, mixed with the ping of elevators arriving and the rattle of dinner trays. The sense of eerie, silent isolation that was ICU was gone down here on the fourth floor. Lucy liked it. She was back in the real world, at least a little bit, and the relief was overwhelming. She was getting better, or they wouldn't have moved her. She wasn't going to die. And now her friends could come visit her.

And they did. En masse. It seemed to Lucy that the entire school, at one time or another, made their way to room 406. It seemed that way to the head nurse, too, who finally put her foot down and said firmly, "No more than two at a time, and that's final!"

Some people were less than tactful. Margie Slater, someone Lucy had always thought of as a very large mouth with a body attached, asked loudly, "So, what are you going to do with all your shoes until you can wear them again, Lucy? I know we wear the same size, and I've always loved those red suede boots of yours." A boy from Lucy's art class spent twenty minutes one afternoon enlightening her about the latest technological advances in wheelchairs, and Lucy's social studies teacher visited briefly to say in what was clearly meant to be a consoling voice, "You know, Lucy, you have a fine mind. As long as you have that, consider yourself lucky."

"Oh, I do," Lucy said. When her visitors left, she always remembered to thank them. Even if what she really wanted to do was smack them silly for the stupid things they said.

But it was Dash Lucy needed to see the most. He didn't show up the first day or even the second. But on the third afternoon he was there, smiling and carrying two books, a CD, and a box of chocolate-covered cherries, Lucy's favorite.

"Sorry I didn't get here sooner. Bike trouble," he explained as he took a seat beside her. Her mother had tactfully developed a need for coffee, and left the room. "Spark plugs. Had to replace them." Dash leaned closer, smiling. He took Lucy's right hand in his. She was grateful it wasn't the one with the ever-present IV sticking out of it. "I miss you. I'm glad you're okay," he said.

Well, not really. She wasn't okay. And she wished someone had washed her hair again. One of the volunteers had washed it for her on Monday, because she'd expected Dash. But he hadn't come, and this was Wednesday, and lying in a bed all day, sometimes with a slight fever, wasn't the way to stay gorgeous. At least she was wearing the new pink quilted robe Tia and Kendra had given her. It matched the walls. Color-coordination seemed like a good idea, even in a hospital room. Maybe *especially* in a hospital room.

"We were really scared," Dash said quietly. "No one was sure you were going to make it. And I'd *seen* the wreck, so I knew how bad it was. Hard to believe you came out of that alive."

Lucy shook her head. "I don't remember the crash, not really." But she did remember that Thursday night at Kendra's. Dash and Jenny . . . dancing. She wouldn't think about it. He was here now. Nothing else mattered. "And I was so out of it when I first got here, I never had a clue that I might not make it. Can't quite grasp that concept, you know?"

Dash nodded. He'd recently had his hair cut. It was very short. He was deeply tanned, and looked healthy and strong. Lucy felt a pang of envy. She'd look like that, too, if she hadn't been stuck inside the hospital for so long. "I guess I look like I've been in prison right? Pale and wan?"

"You look okay to me. So, when are you being sprung? Soon, I hope. The play was great, by the way, although," Dash added quickly, "Norah wasn't nearly as good in the part as you." He grinned. "And it was a lot harder to kiss her."

"What else have I missed?"

"The Azalea Ball."

Lucy groaned. She'd forgotten. The beautiful blue dress silvered with sequins glittering like stars, that she'd bought with the money from her part-time job as a library page, was still hanging in her closet, its sequins probably dull with disappointment because they'd never seen the light of day. "I'm sorry," she said, gripping Dash's hand tightly. "Did you get the rental deposit back on your tux?"

She knew instantly then. She knew because Dash's cheeks flamed and his eyes slid from her face to the flower-curtained window. "You went!" she accused. "You went *without* me." Then, she decided she was being unreasonable. Why shouldn't he go? It was his school, his dance, and not his fault that she was stuck in a hospital bed. "It's okay," she amended hastily, "of course you went. Why not? Did you have fun? What were the decorations like? Tia said she wanted silver stars pasted on the ceiling, but everyone else thought that was too juvenile, so —"

"I didn't go alone," Dash said, his voice low, his eyes still averted.

It took at least half a minute for that to register, and as it did, Lucy realized that if he'd gone stag with a bunch of pals, he wouldn't have said it that way. He'd have said, "Yeah, we all had a good time" or "Well, you know, we're guys, what do we know about decorations?" He wouldn't have said, "I didn't go alone."

Tia and Kendra hadn't mentioned that Dash was at the Azalea Ball. And Lucy hadn't asked. Because she hadn't thought she needed to ask.

The room was very quiet. It often was at four o'clock in the afternoon, when a lot of the patients took naps. Lucy wished suddenly that she was taking a nap. Because if she was, Dash wouldn't be here, and he wouldn't be saying what he'd just said and she wouldn't have heard it. "You didn't go alone," she echoed flatly, determined not to let him see that she was hurt. "And the person you went with would be . . . ?"

But she knew the answer even before he opened his traitorous mouth. "Jenny."

"Jenny. Of course. Of course you went with Jenny. She must have been ecstatic when you asked her. My good friend, Jennifer Elaine Cooper."

Dash looked at her then, and said eagerly, "But that's why, see? I mean, I thought it would be okay with you because we're *both* your friends, and it wasn't like I was asking someone new, someone you didn't even know. I thought you'd figure it would be okay if I went with Jenny."

Guess again, Lucy thought bitterly. If I hadn't seen the two of you dancing at Kendra's house, maybe I'd feel that way. But not now. She pretended to think it over and then said aloud in a bright, brittle voice, "You know what? You're right. Since I couldn't be there, I'm glad my friends went and had fun."

Dash wasn't stupid, and she thought for a minute that he wasn't going to buy it. But he wanted to, desperately, so he did. Relief filled his handsome, tanned face, and he relaxed again in the chair. "Well, it wasn't as much fun as if you'd been there."

"Of course it wasn't. I'm the best dancer at Seneca, and everyone knows it." She was proud of herself for not using the past tense. There wasn't any reason in the world why she couldn't dance again. There *wasn't*.

"Everyone asked about you. Everyone misses you like crazy." He smiled again and leaned closer to her. "Especially me."

He'd called her every night since she'd left ICU. She had to keep that in mind.

When he kissed her, the first time she'd been kissed since the accident, she kissed him back. But first she had to erase the image of Dash dancing across the floor of Seneca High School's gym with a radiant Jenny Cooper in his arms.

Chapter 7

It was Jenny who first mentioned "amputation." And though afterwards, she insisted tearfully that it was an accidental slip of the tongue, Lucy wasn't so sure.

It was Jenny who first mentioned "amputation." And though afterwards, she insisted tearfully that it was an accidental slip of the tongue, Lucy wasn't so sure.

Jenny had come with Dash and Kendra to visit on a sunny, muggy Friday afternoon three weeks after the accident. Tia was baby-sitting her younger siblings and couldn't accompany them. Kendra sat on the floor beside Lucy's bed, Dash took a chair next to her, and Jenny, looking more gorgeous than ever now that she boasted a bronze, even tan, stood directly behind Dash, her hands on his shoulders.

Like she's shopping and just found something she wants, Lucy thought angrily. Well, she can't have this little item. To demonstrate that Dash was still *hers* and would be until they decided otherwise, Lucy took his right hand and held it, positioning their clasped hands on the blanket, a clear signal that couldn't possibly escape Jenny's line of vision.

"I hear Elizabeth graduated and is on her way home," Jenny said, removing her hands from Dash's shoulders. But she stayed where she was, leaning slightly against the back of his chair. "She'll be so relieved to see how much better you are. She called our house one night when she couldn't get hold of your mom to see how you were. She really freaked when she heard your legs might have to be amputated."

The word "amputated" hung in the air.

"*What* did you say?" Lucy gasped, her eyes moving swiftly from Dash's face, which looked grim, to Kendra's, white as bone, to Jenny's, now flushing scarlet under her tan as she realized what she had done.

"I . . . I thought you *knew*," she whispered. "Oh, I'm sorry. I thought your mom had told you. But," she added hastily, "they *didn't* do it, Lucy, they didn't have to, so it's okay, right? I mean, they saved your legs and you're probably even going to walk again."

"Amputate?" Lucy whispered the word. She tore her hand free of Dash's. "What are you *talking* about?" Her own face was scarlet. "Where's my mother? I want to talk to my mother!" Tears filled her eyes, and her hands on the pale-pink coverlet shook. Her voice rose to a high treble. "Why didn't someone tell me?"

Kendra jumped up, moving swiftly to the bed to put an arm around Lucy's shoulders. She spoke quietly, reassuringly. "They couldn't tell you, Lucy." She shot Jenny a furious glance, then turned back to Lucy. "Because they knew it would upset you, like you're upset now. That would have been really bad for you, especially when you first came in here and you were in such a bad way. Besides, no one was sure if it would be necessary, not even the doctors. We were all hoping and praying that it wouldn't have to happen. And it didn't, right? Telling you that it was a possibility would have caused you a whole bunch of misery, and for nothing."

The words *were* reassuring. But Lucy knew now, finally, just how bad her legs really were.

"I'm sorry, Lucy, I'm so sorry," Jenny said. Tears shone in her green eyes. "I thought you knew."

Lucy could tell she meant it. Even if her announcement hadn't been one hundred percent accidental, Jen really was sorry. Anyone could see that. Fighting to calm down, taking huge, deep breaths until she felt she could speak normally, Lucy finally said, "No one ever told me, that's all. I never knew it was that bad." She felt numb with shock.

Kendra poured cool water from the pitcher on Lucy's nightstand and gave it to her. Dash held her hand again. Jenny brushed her hair and showed her an ad in a magazine for a new blusher. Slowly, very slowly, the word "amputated" vanished from the room . . . or seemed to.

By the time the three left, promising to return that evening, Lucy was able to smile and wave and say, "See you."

It wasn't until they'd gone that she focused on the other part of Jenny's shocking statement. That Lucy would "probably" walk again. *Probably*? "Probably" meant "could be," "maybe," "chances are." "Probably" did *not* mean "of course the girl will walk again," which was what Lucy had been telling herself. Now, she remembered Dr. Altari's ominous words: "*If you're going to walk again.*" Words Lucy had ignored. Queen of Denial, that was her.

It was time for a heart-to-heart with her mother.

Which Sara tried to dodge when she arrived that evening. She carried a small, terra-cotta pot filled with violets in one hand. A new, very pretty nightgown dotted with tiny pink rosebuds was nestled inside a shopping bag in the other hand. Dressed in a bright-red suit that showed off her youthful figure, looking slightly less worried for the first time in weeks, she took a stab at avoiding Lucy's questions about her condition and, more important, her future.

"Oh, honey," Sara said, depositing the flowers on Lucy's table and handing her the nightgown, "let's not talk about that tonight. We have plenty of time for that. I have a wonderful surprise for you! Let's not spoil it, okay?" And before Lucy could argue, she called in the direction of the door, "Okay, you can come in. She's awake!"

Lucy's sister Elizabeth, tall and blond, a warm smile on her face, strode into the room and straight to Lucy's bed, where she bent to encircle her sister with her arms.

Her hug was warm and loving, and she held on for a long time. When she straightened up, tears glistening in her eyes, she said, "Hey, kiddo, you're looking very stunning these days. I thought you'd be all pale and washed out, like a heroine in one of those tragic novels you love so much. But here you are, looking as perky as Katie Couric. They must be treating you pretty well here."

Except they never tell me anything, Lucy wanted to say but didn't. "I'm fine. I'm glad you're home." She lifted Liz's left hand to stare in admiration at the moderately sized diamond on her ring finger. "So, the wedding's still on, I guess? I haven't screwed anything up with my untimely accident?" It seemed important to let Elizabeth know that Lucy hadn't forgotten the upcoming wedding, set for December. A

Christmas wedding. Injuries from a May accident would certainly be healed by December. She'd be walking down the aisle ahead of Elizabeth, as maid of honor, as planned. Of course she would, in spite of Jen's use of the word "probably." And Dr. Altari's "if." What did they know? Like her mother said, she was strong and healthy . . . almost.

Lucy's mother and sister took seats in the pink vinyl chairs stationed next to the bed. "You bet the wedding is still on," Elizabeth said. "Adam's been terrific since . . . since your accident. The guy is going to make a super husband, as if I didn't know that already. He knew it was killing me not to come home and see for myself that you were okay. I could have, and then taken the finals this summer. I talked to mom about it. But she said that you had plenty of people taking care of you here in the hospital, and that you might need me around more after you left the hospital. I decided she was right. So I took the finals, and now I'm done, and I'm home, and I'm at your service, Ms. St. Cloud."

"Mom couldn't go to your graduation because of me," Lucy said regretfully. "She waited four whole years to see you graduate from college, and then had to miss it."

"*Not* because of you," Sara said firmly. "Because of that truck driver. Who, I might add, is in serious trouble. The police said he'd been taking pills for hours before he hit you, and that he had been involved in two prior serious accidents. I've talked to Mitchell Dwyer, and he thinks we might have a case against the meatpacking company that hired the driver of the truck."

Mitchell Dwyer was the family lawyer, the same man who had informed the shocked and stunned St. Clouds that Lucas had skimped on life insurance. He had done it kindly, as gently as possible. Lucy liked him.

"I'm not a big fan of litigation," Sara continued. "People sue these days for every little thing. But your rehabilitation is going to be expensive, Lucy, and our insurance won't cover all of it. And the company *was* negligent, hiring someone like Sloan, with his driving record."

But Lucy had heard only one word. She seized on it. "Rehabilitation? *What* rehabilitation?"

Sara tried once more to avoid a confrontation. "Lucy, please, Liz just got here. We'll talk about all of that tomorrow."

Elizabeth spoke up. "Mom, you should tell her. She has a right to know. Besides, I want to know, too. You might as well tell both of us at the same time."

Lucy flashed her a grateful look.

Their mother's pretty face flushed a deep red. "I just think the doctors should tell her.

They know more about it than I do. I'm not sure I have it all straight. I don't want to give her the wrong information."

Elizabeth laughed and ran her fingers through short, blond hair like her mother's, waving softly against her cheeks. Her eyes, like Lucy's, were a deep blue, her lashes long and thick. Like her father, she was tall, with an air of competence about her. People, including Lucy, trusted Elizabeth. "Mother, stow the clueless female routine. You've kept this family together against some really tough odds, and you made it possible for me to finish college. So cut it out, and tell Lucy what she needs to know."

It wasn't pretty. According to Sara, amputation had been discussed seriously. But the orthopedic surgeon had fought hard against it. "If it hadn't been for him," Lucy's mother said grimly, "I don't know ... there was so much damage. The vascular surgeon said that your chances of walking again would be improved with artificial limbs."

Sickened, Lucy tried to imagine not having legs. Not having her *own* legs. There was a boy in her social studies class who had played a dangerous game with firecrackers when he was nine years old, and lost. He had an artificial right hand. It was an intricate, metal appliance that made it possible for him to pick up a pencil and write with it.

But legs were different from hands. Could you dance if you had artificial legs? Was that possible?

Sara shook her head. "I was so afraid I would make a bad decision by supporting the wrong doctor." She fixed anxious eyes on Lucy's face. "I hope I did the right thing, honey. I threw my weight behind the orthopedic surgeon, insisted they do everything possible to save your legs. But when I see how much pain you're in . . ." Tears glistened on Sara's lashes.

Lucy reached out to pat her hand. "It's okay, Mom. Honest. If I hadn't been so out of it, I'd have told you to do exactly what you did. Messed up or not, they're *my* legs, and I want to keep them." Lucy managed a smile. "Thanks for being on my side."

"So," Elizabeth said briskly, "what's next? And what's the prognosis? How much longer will she be in here? And exactly what will it take for her to walk again?"

That, too, was not pretty. Lucy's mother tried, in her usual way, to dress up the information in as pleasant a way as possible, using a lot of "maybes" and "possibles."

But underneath all of that, Lucy heard the truth. Jenny had said it first. It was not at *all* certain that Lucy St. Cloud would ever walk on her own again.

She wouldn't believe it. It just wasn't possible that she might not ever walk again or put on a pair of in-line skates or pedal a bicycle or climb a flight of stairs. Or dance. Not possible. The doctors didn't realize how strong she was, that's all. They didn't know her.

But the worst blow came when Lucy learned that she wasn't going to go home when she left the hospital. She was being sent to a rehabilitation facility. "I'm not going home?" Lucy reeled under this blow. Why couldn't any necessary "rehabilitation" be done somewhere in this hospital, or in the privacy of her own home? "But . . . all my friends are *here*. Why can't I do the rehab here?"

"I'm sorry, sweetie. The kind of work you need is too extensive. It requires a special place. The closest one is way too expensive, but Dr. Tolliver tells me the facility he has in mind is very good. And it's only two hours away."

Lucy was horrified. Two hours? "Mom, two *hours*? That's four hours, round trip. Dash doesn't have that kind of time. I'll never get to see him. I need to be nearer than that." She was close to tears. She'd been in this hospital for weeks, and all she'd thought about was going home, being free, being around familiar things.

Her mother shook her head. "I'm sorry, honey. But with the hospital bills and the doctor's fees, Twin Willows is the best we can do for now. Until we find out how cooperative the trucking company is going to be, we have to be careful with money."

Lucy slid down in her bed. "Why do they always name institutions after trees or flowers? Twin Willows, Rose Hill, Poplar Place. Who do they think they're kidding? It doesn't make those places any nicer. I've read about them. And if *I* were naming them, I'd be a lot more honest. Misery Manor. Painful Place." She was bitterly disappointed and terrified at the thought of living with strangers. "Horror House."

Elizabeth laughed. "You know what, Luce? I think I've been worrying over nothing. I think you're going to be okay. When I call Adam tonight, I'm going to tell him that your color is great and your sense of humor is intact. He'll be relieved."

But by eleven o'clock that night, long after Lucy's mother and sister and friends had gone home, all of them commenting on how much better the patient looked, Lucy's fever had shot back up to one hundred three. An urgent call had to be placed to her orthopedic surgeon.

No one who visited her that day had guessed that the high color in her face, which made her look so healthy, signaled the onset of a rapidly rising fever due to yet another infection.

Chapter 8

Lucy spent the next three weeks back up in ICU, too unaware to be disheartened by the transfer. In all, she underwent three more surgeries on her legs before the doctors decided the risk of infection had passed.

"You're being really brave, Lucy," Dash said during one phone conversation. "Everyone thinks so."

Lucy almost laughed aloud. *Brave?* No way. That was so far from the truth. When she wasn't medicated, she was terrified every single minute. Terrified of the surgeries. People died on operating tables, didn't they? Terrified that she wouldn't get well, that she'd never walk again. Terrified of the pain.

"I haven't even seen you cry once."

This was true. No one had, except her mother. But that wasn't because she was brave.

It was because she was afraid that once the tears began flowing, they'd never stop. But sometimes, late at night, she thought what if? And she cried then.

And crying wouldn't change anything. Crying wouldn't keep that tractor-trailer out of her path. It wouldn't return her perfect, healthy legs . . . and it wouldn't take that look off Dash's face. Even when he was being sweet, she could see it in his eyes. She could see that he was thinking, You're different now, Lucy, and I don't have a clue how I'm supposed to deal with this. Recently, the look had also said, Tell you the truth, I'd rather be any place else on earth than this hospital room.

Well, who wouldn't?

But Dash would never say those things aloud. Not with Lucy lying in a hospital bed.

Her pride urged her to send him away for good, tell him not to visit her anymore. But she couldn't bring herself to say the words. And Dash wasn't that good at reading eyes. If he was, he would have seen the daggers of jealousy she was sending his way that night at Kendra's house, he would have left Jen and asked Lucy to dance, and the accident never would have happened.

The thought shocked her. Did she blame Dash? Tia did, Lucy knew that. Everyone knew it. Tia was never shy about sharing her feelings with the accusing looks she sent Dash's way, and Jenny's, too. Sometimes, when they were all there together in Lucy's room, the atmosphere became so strained, Lucy felt like screaming at Tia, "Stop it, stop it! Can't you see you're just making things worse? I can't blame Dash, because if I do I won't be able to forgive him and then I won't have him anymore, and I *need* him, Tia! On top of everything else, I don't want to lose Dash, too."

It was when Lucy wondered, secretly, privately, if she herself blamed Dash for the accident that she felt most like crying. And did.

Elizabeth came to see her every day. She was working now, in a law office downtown, and planning her wedding. If she had no other free time during the day, she spent her lunch hour, armed with a bologna sandwich and a banana, in Lucy's room. She never talked about Lucy's condition or her prognosis, but kept the conversation light, centered mainly on the July weather, which according to her was perfect, and on the thousands of details that went into planning a Christmas wedding.

Lucy loved seeing her sister, but on one particularly bad day she interrupted Elizabeth to say abruptly, "You'd better count me out of your wedding."

The remark took both of them by surprise. Until then, Lucy had clung to the belief that the wedding was so far away, she had plenty of time to get back on her feet. No way she wouldn't be walking down the aisle ahead of Liz, carrying a nosegay of peach-colored rosebuds and wearing the short, peach-colored dress Liz had picked out for her. Not be in Elizabeth's wedding? How could she even think that, let alone *say* it?

Elizabeth paled. The sandwich on its way to her mouth halted in mid-air.

Lucy already regretted her words. But . . . it was *true*, wasn't it? Maybe it was time they both faced it. No one had said she was being released from the hospital any time soon, and now she knew that even when they did release her, she wouldn't be going home. Who knew how long rehabilitation would take?

The sandwich dropped into Elizabeth's lap. She shook her head. "Count you out? Don't even *think* that, Lucy! I'm not getting married without you in my wedding party. I won't!"

But Lucy couldn't let go of it. Elizabeth and Adam had a right to go forward with their wedding as planned. The accident hadn't been their fault. "I'm just saying, you should ask someone else to be your maid of honor, just in case. They'll need time to plan. Then, if I'm okay by

December, you'll just have one extra attendant, that's all. You can keep Tim on tap as an extra usher."

Elizabeth clearly wanted to continue arguing, but Lucy was saved by the arrival of Nurse Bassett, armed with a luncheon tray.

Lucy almost fainted with relief when Elizabeth, seeing the lunch tray, glanced at her watch and said regretfully, "Oh, Lucy, I've got to get back to work. I'm sorry. But" — bending for a hug and a kiss on the cheek — "we'll continue this discussion later, I promise." As she straightened, she added firmly, "No Lucy, no wedding, period. No room for negotiation there, kiddo. If Adam and I have to postpone for awhile, then that's what we'll do. He'll understand."

Lucy didn't think so. Adam was nice, but he'd been waiting two years to marry Elizabeth.

Lucy was scared. She was so scared. And who could she tell? Dash, who was already having trouble adjusting to this new and different Lucy? He came to see her, and he laughed, and he talked just like always, and his kiss was as warm as ever, but there was *that* look in his eyes. No, she couldn't tell Dash.

And she couldn't tell her mother, whose face hadn't eased into its old expression once since the accident. The new, noticeable lines drawn across her forehead hadn't gone away. If anything, they'd intensified, as if someone had gone over them with a felt-tipped pen.

She had always told Elizabeth everything. But how could she talk about her terror to her sister now, when Elizabeth was so caught up in the excitement of a new job and an upcoming wedding? And Lucy wasn't about to confide in Kendra, who kept saying with admiration, "Lucy, I can't believe you're still making me laugh. I know I wouldn't have a sense of humor if I were in your . . . place." Lucy knew Kendra had almost said "if I were in your shoes." She'd caught herself just in time.

She wouldn't tell Kendra.

She couldn't tell Tia, either. Because she knew that Tia, too, was scared. Scared that Lucy wouldn't regain the use of her legs, and scared that if that happened, everything between them would change. No more jogging together. No more fun hours at the roller rink. No more dances. The long walks they both loved would become a thing of the past, along with everything else involving the use of two good, sturdy legs. Lucy wouldn't even be able to drive to Tia's house. Everything would change.

Lucy was deep in sleep when Dash appeared in the doorway, a book for her in his hands.

Though there was pain in his eyes when he looked down on Lucy, sleeping with her hands tucked underneath her left cheek, there was unmistakable relief as well.

He left the book on her bedside table and hurried from her room, his footsteps carefully quiet so he wouldn't wake her.

Chapter 9

The following evening, Lucy talked to her mother about rehab. "I don't see why I can't just stay home and have someone from the hospital come to the apartment to help me do my exercises. Why can't I do that?"

"Oh, I wish we could, honey," her mother said, toying with the edge of Lucy's pink blanket. "But it just wouldn't work. First of all, there's no wheelchair access to the building, and second, I'm gone all day. Who would take care of you?"

Lucy winced. If there was one thing she hated more than anything else — more than the pain, the pills, the smell of the hospital, which she still hadn't become used to — it was the knowledge that she could no longer "take care" of herself. She was sixteen years old and had to be cared for like a baby. Carried everywhere. Couldn't even get up and go to the bathroom alone, like a normal person. Humiliating.

"We want you in a nice place where you'll get all the attention and care that you need," her mother added. "It won't be for that long, Lucy. The doctor says your legs are mending nicely." She sighed heavily. "Finally." She smiled at Lucy. "And she said if you want, you can always have plastic surgery later, for some of the heavier scarring."

Lucy shuddered, as much at the thought of her legs being scarred as at the thought of more surgery. Just exactly how were her legs going to look? Would she be able to go out in public in a bathing suit? In shorts? In a miniskirt? Her dress for the wedding was two inches above the knee. I looked pretty good in that dress, she told herself. *Before.* What about now?

"I want to see them," she demanded suddenly. "My legs. I want to see what they look like. The nurses never let me see when they change the dressings. It's not like I'll be shocked or anything. I can deal with it. I'm ready."

Her mother paled and let go of the edge of the blanket. "Oh. Well . . ." She glanced around the room a little wildly, apparently hoping someone would suddenly appear out of nowhere to deal with Lucy's request. When no one did, she added, "I don't think anyone is deliberately keeping things from you, Lucy. Really. I don't."

Which meant, of course, that she did. And that she approved.

Lucy laughed. "Oh, please, Mom! Give me a break. The CIA could take lessons from these people. No one tells me anything." Her voice rose. "So don't tell me no one's keeping anything from me, because I know better!"

"Lucy, please, calm down."

Lucy's voice gathered strength, "And I *want* to see what that truck did to me."

A nurse heard her shouting and came running, tiny paper cup in hand. Two fat capsules bounced inside the cup as she held it out to Lucy and reached for the water pitcher with her other hand.

"No!" Lucy screamed. One arm flew out and sent the cup sailing across the room. "You . . . take these bandages off . . . right now . . . and let me see for myself what I'm dealing with! I'm not taking another pill or going through another procedure or eating another bite until you show me my legs." And she meant it.

While her mother hurried off to confer with the doctors, the nurse brought Lucy a damp washcloth to wipe her face. "You shouldn't get so upset," she said. "It's not good for you."

"Not being told the truth isn't good for me!" Lucy shouted.

"You don't need to be sarcastic." The nurse was very young and very blond and she had two healthy, undamaged, unscarred legs that carried her about the room quite nicely. Lucy hated her.

When Sara returned with two doctors in tow, Lucy knew she'd won. Clearly, Sara didn't want the unveiling, and she wouldn't have looked that unhappy had the doctors refused to do what Lucy wanted. They must have agreed that it was time.

Lucy felt sorry for her mother. But I have to have this, she argued silently. I have to *see*.

She knew both doctors. Dr. Tolliver had performed two of her surgeries, and Dr. Helene Smythe-Collins the others. Lucy liked the woman, who was taller than Dr. Tolliver, with iron-gray hair and warm blue eyes. Dr. Tolliver's visits after the operations were always brisk and brief. But Dr. Smythe-Collins often stayed to chat for a few moments.

"You're absolutely sure you're ready for this?" Dr. Tolliver was short and round and rosy-cheeked, and reminded Lucy of pictures she'd seen of leprechauns. But Lucy had learned that he wasn't as jolly as he looked, and his tone of voice now was cool. "We had planned to wait until just before your discharge. Give the wounds plenty of time to heal." He inclined his graying head toward Sara. "Your mother would still prefer that we wait. You refuse to honor her wishes?"

If he hadn't used that tone of voice, Lucy might have changed her mind. But he made it sound like she was being a very bad little girl. As if she'd broken some silly rule, maybe kept her light on too late at night or played her radio too loud or spilled lime-green Jell-O on the clean white sheets.

Still, the doleful expressions on all four adult faces in the room scared her.

"I want," she said evenly, "to see my legs." To Sara she said, "I'm sorry if that upsets you, Mom. Maybe you could go downstairs and get a cup of coffee or something while we do this. Because" — fixing a level gaze on Dr. Tolliver's disapproving face — "we *are* doing this, aren't we, doctor?"

He shrugged and pulled a straight-backed chair up to Lucy's bed. Then he sat down and folded the blanket and sheet back, away from Lucy's bandaged legs. Dr. Smythe-Collins walked to the opposite side of the bed, flashing Lucy a reassuring smile as she reached for Lucy's right leg.

"I'm staying," Sara said firmly. She walked to the head of the bed to put an arm around Lucy's shoulders. "I'll be right here, honey."

Lucy heard the unspoken words, In case you need me . . . and you *will*. She swallowed hard.

Maybe she was making the worst mistake she'd ever made.

No. The worst mistake she'd ever made was running out of Kendra's house That Night. But she'd survived the crash, hadn't she? She could survive this, too, whatever *this* was.

The unwrapping seemed to take forever. "Is there *any* gauze left in this hospital?" Lucy joked shakily. No one responded, though her mother squeezed her shoulder.

She could see now that the unrolled layers folded loosely on the bed were becoming increasingly thicker, and that the bulkiness of her injured limbs was diminishing. Only a thin, gauzy covering from ankle to thigh remained. Maybe she *wasn't* ready. There had to be scars. They'd be ugly. Did she really want to see them?

Her mother leaned closer and breathed into Lucy's ear, "It'll be okay, honey, it will. Just keep in mind that you can have plastic surgery whenever you're ready."

Praying for strength, Lucy bit down hard on her lower lip and kept her eyes on the doctor's strong hands as the last layer of white was peeled away.

Both legs were revealed at exactly the same moment. They stretched out before Lucy on the smooth white sheet, surrounded by winding ribbons of wrinkled white gauze. But *this* isn't what I wanted, she thought dully, staring.

Not *this*! Take them back and get me something else.

"We can cover them up again," Dr. Tolliver said in a surprisingly gentle voice. His hands were already reaching out to the nurse for a fresh box of gauze.

Lucy found her voice. "No! No, not yet. Wait ..."

She looked. And she didn't look away, though she wanted to, desperately. A vision of smooth, golden-tanned, strong legs stretched out on the lawn in front of Seneca High flashed through her mind. *Her* legs. How long ago had that been? May ... two days before the accident.

The vision faded. The legs lying before her now were not smooth, were not golden, were not strong.

"Lucy, please ..." her mother murmured, putting an arm around Lucy's shoulders.

"No! Let me look!" She forced herself to study the sight she had begged for. It wasn't just the fiery-red color that shocked her. She thought dazedly of fabric caught in a zipper. The "teeth" were the stitches ... hundreds of them.

"We're not plastic surgeons," Dr. Tolliver said, a bit defensively. "We did the best we could. The important thing was to save your legs, and we did that."

And Dr. Smythe-Collins added gently, "Plastic surgery will help, Lucy, I promise you."

"The stitches will dissolve, honey," her mother said into Lucy's ear. "You won't have those much longer."

Lucy did laugh then, aloud, a high, tinny, hysterical sound. She had thought it would be okay. She really had. She had believed, all along, that she would walk again, that her legs, would heal and look, if not perfect, at least . . . not revolting. But these legs would never hold her up! How could they?

No one said a word for several minutes. When Lucy could finally speak, all she managed was, "They're . . . they're so *thin*."

"You haven't been using the muscles," Dr. Tolliver said. "They've grown weak, which changes the contours of your legs. Don't worry, rehab will help you build them back up again." He actually patted her right leg. Lucy shuddered. How could he bare to touch it?

Even if by some miracle she was walking again by December, she would never, *ever* wear the pretty peach dress that Elizabeth had picked out for her. It was short. It would hide nothing.

"Wrap them back up," she said, her voice husky. Then exhausted, she lay back against the pillows.

Chapter 10

The following day, Lucy began hoarding her pain pills. She made a show of seeming grateful, and pretended to take them. Then, when the nurse left, she spit the capsules back out, wrapped them in a tissue, and thrust them into the very back of her nightstand drawer. No one ever checked the drawer's contents. The pills were safe there until she'd made up her mind, one way or the other.

She didn't have a plan. She hadn't really thought things through yet. All she knew for sure was, the sight that had met her eyes yesterday after those bandages came off had robbed her of all hope. No matter what anyone said to keep her spirits up, life in a wheelchair seemed certain.

She couldn't bear the thought.

Lucy knew that other people had suffered the same kind of tragedy. And she knew that they still managed to live full and rewarding lives. No one had to tell her that. She'd seen the movies, read the books, and had found them inspiring.

But *she* couldn't live that kind of life. It just wasn't who she was, or who she could be.

Trapped in the wreck, she had begged not to die. And she had meant it. Dying had seemed like the very worst thing, then. Now, it didn't. There were things ahead of her now that seemed much worse than dying.

So she hoarded the pills. In only two days, she had a hefty handful nestled in a dark corner of the drawer. But she didn't know if it was enough. She wasn't sure how many she needed, and didn't know how to find out an exact number.

Then there was the pain. She'd forgotten how it could be without the medication.

On a rainy Monday, as Nurse Bassett handed her her morning pill, Lucy asked casually, "These can't kill me, can they? I mean, I take so many. Don't they build up in your system or something? Seems to me I read something about that somewhere."

The nurse nodded. "You're talking about drugs that last longer in the system than others. Not to worry. You'd have to take quite a few of these at one time to do serious damage."

But she didn't say how much damage, and

she didn't say how many pills "quite a few" was. Lucy needed to know that, but she couldn't very well ask. All she could do was keep stashing the pills in her drawer until she thought she had enough.

Unfortunately, the number of visitors in Lucy's room increased dramatically during the next few days. She knew it was because Tia and the others had told everyone from school that she would be going away soon. They all wanted to say good-bye and wish her well. Though she didn't feel like visitors, she accepted the visits. Whether she went away to rehab or decided to swallow her stash of pills, good-byes seemed appropriate.

Outwardly, she was calm, though easily irritated because of the pain. Inside, she was writhing with fear and indecision. She couldn't believe she was actually contemplating an end to her life. She had never thought of herself as cowardly. Hadn't she been the first one in third grade to climb all the way to the top of the water tower? Hadn't she suffered eleven stitches in her left elbow without a peep when she was thirteen after a fall during a bicycle race? Hadn't she gone to school every single day after her father's funeral when all she really wanted to do was dive into her bed and hide beneath the covers?

She wasn't a coward. *Wasn't.*

But she couldn't ... could *not* ... spend her entire life in a wheelchair.

The constant flow of visitors was difficult for Lucy. She had to make conversation, even laugh at jokes, had to pretend to be normal. What hurt the most, and added to her conviction that the pills were not such a terrible idea, was the sight of all those healthy legs walking around her room. It was late July and hot. The girls wore shorts or miniskirts, the guys cut-offs. Lucy lay in her bed and watched with envy as strong, healthy, tanned limbs bent and crouched and stretched effortlessly. Tom Winthrop, a fellow track member, kicked out jokingly at Kendra when she teased him about his too-short haircut, and Lucy felt a fierce pain in her chest. How easily Tom moved that leg!

She knew none of them understood how wonderful that was ... that a brain would tell a leg or an arm to do something and it would obey instantly. They all took their physical movements for granted, just as she always had. How could they know what it felt like to have limbs that just lay there, motionless, heavy and useless, as if they were made of stone?

And then there was the way all of those legs looked. The girls' legs were smooth as silk, most of them a glowing bronze, the boys' hairy and strongly muscled and just as tanned. No ugly, puckered skin with black "zippers" zigzagging up and down and back and forth anywhere in the room ... except underneath Lucy's sheets. Joey Cornish had a small scar on his kneecap, Lucy noticed, so tiny no one would even see it unless they were scrutinizing, as Lucy was, every leg in the room for imperfections.

It was as if all the legs were shouting at Lucy, You'll never look like this again, and you'll never do any of the things we do, either!

She could hardly bear it.

"When you get home from rehab," Kendra announced happily, "we're planning a picnic in the woods behind Joey's house. Tia and Jenny and I will fix all of your favorite foods, including that mayonnaise chocolate cake you're so wild about."

Lucy pictured her ruined legs. If she didn't take the pills, and went to rehab instead, she vowed not to leave there, no matter how much she hated it, until the weather had turned cold. That way, she could wear jeans without anyone commenting on how hot she must be and asking her why she hadn't worn shorts like everyone else. But — her heart sank — it didn't get that cold until October. She would have to stay in rehab for three whole months. That was way too long to be so far away from home ... from Dash.

She decided to tell him about her legs. The

thought scared her, but two things persuaded her. The first was, she wanted to be fair. Dash had a right to know. Legs that looked like hers hadn't been part of the package when he first asked her out. Things had changed. Things had changed a *lot*, and he shouldn't be kept in the dark.

The second thing was, she *needed* to tell someone. She hadn't talked about what she'd seen with anyone, not even her mother. Talking about it would have made it so much more real.

But she had to tell Dash. She didn't know how, exactly . . . what words could she use to describe what she'd seen? Her mother and the doctors had assured her that her legs would look better after a while, that there was always plastic surgery for the worst of the scars. So maybe she could tone down what she told Dash, not be too graphic. She had a tendency to exaggerate. This would not be a good time to do that. But she had to be honest. She needed to gauge his reaction. That wouldn't mean much if she sugarcoated the truth.

On Wednesday afternoon, the weather was gray and rainy outside her windows. Lucy waited until everyone else was leaving. Then she asked Dash to stay. She ignored Jenny's comment as she left the room that she'd see Dash later. Why shouldn't Jenny see him later? They were friends.

"You need to know something about my legs," Lucy said when Dash was seated beside her bed and holding her hands in his. She was pleased that her voice was steady, belying how nervous she was. "I mean, something besides the fact that no one knows if I'll ever walk again. Something else."

"You'll walk again," he said confidently, squeezing her hand. His strong, square face was very tanned, his blond hair almost platinum from hours spent in the sun. His eyes in the midst of all that bronze looked very blue and matched perfectly his knit shirt. "Nothing could keep you down for very long, Luce. Everybody knows that. It's one of the things I love about you. And it's why I'm not worried."

Lucy shifted uncomfortably in the bed. "That's not what I want to talk about. I'm talking about the way . . . the way they look. My legs. I saw them. No one wanted to show me, but I made them do it." Her eyes had been on her blanket, but now they moved to Dash's face and she looked directly into his eyes. "It's bad, Dash. It's really bad. They were so smashed up, and then there were all those surgeries, all that stitching up." Then, because that didn't seem to be enough, she described more explicitly what had happened to her legs and what they looked like now.

She had to give him credit. He didn't shudder or draw away. If he paled just a bit, it was hard to see beneath that deep tan. "Well, they'll fix all of that, Lucy," he said in that same confident tone of voice. "Don't worry about it. Anyway," he added, grinning at her, "beauty's only skin deep, remember? Who cares what your legs look like, as long as they work?"

She took another stab at making him see the truth of it, but he wasn't listening. He wanted to talk about the upcoming school year, and he wanted to talk about it as if nothing in the world had changed. Lucy let him. Dash talked on and on about their lives as if everything were still the same. She let herself believe that it was, just for a little while.

He certainly kissed her the same way. Her legs might not work, but there wasn't anything wrong with her lips. Or her arms, which folded around his neck tightly, just as they always had. She allowed herself to be held comfortingly against Dash's warm, safe, chest, and she let herself think, just for a minute or two, that maybe he was right, maybe nothing *had* changed, maybe everything would be just fine.

It wasn't until he'd left and she was alone in her room again that she thought uneasily, But you never thought beauty was only skin deep, Dash. If you did, you'd have dated some of the plainer girls at school, and you wouldn't have been so cranky on the nights when your hair wouldn't lie just so on your head, and you wouldn't have made those cruel comments when the Nelson twins, who are both very overweight, walked by in the halls.

Dash had sounded sincere when he'd said that beauty was only skin deep. But nothing he'd done or said since Lucy had met him proved it was really what he believed.

And too, he hadn't actually seen her legs. He had said, "Come on, how bad can it be?" So, even though she'd described as accurately as she could without being totally gross exactly what she had seen when the bandages came off, it was obvious he was in denial. Just as she had been until she saw the damage with her own eyes.

Or maybe it was just that Dash's imagination wasn't finely honed to the point where he could picture what she was describing.

What difference did it make, anyway? How her legs looked? The really important thing was, they were never going to work properly again. If they never looked any better, she could always keep them covered. But if they never did what she wanted them to, she'd be helpless.

As for Dash, she could see him dating a girl who wore jeans and long skirts to hide scarred legs. He wasn't a leg man. What she couldn't see, though, was Dash dating a girl in a wheelchair. Dash was normal and healthy, he was athletic, and he loved to dance. So did she. The difference was, he *could*. She couldn't. Impossible to believe that the legs she'd seen yesterday would ever again support her weight on the dance floor . . . or anywhere else.

Chapter 11

Lucy's ongoing depression deepened whenever anyone mentioned Twin Willows. It was maddening, the way the nurses talked casually about the rehab hospital, as if Lucy were going off to summer camp.

"You'll meet other kids your age who are in the same fix," Nurse Bassett said as she unhooked one of Lucy's IVs. The need for steady doses of antibiotics had ended, and Lucy's arms were now free of all embedded needles. The sense of relief as the last one was removed was enormous. "That's always a help," the nurse added kindly. "Talking to other people who understand what you're going through."

The younger blond nurse, whose name was Kelly Downs, chatted on inanely about what kind of clothes Lucy should have her mother pack for her.

"I'm not going off to college," Lucy snapped,

annoyed more by the sight of Kelly's healthy, tanned legs beneath the too-short white uniform than by the nurse's friendly chatter. Lucy knew the pain was shortening her temper. But she stubbornly refused to dip into her cache of pills again. There was so little time left. She was going to have to make up her mind soon. Almost every night she cried herself to sleep, though no one knew that. "I'm going to another hospital, Kelly, where I'll be in a wheelchair. What I'm going to be wearing isn't on my list of priorities right now."

Nurse Downs stopped smoothing and straightening Lucy's sheets. "Yeah, you're right," she said slowly, deliberately. "Probably isn't room on that list for wardrobe, what with self-pity taking up so much room." She turned and left the room.

"Hey, what about my water pitcher?" Lucy, flushed with anger, called after her. "It's empty!" But Downs was gone.

Her comment disturbed Lucy. When Tia and Kendra, minus Jenny, arrived that afternoon, they'd barely taken seats when Lucy asked abruptly, "Do I act like I feel sorry for myself?"

"No, of course not," Kendra replied immediately.

"Yeah, you do," Tia disagreed. "But so what? Who wouldn't? Why? Did Dash say something?"

That caught Lucy off guard. She frowned. "Dash? No, it wasn't Dash." Then, uneasy, she followed up with, "Why, did he say something to you? Did he tell you he thought I was feeling sorry for myself? Because if he didn't tell you that, why would you think that I'd heard it from him?" The only conversations she'd had with Dash since she'd told him about her legs had been over the telephone. They'd been brief and unsatisfying. He hadn't been to visit at all, saying he was "really, really busy." Right. Maybe she'd made a terrible mistake telling him. Too late now.

But Tia shook her head. "No, I didn't mean that. Dash hasn't said anything to me. He barely speaks to me."

"That's because he knows you blame him for Lucy's accident," Kendra said matter-of-factly. She was perched on the foot of Lucy's bed, looking very summery in brief white shorts and a yellow tank top. She was very tanned. Especially, Lucy noticed with envy, her legs, bare except for a pair of white strap sandals. "You've done everything but come right out and accuse him and Jenny, Tia. So why would Dash talk to you?"

"I don't *care* if Dash talks to me." Tia, in a short, very full, white skirt and a red short-sleeve T-shirt, her thick, dark hair fastened with a loose ponytail, stood beside the head of

Lucy's bed, glaring at Kendra. Of Lucy, she asked, "If Dash didn't accuse you of self-pity, who did? Someone must have. You wouldn't have come up with such a dreary thought all by yourself."

"I come up with lots of dreary thoughts these days," Lucy said with a sigh and a laugh. She wished her friends had worn jeans. Was that why Downs had accused her of self-pity? Because she envied other people their strong, healthy legs? She couldn't help it. "But you're right, I didn't come up with this one. One of the nurses did." She sighed again. "She's right. So are you, Tia. I have been feeling sorry for myself. I can't face the thought of going so far away to rehab." Maybe she wouldn't have to face it. She had the pills, hiding in the drawer. Her cache hidden inside the tissue had grown. She might even have enough. . . . Tears stung Lucy's eyelids. "All I want to do is go home. I want everything to be the way it was before."

As Lucy's tears spilled over, Tia plucked a tissue from the box on the nightstand, and used it to gently wipe Lucy's cheeks dry. Her own dark eyes were suspiciously bright. "Sure you do. Anyone would. That's not self-pity, Luce. It's just . . . normal."

"You think?"

"I don't think, I know. I'd feel exactly the same way. But look, we'll all drive up to see you every chance we get. We won't let you rot in that place, I promise."

"It's a four-hour trip, both ways," Lucy pointed out. They might come at first, maybe even more than once. Twice, maybe. But then the trip would become a drag and they'd be busy with their own lives and they'd forget how much Lucy needed to see them. She'd be alone, then. Really alone.

The more she thought about it, the more sense it made to take charge of her own life, swallow the pills before it was too late. She knew everyone would hate her for it. Her mother, Elizabeth, even Tim, Dash and her friends, all would think her a coward and despise her for taking the easy way out. They would never understand. She'd never even thought of doing such a horrible thing as long as she'd had hope that her legs would eventually be as good as new. The old Lucy was already dead, anyway. She'd died in the accident. If people really loved her, they'd understand why she couldn't keep going as this new and helpless Lucy.

"Your hair needs brushing," Tia said then, turning toward the nightstand.

Lucy drew in her breath sharply as Tia pulled open the nightstand drawer and reached inside, searching with her hand for Lucy's hairbrush.

But she found only the brush, not the tissue-wrapped cache of pills.

Lucy exhaled in relief as Tia's hand emerged holding the hairbrush. "A four-hour trip is nothing," Tia said as she began brushing Lucy's hair in smooth, rhythmic strokes. "Maybe we'll all stay overnight in a motel or something. Make a holiday out of it. Wouldn't that be fun, Ken? Then we could visit Lucy two days in a row before coming back here."

Lucy brightened a little. But her mood changed again quickly as Kendra answered with a distinct lack of enthusiasm, "Yeah, sure. If Dash and Jenny want. They always seem to be busy lately. You'd better check with them first."

An uneasy silence filled the room. To erase it as quickly as possible, Lucy asked, "What could they be busy with? It's summer. No more track, no classes, and Dash's job at the market is part time. Jenny doesn't even have a job." She fixed her eyes on Kendra's face, willing Kendra to look at her instead of the blanket, which she seemed to be studying carefully. "Ken! What is it exactly that's keeping my boyfriend and my friend so occupied these days? And now that you mention it, why didn't they come with you this afternoon? Where are they?"

"Dash is working," Kendra answered, her eyes still on the blanket. "And Jenny had some shopping to do, she said. Forget about them, Lucy. They'll come with us when we visit you at Twin Willows, I promise. They *will*."

Tia gave Lucy's hair one final swipe with the brush and yanked open the nightstand drawer. Perhaps because the discussion about Dash and Jenny had irritated her, she pulled too hard. The metal drawer flew free of its base and fell to the floor with a sharp, clanking sound.

Lucy gasped as its contents spilled out across the white tile.

"Sorry," Tia said, and knelt on the floor to scoop everything back into place. Her thin fingers worked quickly, nimbly, collecting the emery boards, the comb, the pale-pink lipstick Lucy only bothered to apply when Dash was expected, the pen, the tiny black address book . . .

Lucy, watching her, couldn't breathe. There it was at Tia's left elbow, the small, neat puff of white tissue, its edges still folded securely around her hoard. If those edges unfolded, Tia would see . . . she'd know . . . she'd be disbelieving at first, then livid. . . . She'd tell someone, and then Lucy would be dispatched in haste up to the psych ward. Everyone would know.

A pack of gum, a small box of breath mints, Lucy's toothbrush in its plastic holder, the red-and-white striped tube of toothpaste, and now, finally, Tia's hand reached for the white bundle.

Please, Lucy prayed, please . . .

Everything should have been all right then, because Tia had already picked up the tissue without disturbing its edges and was about to deposit it in the drawer. Since that was the last item, she would have then replaced the drawer and closed it and Lucy would have heaved a sigh of relief. Except that it wasn't, because at that precise moment, Lucy's brother Tim stuck his head in the doorway and called out, "I brought pizza, Luce."

The sudden, unexpected voice startled Tia. Still kneeling, she dropped the bundle.

The edges unfolded and fat white capsules spilled out around Tia's full, white skirt.

Tia's head whipped around. Her eyes met Lucy's. And Tia understood the truth instantly.

In the next moment, Lucy realized that for the rest of her life, however short or long that might be, she would owe Tia Perez a debt so enormous, it would be impossible to repay. Because Tia, in one swift, unobtrusive movement, covered the pills with the folds of her skirt.

Kendra, who had turned her head toward the doorway at the sound of Tim's voice, had noticed nothing out of the ordinary. And even if Tia hadn't moved so swiftly, Tim was too far away from where she knelt to spot white capsules rolling across white tile or along the folds of a white skirt.

Only Tia knew.

And Lucy.

"Pizza would be great," Tia said in a perfectly normal voice. "But we'll need something to drink. Lucy's water pitcher is empty. Ken, how about if you two run downstairs and grab us all some soda?"

Kendra didn't argue, and when Tim had deposited the warm, aromatic pizza box on a chair, the two left.

Tia wasted no time. Scrunching up the folds of her skirt to hold the pills captive, she stood up and faced Lucy. Her brown eyes were black with anger, her olive cheeks flushed. "I don't *believe* you!" she hissed, moving close to the head of the bed. "Tell me I'm wrong, Lucy. Tell me I'm crazy. Tell me some nurse screwed up and dumped these pills in your drawer by mistake."

Lucy said nothing. But she found herself wishing that almost anyone other than Tia had found the pills. A nurse, a doctor, even Dash. They might not have looked at her with as much contempt as Tia, who hated cowardice almost more than anything.

Then she reminded herself that someone *else* might not have covered for her. She would be on her way to the psych ward right this very minute.

"This is why you've seemed so weird lately,"

Tia said darkly. "Because you weren't taking your pills. You were hoarding them. You weren't being weird, you were in pain, you idiot!" She whirled and disappeared into the bathroom. Lucy heard a flushing sound. When Tia came back out, her expression grim, her skirt was hanging in a normal fashion. The pills were gone.

"I hadn't decided to take them," Lucy said in a small voice, "not yet. You probably won't believe that, but it's true. I just . . . I just needed to know I had them, in case . . ." her voice trailed off.

"In case *what*, Lucy? In case you decided to be a total moron?" Tia, angry tears in her eyes, plopped into the chair beside the bed, regarding the patient with a steady, accusing gaze. "God, Lucy, if there's one thing I never thought you'd turn out to be, it's a coward."

Lucy's defenses sprang into action. "You think it's okay for terminal cancer patients to plan their own deaths, in their own time. You've said so."

Tia leaned forward in her chair. "You're *not* terminal, Lucy. You don't have cancer. You had an accident, that's what you had, and it wrecked your legs. But they're going to get better. At rehab."

"You haven't seen them. If you'd seen them, like I have, you'd know that's not true. They're *not* going to get better. Ever. It's not possible. They're . . . they're disgusting. Nobody could walk on those legs. Nobody."

"You're not even going to try?"

Terrified that Tim and Kendra would return and overhear, Lucy said hastily, "Well, I guess I have to now, don't I? I don't have any choice. So you can quit worrying. I already told you I hadn't decided yet, and I probably wouldn't have done it even if you hadn't flushed the pills. But now that you have, we can end this conversation."

Tia stretched out both arms. Her hands were closed fists. When she opened them, fat, white capsules seemed like eggs in a bird's nest in the palms of her hands.

Lucy's jaw dropped. "I thought you —"

"I was going to. Then I figured if you really wanted to do something so stupid, you'd find a way. So I decided the pills aren't the problem. *You're* the problem, Lucy." Tia dropped the capsules onto Lucy's blanket. "There. If you really don't care how your mom would feel, how hurt and angry Elizabeth and Tim and all of your friends would be, then go ahead." Tia kept her eyes fixed on Lucy's, and Lucy didn't have the courage to look away. "But," Tia continued, "I just keep thinking about how scared we all were when we thought you were going to die. That's why I'm so mad at you now. Your mom kept praying. I could hear her. What she said was, Please, please, let my little girl live, don't let her die. I cried just listening to her. That's what we *all* cared about, Lucy. That you would get to live. And you did. You *did* get to live, when all the doctors said that you probably wouldn't. I can't tell you how glad everyone was that you were going to make it. Everyone was smiling and hugging one another out there in the waiting room when we got the news, and some of us were crying, but we were crying from relief, that's all." Tia's angry tears spilled over, wetting her cheeks. "And now it's like you don't even care, not if you'd go ahead and do something so stupid and hurt us all over again! You're my best friend in the whole world, Lucy. You can't leave me. I need you here. You don't even *know* for a fact that you'll never walk again. You can't know that, not for sure. You could at least try."

Lucy had never felt so selfish in her life. Not even when she'd thrown a fit about her mother selling their house after her father died. All she'd been thinking about lately was her own misery. She'd been so discouraged, so scared, she hadn't allowed herself to think of what that kind of cop-out would do to her mother . . . or anyone else.

Her own eyes filled with tears. She looked at Tia with a plea for understanding. "I just . . .

I can't . . . a wheelchair . . . forever . . . Tia, I can't . . ."

The anger left Tia's eyes. "I know it stinks. But you don't know that it will be forever. Can't you at least try? I'll help, I will, any way that I can. We all will. Just go to rehab, okay and give it a shot? If you really, really hate it, I'll drive up and spring you myself, I promise."

Lucy was crying openly now, too. "I'll go, Tia. I'll hate it, I know I will, but I'll go. And I'll try. I *will*." She flicked at the capsules with a finger. "Flush them, go ahead, flush them now, before Tim and Kendra come back. I don't think I would have taken them, anyway. I hate cowards, too, y'know. And thanks, Tia, for not saying anything when you saw those pills." Alarm flared in Lucy. "You're not going to tell my mother, are you?"

Blotting her own tears with a tissue, Tia smiled weakly. "Tell her what? That her daughter is an idiot? That would be redundant. I'm sure she already knows."

And then Tia was hugging Lucy, who was crying and laughing, promising that she would never, never think of doing such a dumb thing again, no matter what. She was pretty sure she meant it.

"Hey, what's the deal?" Tim asked as he and Kendra entered the room carrying sweating cans of soda. "Somebody die or something?"

Lucy laughed as she dried her own eyes. Tia jumped up, both fists closed around the pills, to run to the bathroom. When Lucy heard the flushing sound again, she let out an accepting sigh. Then she turned her attention to Tim and Kendra.

"No," she said, her hand unsteady as she reached for the soda, "that's just it. Nobody died. And nobody's going to." Then she checked to make sure they'd brought diet soda. She had no intention of arriving at that horrible rehab place weighing two hundred pounds.

Chapter 12

Lucy was discharged from Vassar Brothers Hospital and sent to the Twin Willows rehabilitation facility on a hot and muggy Wednesday morning in early August. The weather didn't help her dark mood. The sky was a dismal gray, and the light rain falling from it, sending up vapor from the steamy sidewalks at the entrance, reminded her of the fateful night when she had rushed from Kendra's house.

As an orderly carefully deposited her on the rear seat of her grandfather's station wagon, she realized that she hadn't been in a car since that night. She wished it were a bright, dry, sunny day. If it were, any memory she had of that night would stay hidden in her subconscious or wherever it was that bad memories lurked.

Her teeth clenched in dread of the long ride ahead.

With mixed feelings, she'd said good-bye to the hospital staff and to those friends who had come to see her off. The relief at being discharged after two months was tempered by anxiety about where she was going. If only she were being taken straight home!

She took the bouquet of pink and sky-blue Mylar balloons the staff had given her, and the box of candy Dash had brought even though she'd told him she was trying to keep the calories down, and the book from Jenny, and the magazines from Ken and Tia. She forced a smile when she'd been deposited in her wheelchair, and thanked everyone for all they'd done for her during her stay. Because that was what you did when you left a hospital, if you had any manners at all. Even Dr. Tolliver came by to wish her luck. And Dr. Smythe-Collins patted her shoulder and said, "We expect great things from you, Lucy. Don't disappoint us, okay?"

Lucy said, "I'll try not to." But she was thinking how she hated the way her wasted, skinny legs dangled uselessly beneath the long, flowered skirt she had insisted upon. Kelly Downs had helped her dress. Like a million other small tasks, dressing herself was something Lucy had always taken for granted. But she had learned how impossible that was when you couldn't stand up. It had enraged her. She was angry all the time now, rage replacing the depression. "Your legs won't always be like this," Kelly had assured her as she tied a totally unnecessary Doc Martens boot on Lucy's left foot. "Or look like this, either. You wouldn't believe what they can do these days for injuries like yours."

No, Lucy had thought, I probably wouldn't believe it. How could anyone make the dead weights that hung from her hips work again?

Dash's good-bye kiss had been long and sweet and thorough. They knew it would have to last. He had promised to visit her in rehab, although he had added warningly, "Got a job, though, darlin', can't be taking off too much time or they'll get somebody else. Got to be saving for college, right?"

College. Lucy wondered if she would ever get there. She'd been planning on it since sixth grade. And if she was able to go, would she have to settle for a school that was wheelchair-accessible but didn't have the courses she wanted? Just another item added to the long list of things she wanted but couldn't have now.

She didn't want to think about that. She was too nervous about rehab to think about anything else.

Her grandparents were transporting her to the new hospital because her mother had an important meeting at ten-thirty. "It could mean a really hefty commission, Lucy," Sara had explained the day before, "and I can't afford to turn that down just now. Grandma and Grandpa will drive you up to Twin Willows, and help you get settled. I'll be up to visit the first chance I get."

Lucy didn't mind. Her grandparents were cool. And the back of the station wagon would give her more room to stretch out.

Though the trip hadn't excited her, she had looked forward to being outside again. It had been so long. One warm, sunny afternoon, Kelly Downs had wheeled Lucy out to one of the patios and let her sit in the fresh air for a while. But Lucy had been so painfully conscious of curious stares from other patients and visitors, she'd been unwilling to venture out a second time.

It would be good to feel the air on her face, rain or no rain. To that end, she cracked the rear window open a little, unmindful of the mist that blew in through the opening. She breathed it all in, forgetting for a moment her dreaded destination, feeling nothing but grateful for the moment to be out in the real world once again.

But they had only driven a few hundred yards away from the hospital when the motion of the car, the sound of the tires hitting the wet pavement, and the haze outside the windows, all of it so eerily familiar, filled her with sudden terror. She could feel an overwhelming fear swelling inside of her, rising like icy water throughout her body. She had never felt anything like it before. Her stomach turned over, her muscles tensed, and her heart began beating rapidly. Her breath quickened to short, painful gasps. Then her stomach actually began to hurt, cramping and aching as if some giant vise were squeezing her insides together. She had to put her hands on her stomach and press against it in an effort to soothe it. She felt as if she was dying, and it occurred to her that perhaps she was. They'd discharged her too soon. Her body wasn't ready.

Her grandmother, in the front seat, heard the sharp change in Lucy's breathing and turned her head to see. "Lucy? What's wrong? Are you sick?"

Lucy didn't *know* what was wrong. She only knew she had to get out of the car . . . had to . . . couldn't breathe in here . . . couldn't. But how could she get away when she couldn't even walk? Couldn't throw the door open, couldn't jump out, couldn't run. "I . . . don't . . . know," she gasped, one hand moving from her stomach to her throat because her throat was suddenly closing on her. Breathing was becoming impossible. "Got to . . . get out of . . . the car!" Desperate, frantic, she reached behind her to yank at the door handle.

"Sweetie, we just started," her grandfather protested mildly. But when he glanced quickly over his shoulder and saw the look on Lucy's face, he slammed on the brake. The car skidded slightly, causing Lucy to gasp in terror, before coming to a full stop on the side of the road. "What is it?" her grandfather asked. "What's wrong?"

"It's all right," Lucy's grandmother said, reaching into her purse. "I have something to give her. Dr. Altari was afraid this might happen." A moment later, she thrust a small, yellow pill at Lucy. "Here, honey, take this. Hand me the thermos of water, Jake."

They waited by the side of the road for the small, yellow pill to take effect.

When Lucy's breathing had regulated itself and the pain in her stomach had subsided, she asked shakily, "What *was* that? It was almost worse than anything in the hospital. I felt like I was dying."

"Panic," her grandmother said, taking the thermos Lucy handed her. "You had a panic attack. The doctors warned me that it might happen the first time you were in a car again. I should have given you the tranquilizer before we left. I'm sorry, honey."

Now that she was calmer, Lucy was able to say a bit breathlessly, "Not your fault. Who knew? It . . . it won't happen again, will it?" The attack had left her completely drained. "Like every time I get into a car?"

"No, not likely. The doctor gave me the impression that it might happen the first time you rode in a car. But he sounded like it would just be a one-time thing." She waved a crystalline packet containing three or four more of the yellow pills in the air. "But if you feel it coming on again, you just say so and I'll give you one of these."

The attack, as horrible and frightening as it was, served a purpose. It left Lucy so exhausted, she fell asleep shortly after they began traveling again.

When she awoke, the car was turning up a long, wide, curving driveway leading to a huge, white-brick, four-story building sprawled at the top of a grassy green slope. Lucy blinked in sleepy confusion at the sight of countless, occupied wheelchairs dotting the slope. Some of the occupants were reading, some were working on handicrafts, some were writing. A few waved at her as the station wagon passed on up the hill.

Lucy guessed, then, where they were. But as if to confirm her guess, her eyes, still heavy from sleep, darted over to the large, white, wooden sign perched on the grass on her right.

Twin Willows Rehabilitation Facility, Twin Willows, N.Y.
Welcome.

Ready or not, she had arrived at her new home.

Part Two

Part Two

Chapter 13

The building Lucy was wheeled into was old.
Her grandfather told her it had been a summer
resort for years before being sold to a medical
organization. The lobby was high-ceilinged and
spacious. It was clean, but dimly lit. Dark wood
paneling covered the walls. The floors were
scuffed, bare hardwood, the ceiling white tile
squares. Comfortable-looking furniture, a tweed
sofa and two matching chairs, rested against
one wall.

Lucy saw no one as the attendant wheeled
her to a tall, semi-circular desk at the far end of
the lobby. Her grandparents trailed along behind. It was quiet inside the building, and it felt
damp, as if it had just been washed. Lucy told
herself that was probably because of the
weather. She smelled bacon ... from breakfast?

She paid no attention to the preliminaries of

being signed in as a resident of Twin Willows. The man behind the desk, tall and thin, dressed in a white knit shirt and white shorts, seemed nice enough, but she let her grandparents sign the forms and tend to the details while she glanced around her pessimistically. Not enough light. Too damp. Too big, no feeling of coziness. I'm not going to like it here, Lucy told herself clearly. She was assailed then by a wave of loneliness so strong that, had she been standing, it might have knocked her to the floor.

"Come along, then," the man said, his voice matter-of-fact, as if he were totally unaware of Lucy's state of mind. "We'll get you settled in your room before lunch. That's at twelve. Your grandparents can finish the paperwork down here, and then they can stay and eat with you if you want." In a kinder voice, he added, "I know the first day is always hard. It gets easier, I promise."

How would *you* know? Lucy thought rudely. The man, who was tall and skinny, had two perfectly good, though bony, legs. His white shorts and knit shirt made Lucy think again of summer camp. Last summer, she had been a counselor at a great camp in the Catskills. She had planned to do that again this year, to earn college money. But . . .

Why think about it? It hadn't happened. Wouldn't happen. Maybe never again. To stop thinking about all of the things that might not ever happen again, Lucy concentrated on lunch. It surprised her that she was hungry, but she was. Of course, this *was* a hospital, so it probably served hospital food. Maybe that all by itself would curb her appetite and she wouldn't have to start counting calories.

They saw no one in the elevator, which creaked like the floors in an old house as it rose, and no one in the hall on the third floor, where they stopped.

"Are you sure there are other people here?" Lucy asked the clerk as he pushed her chair down a wide, dim hallway lined with numbered doors. "Where is everyone?"

He laughed. "Oh, you'll have plenty of company. We're booked solid right now."

As if it were a hotel.

"We have quite a few patients your age, as a matter of fact. They're at morning activities."

Lucy bit back a sarcastic remark. If the others were wheelchair-bound, like her, just how "active" could they be? What were they doing, weaving baskets? Certainly not swimming, or playing tennis, or running track or bicycling or jogging. Not *those* activities.

"But they'll be at lunch. You'll meet them all then."

The thought was frightening. She was going to be introduced to a whole horde of strangers at one time? What were they going to do, wheel her into the center of the room and announce her arrival as if she were the new attraction at the circus? She didn't feel like meeting anyone. Not yet.

Maybe he just meant they'd all be having lunch at the same time. She was glad again that her grandparents would be staying. She could talk to them, ignoring everyone else and pretending she wasn't the new kid on the block.

She sat in her chair in the middle of the room and glanced around. "I guess they didn't waste a lot of money on decorating." There was a single bed draped to the bare, hardwood floor with a pink bedspread. A dark wooden nightstand stood beside the bed, and a wide dresser in the same dark wood was parked against the opposite wall. There were a few pictures of gardens and fields on the walls.

A metal pulley arrangement hung from the ceiling over the bed. Lucy guessed that was to help a patient — that would be *her* — pull herself up after awakening. The nightstand held only a small lamp with a pink shade, and a round, white plastic clock. There was no telephone. She would have to make her way to the pay phone she had seen in the hall to call her friends. One white-curtained, tall window was half open, with an old-fashioned wooden screen inserted to keep out insects. The window was too narrow to allow an abundance of light, giving the room a dim, hazy atmosphere.

She smelled pine-cleaning solution and something else . . . medicine, she thought distastefully. It reminded her of the other hospital, and the surgeries and the infections and the pain. "It looks a lot like one of the cabins at summer camp."

Her attendant, whose name tag read PETE, laughed. "It's not the Hilton," he admitted ruefully. "But," pointing to a door on his right, "there's a bathroom right here, fully equipped. And the food is pretty good."

I don't want the food to be good, Lucy thought but didn't say. "When do they start torturing me?"

"Not on your first day. They help you get acclimated first."

Acclimated. As if the climate itself was actually different here. "So that means tomorrow?" The sooner she started therapy, the sooner she'd get out of this place.

"Right. If you want, I'll stay with you until your family comes upstairs." He peered down at her from behind thick-lensed glasses. "Unless you want to be alone." He said this last hopefully, so Lucy assumed he had things to do.

She waved him away. "Move me over to the window, and I'll just study the scenery until my grandparents show up. Go ahead. I'm a little too old for a baby-sitter."

A voice from the doorway said indignantly, "Hey, that's *my* line! One of the first things I said when I got here. Copycat."

When Lucy turned her head, she met the eyes of a pale, overweight boy in a chair identical to hers, his hands on the wheels, an amused smile on his face. He wore jeans and a red shirt, and she could see that his legs hung limply, no more useful than her own. "Anthony Manning," the boy told her. He wheeled expertly through the doorway to arrive at her side. "I'm the resident smart mouth. You're not here to usurp my place, are you? I can't stand competition."

"Tony Manning," Pete said, "meet Lucy St. Cloud." A look of barely disguised relief on his face, he told Lucy, "I'll leave you in good hands. Tony's been here six months. He knows all of our dirty little secrets. But believe only half of what he tells you. The other half is pure fiction." He reached out and shook Lucy's hand. "Good luck. Try to trust us, okay? We know what we're doing."

"Do they?" Lucy asked Tony Manning when Pete's long legs had carried him out the door. "Know what they're doing?"

He shrugged. "You're asking me? Didn't Pete just say I'd been here half a year already? That's six months too long. If they did know what they were doing, wouldn't I be home by now, vegging out in front of the tube? We have cable. They don't have it here." He wheeled back and forth for a few minutes, then began twirling his chair in lazy circles around the floor.

Show-off, Lucy thought. She could barely steer hers in a straight line. "Six months ..." she breathed in alarm. *Six*? In six months, Elizabeth would be married and Dash and the others would be halfway into their junior year. She couldn't be in this place that long. She'd die.

"So what's your story?" He stared at her boldly, as if there were no possibility that she might not want to confide in him. "Car? Train? Plane? Diving accident? A bad bungee jump?"

Well, why not? She was going to have to answer questions sooner or later. People could see with their own eyes that something had happened to her. They'd want to know what. "Car. Van, actually. I had an argument with a very large tractor-trailer rig. I lost." Just saying it made her angry again at the truck driver.

"I can see that. They tell you you'd walk again?"

The question was put so bluntly, Lucy felt as if he'd slapped her. "Boy, you don't waste any time, do you?"

"I'm not very tactful." His eyes were a pale blue. Lucy had an eerie feeling they might turn icy when this boy was mad, though she couldn't have said where the feeling came from. He didn't seem angry at all. "One thing I learned during my weeks in the first hospital was not to waste time. You never know how much you really have. So did they? Tell you that you'd walk again?"

She couldn't bear to admit that they hadn't actually said that. The doctors and her mother had used words like "hope" and "possibility" and "all things considered" . . . but no one had actually *said* that she would definitely, absolutely walk again. "Sure," she answered lightly. "They said I would. But I have to have therapy first."

He nodded knowingly. His hair was sandy brown and needed cutting. He wouldn't have been bad-looking if he had looked healthier. There was the excess weight, and his pallor made him seem old and tired. But Lucy was sure he was about her age. "Uh-huh. That means they didn't give you any guarantees. I know the feeling. When I first came here, they kept telling me if I'd just work harder, I'd be on my feet again in no time. Took me months to figure out that wasn't going to happen. Ever. No one came right out and told me. I just knew."

Lucy's stomach dove. He was going to be in that chair for the rest of his life? "What happened to you?"

"Drunk-driving accident. Prom night. Last year. My date wasn't as lucky as I was. She died."

He said it matter-of-factly, but Lucy gasped. "Oh, my god. I'm sorry. I hope they got the driver."

"Oh, they did. He ended up in this chair." Tony smiled ruefully at the shocked expression on Lucy's face. "Don't sweat it. I've learned to deal. There's a shrink upstairs on the fourth floor, Dr. Giardello. She sees a lot of me. Been a big help. You'll see her, too. Everyone has to. She'll ask you all kinds of questions about what happened to you, and how you feel about it." He drew his chair closer to Lucy's and leaned forward. "If you ever want to get out of here, tell her you're not angry. Tell her you understand that these things happen, and it could have been a lot worse, you could have died, and you're grateful you're alive and the whole thing has taught you what's really important." He sat back in his chair. "They like it when you say things like that. They write it in your file. If stuff like that is in there, you'll get out sooner. Trust me."

His words made Lucy uneasy. "Can't I just leave when I want to? You make this place sound like a prison. It's not."

Tony laughed. "Depends on your point of view. Your family won't want you released until you're good as new, 'cause it's too big a nuisance having someone in a wheelchair around the house . . . the doorways aren't big enough, and what if you have stairs, that kind of thing? It's a pain. So it's not really whether or not *you* think you're ready, it's when the people on the outside are ready for you. Of course," he added slyly, "since you're going to walk again, there's no problem."

He didn't believe she would walk again. Because that was her greatest fear, Lucy asked sharply, "Is that why you haven't been discharged? Because your family isn't ready for you?"

His face clouded over, and she was sorry immediately. "Not exactly," he answered, turning his chair toward the door. "Those of us who, unlike you, will always need help, stay until our insurance runs out. Then, ready or not, we're out of here. I have another two months. Lucky me." Then, without saying good-bye, he wheeled to the doorway and was gone.

Lucy's grandparents arrived a minute or two later, announced lunch, and they all went downstairs to the cafeteria, which was in the basement. Lucy saw no sign of Anthony Manning, and was relieved. They hadn't got off to a very good start. She didn't tell her grandparents about him. They'd assume she had made a friend already. She didn't think she had.

The cafeteria was brighter than her room upstairs, cheerfully painted yellow and white, with long, metal tables lower than normal to accommodate wheelchairs. It had wide windows and it smelled of pizza and coffee, and it was crowded. Everyone was not chair-bound, Lucy noticed as her grandparents wheeled her to a table, then went to get their meal. Crutches and metal walkers were stationed behind chairs like bodyguards, resting until they were needed again. The sight of them filled her with fresh hope. She wouldn't mind using crutches, or even a walker, if it meant leaving this chair. There were people walking, too, without any physical aid, and she knew they weren't staff because they weren't wearing the white knit shirts. Some walked with the uncertain gait of a toddler, telling her they were learning the skill anew, just as she would have to. But they *were* walking.

A pretty girl no taller than Tia, with crew-cut blond hair, was seated at the table Lucy's grandparents selected. She had huge blue eyes and clear, smooth skin . . . but only on the left side of her face. When she turned to smile at Lucy to say hi, she revealed a long, jagged scar on her right cheek from just under her eye to her jawbone. It didn't look red or raw enough to be new.

Before Lucy could say hello, her grandparents returned to the table, bearing a tray filled with pizza and cold drinks. They greeted the girl and asked her name.

"Robin Papajohn. Motorcycle wreck," though no one had asked. "Head injury, but that turned out to be minor. It's not what put me in this chair. I also, it turned out, did a number on my lower spine. I can still use my arms, though. Anyway, the head injury is why I had to have my head shaved." She smiled. "That's why I look like a lawnmower ran over me. I used to have long, naturally curly tresses, like Nicole Kidman, if you can believe that. It's true. But I think it's growing back straight."

Lucy returned the smile. "Maybe not. It's really too short yet to tell. It could curl back up as it comes in."

Robin's smile widened. "You think?"

"Sure. Anyway, it looks cute. You have such a small face. If my hair were that short, I'd look like a guy."

"Oh, no you wouldn't! You're too pretty."

"Thanks." Lucy lifted her slice of pizza. It was piping hot, and dripping tomato sauce. No resemblance to hospital food whatsoever. There went her diet. "I guess you probably know Anthony Manning, right? I just met him. I don't think he liked me very much."

Robin sipped from her water glass. "Tony pretends he doesn't like anybody. That's just how he is. I think it's because no one in his family ever comes to visit. They're mad at him for screwing up his life. And he was madly in love with the girl who died. The one who was with him in the car? They'd been dating since eighth grade. They'd gone to the prom and were on their way home when the accident happened. He says he's dealing with it, but we all know he isn't. Tony steals sleeping pills from other patients so he won't have nightmares."

This was such a completely different picture of Tony Manning than the one Lucy had been imagining, that she couldn't think of any response. Sadness enveloped her and she fell silent, lost in dismal thought, eating slowly.

Her grandparents began talking about the center, filling Lucy in on the information they'd gathered when they signed her in.

She wanted to listen. They were probably telling her things she needed to know. Not that anything they said could make her feel better about this strange new place. But all she could think about was how Tony Manning must have felt when someone told him his girlfriend was dead and it was his fault.

Chapter 14

In a day filled with difficult moments, the worst for Lucy came when her grandparents left her alone at Twin Willows. As the station wagon pulled away, her grandmother's thin, freckled arm waving out the window, Lucy had to struggle against threatening tears. She didn't want anyone in this new place to see her crying.

"It'll be okay," Robin said gently. She had accompanied Lucy outside, claiming she needed some fresh air. But Lucy guessed that she was really there because she knew how rough the moment would be. Nice of her. "Will your family come to visit?" Robin asked. "Mine does, every weekend. It's a long drive from White Plains, but my mom never complains. And she always brings Snickerdoodles. I'll share."

Lucy swallowed her tears and cleared her throat. "What's a Snickerdoodle?"

"Sugar-and-cinnamon cookies. They're to die for. Where are you from?"

They filled each other in on basic background information as they wheeled their chairs back inside and into the elevator. To Lucy's surprise, she learned that Robin's father had been driving the motorcycle that skidded on a wet highway and flung father and daughter into a stone culvert beside the highway. Although at first Robin's head injury had seemed serious, it was actually the spinal injury that had put her in the wheelchair. That sounded far more ominous to Lucy. The brain could heal itself sometimes. The spinal cord couldn't. "Your father was driving the motorcycle? For real?"

"Yep. He used to love his bike. He hasn't ridden it since the accident." Robin sighed heavily as they exited the elevator. "I just wish my dad would stop feeling guilty. It wasn't his fault. He wasn't going too fast or anything. The bike just skidded, that's all." She stopped her chair in front of room 302. "I think he feels the worst about what happened to my face. He used to tell me all the time that I looked just like Heather Locklear. She's one of his favorites. He doesn't tell me that anymore. But one of the doctors here told me I can have the scar taken care of later." Robin shrugged. "It doesn't matter. I'm too busy trying to get out of this chair to worry about what I look like. My dad won't look at me, though. He must have the pattern on the curtains in my room memorized, because he stares at them instead of looking at me. I guess my face reminds him. He doesn't want to be reminded." In a different tone of voice, Robin said, "This is my room. 302. You're just down the hall, right? So, will your family come to visit?"

"I'm in 307. They will if they can. But my mom's in real estate and weekends are her busiest times."

Robin opened the door to her room. "What about your dad?"

"He died." Lucy began wheeling away. "Come down and see me when you feel like it."

"I will."

Exhausted from the long trip, Lucy wanted to take a nap. Another bad moment, because she couldn't figure out how to get herself from the chair into her bed. In the other hospital, there had always been an attendant to help her. She had hated that, being lifted in and out of bed like a baby, had hated feeling helpless. But now she realized just how helpful that had been, and wished that she had been more appreciative.

There was a small, round button set into the wall beside her bed. Pete had said it was to be used to summon help. Didn't she need help now? She wanted to sleep, and there was no way she could climb into that bed on her own. But when Pete had said "help" he'd probably been referring to a medical emergency of some kind. Like if you'd fallen and couldn't get up. All she wanted to do was get into bed. That could hardly be classified as an emergency.

Was she supposed to manage this feat on her own? On her first day there? Maybe she was supposed to use the pulley hanging from the ceiling. But she couldn't reach it unless she was already *in* bed. Which she wasn't. Which was the problem.

She was still sitting in her chair, staring bleakly at the button, when a voice she recognized as Tony Manning's said from behind her, "I agree, it stinks, not being able to do it yourself. Pete says we should be grateful there are places like this to help us. Personally, I'm not big on looking at the brighter side of things. Too depressing."

Lucy spun her wheelchair around to face him. She couldn't help laughing. "Looking on the brighter side of things is depressing? That sounds weird."

"True." Tony shrugged plump shoulders. "But you get my drift, right? Doesn't it fry you when people who have two good legs try to point out how lucky you are to be alive? They only do it because they can't stand it when you're depressed. Bums them out." He rolled his chair over to park beside her. "You know, like one of the yankers yesterday, he said that instead of being pissed that my family doesn't visit, I should be grateful that they have insurance. What he really meant was, I should be grateful I'm not in prison for DUI, but he was too polite to say that."

"Yankers? What's a yanker?"

Another shrug. "My word for the physical rehab people. The therapists. They yank at your legs like they're pulling taffy. I myself have never pulled taffy, but I've seen it done in old movies. It always looks like fun. Physical therapy is not fun. At least those people in the movie got candy out of all their hard work. I myself get something far less desirable."

"What?"

Tony's round face twisted into a grimace. "Pain. Big time. You'll have it, too."

"I've already had it. Still do, but it's not as bad. As for the yanking, I'll do whatever it takes to walk out of here."

"Yeah, sure. We'll all walk out on our own steam. And Demi Moore is gonna ask me to star in her next movie."

Annoyed by his skepticism, Lucy asked bluntly, "Why *aren't* you in prison?" It seemed a fair question, though Lucy knew she would never have asked it if he hadn't made her mad.

"Tammy's parents asked the prosecutor not to press charges. They said I'd be paying for the rest of my life as it was." His voice hardened. "I think maybe they were right."

Tammy. The girlfriend who had died in the accident. "I guess Pete's right, then," Lucy said, not willing yet to forgive him for doubting her ability to walk again. "You *were* lucky. Her parents could have been angry enough to want you rotting behind stone walls." She glanced around her. "These walls aren't stone."

He shrugged again. "Not that it makes any difference. They might as well be. Have you met Jude?"

"No. Just Robin. Who's Jude?"

"Jude Fairfax. Dove off a diving board and landed twisted up like a pretzel. He's learning to walk again, but he still uses his chair a lot. He gets tired, hauling that metal walker around. Says it's like carrying a couple of bowling balls around all day. He says the chair is easier."

Lucy didn't want to be linked with someone who thought the chair was easier. She said firmly, "I don't really need to be here. I could have done my therapy at home. If my mother wasn't working so many hours —"

Tony's laugh was harsh. "Sure. You bet. You sound like a new inmate in a prison movie. They all say they're innocent, that they don't belong there. *That's* never true, either. If you're here, it's because you have to be."

Lucy would have lost her temper and lashed out at him in anger then if a short but sturdy-looking woman in white shorts and knit shirt hadn't appeared in the open doorway to ask, "Anyone in here need anything?" When Lucy said she wanted to take a nap, the woman promptly strode into the room and set about the business of getting Lucy into bed. She calmly told Tony to take a hike.

"I wish. If I could take a hike," Tony responded just as calmly, "I wouldn't be in here, would I?" But he left without argument, telling Lucy he'd see her at dinner. "Grilled chicken tonight," he added as he wheeled his way to the doorway. "It's actually edible."

When he had gone, Lucy asked the aide, whose name tag read JEANNINE, "Am I going to have to wait for someone every time I want to get in or out of bed?"

Jeannine pointed to the large metal ring hanging from the ceiling pulley. "Nope. We'll show you what to do." She smiled down at Lucy. "That's what we're here for, to show you how to do for yourself. We know how important that is, getting your independence back."

"How long will that take?" Lucy asked, grateful to be out of the chair and lying flat. Her back ached.

"That depends on you. It always depends on the client."

Tactful of her to say "client" instead of "patient." It made Lucy sound less like an invalid. She would have thanked the woman if she hadn't already been falling asleep.

Dinner wasn't the nightmare she'd dreaded. Jeannine arrived at five-thirty to show Lucy how to get out of bed using the pulley. Then she helped her into her chair, saying, "You'll get the hang of it quick enough. Just don't jerk real fast or you'll pull a muscle. That hurts. But I'll be here to help you until you've got the movements down."

Robin had saved her a place at one of the tables in the dining room. Tony, already forking a huge bite of grilled chicken, was sitting on the other side of Robin. A thin, short, broad-shouldered boy with dark-red hair sat beside him. Jeannine brought Lucy's wheelchair to a halt in the space between Robin and Tony. Lucy could feel the dark-haired boy scrutinizing her carefully. She noticed he wasn't sitting in a wheelchair. A metal walker was parked by his side. Her cheeks felt warm. "It's rude to stare," she said sharply. "You'd think someone in this place would know better."

He laughed. "Sorry. You're right. I was just admiring your cheekbones."

"Jude's an artist." Tony stabbed at his chicken again, but before taking another bite, he added, "So he doesn't really need to walk again. All he really needs are his hands."

"Jude Fairfax," the boy said, leaning across Tony to thrust out a hand to Lucy. She took it, found it strong and warm. When he retrieved it, he said, "And I do need to walk again. I have plans to travel, see the world. So I'll have something interesting to paint. I want to travel on foot, not in a wheelchair."

Lucy noticed that Jude turned to look at Robin then, with what looked like affection. Love, maybe? She wondered if Robin felt the same way. Too early to tell.

There were probably lots of romances here in rehab. Wouldn't people shut away from the "real world" naturally turn to one another for comfort? Who could blame them? But she couldn't help wondering if romances that began in rehab lasted afterwards, when people were leading normal lives again. Jude might be leaving soon. Would he remember Robin when he was back out in the world?

She couldn't wait to get back upstairs and call Dash, partly because she needed to hear his voice, but partly because she also needed to connect with the "outside world."

She hadn't even been at Twin Willows a full day yet. It felt like forever.

Chapter 15

Dash wasn't home when Lucy wheeled to the pay telephone in the deserted third-floor hall and dialed his number that night. That wouldn't have disturbed her if Jenny had been home when Lucy next tried her number. But Jenny was out, too, which made Lucy uneasy. But when Tia and Kendra weren't home either, Lucy relaxed and told herself all four were out together somewhere. Having fun, of course. She was about to try her mother when the phone rang. Lucy jumped, startled. The sudden movement sent a sharp shaft of pain up her right leg. Wincing, she picked up the receiver.

And her heart jumped for joy as Dash's voice said, "Could I please speak to Lucy St. Cloud, if she's not in therapy or something?"

"Dash! It's me. I was just trying to call you. Where are you?"

"At Ken's. We're trying to figure out how

soon we can come and visit. Would Saturday be okay?"

Saturday. This was Wednesday. Saturday seemed a century away. "Sure. Robin said visitors can stay all day on the weekend, so you don't have to worry about getting here at the right time. I can't wait to see you."

"Robin? That a guy or a girl?"

Lucy smiled. He still cared enough to be jealous. "A girl. She's nice. I'll introduce you when you get here. You'll like her."

"I like *you*. Can't wait to see you." They talked for a while longer, Lucy filling him in on what she had learned so far about Twin Willows. Then Dash said, "Listen, I gotta go and tell everyone Saturday's okay. We need to make plans. See you then, but I'll call you tomorrow night. Take care. Love you. Bye."

The conversation had been much too short to suit Lucy, who faced the long, quiet evening ahead. She went into her room and sat by the window, looking out. Dusk was falling, covering the rolling, green campus with an eerie, purplish mist. If this were Seneca High, Lucy thought yearningly, couples would be walking along hand in hand, laughing and talking, carrying books and wearing backpacks. But this campus was deserted. There wasn't anyone walking along the wheelchair-wide cement paths because hardly anyone at Twin Willows walked.

She was *not* going back to school in a wheelchair.

"So, how was your first day?" Tony Manning's voice asked, again from the doorway.

Lucy wheeled to face him. "Don't you ever knock?"

"No. Anyway, your door was open."

"I was hoping for a breeze from the hallway. It's stuffy in here."

Tony wheeled into the room to park his chair opposite hers. "That's because it was empty for almost a month. The girl who was in here before you . . . left."

Lucy knew by the way he said it that there was more to the story. Curious, she asked, "She learned to walk again? How long did it take her?"

His cheeks flushed. He looked different with color in his face. Healthier. Lucy could see that he wouldn't be bad-looking if he lost weight and got more fresh air. He glanced toward the window as if he were checking out the weather. "Forget it. I shouldn't have said anything."

"Well, you did. So tell me the rest of it. Did she or did she not learn to walk again in here?"

"No." He continued to stare out the window. "Her name was Holly Buford. She just had a bicycle accident, that's all it was, but she wasn't wearing a helmet and her head slammed into the curb when she landed. Broke her neck, I think. She was so depressed when she got here she was under a suicide watch for a while. Then she seemed to get better and —"

"Tony!" Robin's voice interrupted. "Why are you telling her about Holly?" Robin sat in the doorway, her blue eyes accusing. "Lucy just got here. You don't need to be scaring her."

Lucy motioned Robin inside. "No, it's okay. I want to hear the rest of it. Go ahead, Tony."

"Her physical therapy wasn't working. Sometimes it doesn't. They should have told you that, Lucy. Someone should have told you it doesn't always work. And Holly didn't have very much to work with."

"What happened to her, Tony?" Lucy demanded.

"She got pneumonia. That happens, too, when you're lying flat on your back all the time. They took her to another hospital, but I guess she had it really bad. She died."

Lucy gasped. "Died?" Her eyes flew to Robin's face. "She's dead?"

Seeing how stricken Lucy was, Robin wheeled swiftly over to put an arm around her. "Tony's making it sound like pneumonia happens a lot here. It doesn't, Lucy. By the time we get to Twin Willows, most of us have already beaten that threat. Holly just wasn't very healthy when she got here, that's all. Don't think about it, okay? Anyway, you can sit up, so you don't have to worry about it that much. Holly couldn't sit up, because of her spine. That's why her lungs filled up with fluid."

In spite of Robin's comforting words, Lucy was thoroughly shaken. The girl who had been in this room before her had *died*? "How old was she?"

"What?"

"How *old* was she? I mean, some of the people I saw in the cafeteria were middle-aged, and some were older than that. They have lots of different ages here. How *old* was Holly?"

Robin's voice was subdued. "Sixteen."

"Oh, jeez." Her face white, Lucy sagged in her chair.

Seeing her pain, Tony said sincerely, "I shouldn't have brought it up. Sorry, Lucy. Anyway, like Robin says, you're in much better shape than Holly was when they brought her in. It's not the same thing at all."

But, though Lucy had never laid eyes on Holly Buford, she knew she would feel the girl's presence in this room every moment she was at Twin Willows.

She found that thought so unsettling that she agreed to go down to the recreation room and play cards with Tony and Robin, when what she really wanted to do was ring for an attendant to help her into bed, slide beneath the covers as if she were burrowing to safety, and stay there until her mother said she could come home.

When she did get to bed, with Jeannine's help, and the building fell silent but for the faint strains of music coming from other rooms, Lucy lay staring up at the ceiling. Quiet tears slid down her cheeks as she tried to shut out the soft whisper of Holly Buford's voice in her ear, "You know, Lucy, there are only two ways to get out of this place. Learn to walk again. Or die. Those are your choices."

I don't *know* if I'll be able to walk again, Lucy answered silently, letting the tears flow freely. But I do know I don't want to die.

Which was why she made no protest when a husky man in his thirties, who said his name was Tom, came to get her the next morning shortly after breakfast and wheeled her downstairs to a small, peach-walled physical therapy room. There were, he told her, half a dozen other therapy rooms in the facility. "Latest equipment," he said proudly as they left the elevator. "The decorating might not be anything fancy, but they don't skimp on equipment here. We've got bigger rooms, medium-size rooms, rooms with a dozen tables in them. But we always use the smaller rooms to begin with, until people get used to being here."

And she didn't argue when she found herself lying flat on a hard, narrow table while Tom began, gently at first, then not so gently, to stretch her legs. They were wrapped now in snug, elastic, beige stockings designed to promote healthy circulation. Lucy hated them. They were ugly and constricting. She wore them only because she had believed Dr. Altari when he said the stockings would help.

She was so determined that first morning, she didn't even cry out when the first twinge of pain came, or the second, or the third. As the exercises intensified, so did the pain. Lucy bit down hard on her lower lip and reminded herself of Holly's whispered message.

"I'm taking it easy on you today," Tom said at one point, "this being your first day and all. You haven't moved these legs in a long time. We don't want to overdo, or you'll be a basket of aches tomorrow."

A basket of aches. Cute terminology. Not very appropriate for the pain she was feeling. Lucy's heart sank. If he was "taking it easy" on her today, that meant that her tomorrows would be even more painful than today.

How was she going to stand it?

She would. She just would, that was all. She had to.

She did balk, however, when Tom, at the end of their session, suggested a dip in the pool, located in a separate room. Lucy paled. "Oh, no. No way. I'm not getting into a pool in front of everyone. I'd have to take off my stockings." She couldn't believe he expected her to reveal that sight to everyone. He couldn't *make* her do that, could he? He wouldn't.

"Yeah, so?" the tall, ruddy-faced young man gazed down at her. "You're right. If you leave the therapeutic stockings on, they'll get soaked. So take them off." Then comprehension dawned in his eyes, followed immediately by a look of surprise. "You think you're the only one in here with scars?" He shook his head. "Lucy, there are plenty of people in here whose scars are worse than yours. Some from burns, some from accidents. One guy got caught in a threshing machine on his farm. What do you think *his* legs look like?"

"I don't know what a threshing machine is. Anyway, you haven't *seen* my legs yet."

"I've seen pictures. They send them to me with every new patient."

Lucy couldn't remember anyone taking pictures of her legs. When had that happened? "I am *not* getting into any pool," she said heatedly. "Not unless you bring me a wetsuit that will cover my legs."

He laughed. "A wetsuit? You're kidding,

right?" He lifted her off the table and into her wheelchair, but didn't offer to push her. Instead, he stood to one side, regarding her with thoughtful eyes. "One thing you can't cling to in here, Lucy, is vanity. I'd think you'd understand that. But I'll let you off the hook today. Tomorrow, though, you start hydrotherapy. Those are the rules."

As Lucy wheeled away from the therapy room, she shook her head in disgust. Rules! It *was* like summer camp, after all. Only not as much fun. No fun at all, in fact.

She wanted to go home.

And more than that, she wanted someone to tell her exactly why her wonderful, busy, happy life had been totally destroyed. Wasn't it bad enough that her father had died? She'd had a hard time with that, but she'd kept going, hadn't she? And now this.

Why had this terrible thing happened to her? *Why?*

Chapter 16

There was more therapy on Thursday afternoon for Lucy, but none as demanding as the morning's session. After lunch, which she ate with Robin, Tony, and Jude, Lucy spent the better part of an hour practicing, with Jeannine's help, how to use the pulley and the bathroom. Everything was more difficult than Lucy had anticipated. She was also taught to do exercises on her own while she was lying in bed. They were simple leg lifts and knee bends, but they were almost as painful as the stretching Tom had done. Lucy's grimacing led Jeannine to say, "I know it hurts now, honey. But the more you do these, the easier it'll get."

That was hard for Lucy to believe. The only medication she was taking at Twin Willows was aspirin. Though it did alleviate the pain somewhat, she missed the soft, pink cloud she'd become used to in the hospital. There were times when she missed the shots and the pills so fiercely, she understood clearly how easy it would be to become addicted to the painkillers.

"I wasn't even on them that long," she confided to Robin at dinner. "It scares me that I wish I still had them, sometimes. I don't see how someone gets off them when they take them longer than I did."

Robin, who seemed very pale and tired, shrugged. "I was never on them. With my kind of injury, pain isn't that big a problem. Had a headache for a while, but all I got was aspirin. Very expensive in a hospital, aspirin. My mom finally brought a bottle from home. Cheaper that way."

Lucy noticed that Robin hadn't eaten anything. "Did you guys sneak out and get pizza this afternoon while I was being tortured?"

Robin's laugh was harsh. "Get real. Can you see us all wheeling into a pizzeria? I haven't been out of this place since I got here last January."

January? Robin had been at Twin Willows since January? Longer than Tony.

Dismay swept over Lucy. She had assumed that Robin was new at the hospital, because there was so little Robin could do. She had been here seven months and made so little progress?

Lucy pushed the thought away by focusing on Robin's comment. Why hadn't she been out of the hospital since she arrived? "Aren't we allowed out?" She had planned to ask Dash and the others to take her to the local mall. There was a picture of it in the info book she'd been given when she arrived. She wanted to buy a new sweater. As hot as the August weather was, the hospital was cool at night. She needed something to toss over her shoulders. No way was she going inside the mall. People would stare. She wasn't ready for that. She'd send Tia in to pick out a sweater.

Tony answered Lucy's question for Robin. "We're allowed out. This isn't a prison, Lucy. Problem is, who wants to be bothered with a wheelchair?" He lapsed into an account of the difficulties: "First, whoever takes you has to lift you out of the chair and into the car. That's bad enough, because most people are scared to death they'll drop you and do even more damage than you've already got. Then they have to collapse the chair and put it in the trunk or the back seat. Then, when you get wherever you're going, they have to reverse the process. It's a pain, and hardly anyone wants to go through it."

"How do you know?" Jude asked, his voice friendly enough. "You said your family hadn't been to visit you. So how could you know they'd hate bothering with your chair?"

Lucy thought the remarks rude, but Tony

failed to take offense. "I'm an observer. I've watched other patients when their families come to visit. You can tell the patient is dying to get out of here, out into the real world, and you can see that the relatives feel just the opposite. They've already driven a few miles, maybe a lot of miles, to get here, and all they want to do is sit outside and drink lemonade until it's time to leave. What they don't want to do is hassle with a wheelchair. So they make up all kinds of polite excuses — it's too hot, the traffic is terrible, the patient looks unusually tired, the tires on the station wagon are going bad — anything they can think of to park themselves right here and not move until visiting hours are over. I heard one guy tell his kid he didn't want her to get sunburned and he'd forgotten the sunscreen. Gimme a break!"

"My friends won't mind the wheelchair," Lucy said a bit too defensively because Tony's words were unsettling. "They're athletes, and strong. They'll toss this chair around like it was a Frisbee, and they'll take me anywhere I want to go."

"Well, good for you!" Tony's expression was blatantly skeptical. "Aren't you the lucky one?"

Ignoring his attitude problem, Lucy turned to Robin. "If you didn't go for pizza, why aren't you eating? Don't you like pork chops?"

"I'm just not hungry. Leave me alone, okay?"

Laying her unused fork down, Robin turned her chair and wheeled away from the table and out of the room.

"She gets like that sometimes," Jude told Lucy. "It's got nothing to do with you. She was a dancer, did you know that? Very good, according to her brother Crew. She spent the last four summers in New York City, studying at some famous dance school. Crew said she'd made some really good friends there, from all over the country, and looked forward to seeing them every summer. She's missing them when she gets like this." There was more than admiration in Jude's voice as he added, "Robin's pretty brave most of the time. But sometimes what's happened gets to her, and she can't deal."

It sounded to Lucy like Jude had a real thing for Robin. Had he told her that yet? It might cheer her up. Jude was cute, and seemed nice. Lucy toyed with her own fork, her appetite gone. "Will Robin ever dance again?"

"Oh, sure," Tony said sarcastically, "and I'll play football again and Jude will hike on foot through Europe studying the paintings of the great masters, and you'll — well, I don't know, Lucy — what is it that you did before that you want to do again?"

Angry tears clouded Lucy's vision. "Walk," she said flatly. "I'd settle for just walking again,

Tony." Although she had eaten only a few bites of her dinner, she threw down her fork as Robin had, and wheeled swiftly from the room.

Knocking loudly on Robin's door for several minutes brought no answer, and no sound from inside. Lucy was too tired to go looking for her. Instead, she went to her own room and sat by the window, looking out but not really seeing, waiting for Dash's phone call.

But every time she answered the insistent ring from the hall, the call was for someone else. When the voice on the other end finally did ask for Lucy, the voice was Tia's, not Dash's. Lucy had to ask if Tia knew where Dash was and why he hadn't called, and then was sorry she'd asked because Tia's answer was so evasive. "I think he might be working," was all she said.

They made plans for Saturday, which Tia sounded excited about. But Lucy was depressed when she hung up.

When the night aide who had replaced Jeannine came in to help her into bed, Lucy was already asleep in her wheelchair, her head tilted to one side, her hands folded in her lap.

She awoke the following morning to new aches in her legs and her back. "I was too tired to do the nighttime exercises," she told Jeannine when the aide arrived to fortify the lessons in using the overhead pulley.

"You have to do them, Lucy. The sooner you strengthen those muscles, the faster you'll be rid of the pain. Now let's see you pull yourself up like I showed you."

"I can't. And I can't go to therapy this morning, either. I hurt all over. My friends are coming to see me tomorrow. I want to be really up for them. Anyway, it can't be good for me to do those horrible exercises when I'm in so much pain."

The attendant was unrelenting. "Oh, yes it can. You only hurt because you haven't used the muscles in so long. If you take a day off, it'll just be that much worse the next time. Anyway, if I don't take you down for your therapy session, Tom'll come up and get you. And he won't be happy about it, take my word for it. You'll feel better after you eat breakfast. Come on, now, grab hold of the ring and pull."

"No. I can't. Go away and leave me alone."

Jeannine stood back from the bed, arms akimbo on her hips, regarding Lucy with a stern gaze. "Well, I guess you don't really want to walk again, after all, do you, miss? I mean, it's not that you can't. No one has said that you can't. At least, no one told *me* that. So I guess it's safe to assume that you're perfectly capable of walking out of here on your own steam, am I right? Only that's not going to happen if you don't get yourself up out of that bed right this minute and get down to breakfast. What's it going to be? You going to stay in this bed forever, or you going to do what it takes to get yourself mobile again?"

Lucy let out a heartfelt groan. She shook her head and rolled her eyes toward the ceiling. But when she had made her feelings known, she reached up and out, grabbed the ring, and pulled herself upright.

"Well, there we go!" Jeannine cried, and helped Lucy into her chair.

Robin wasn't at breakfast.

"She's up with the shrink," Jude informed Lucy. "Don't think it'll help much, though. Robin won't tell the truth. She won't tell Doc how bad she's really feeling. She never does."

"Why not?" Lucy picked unenthusiastically at her scrambled eggs.

"Because she's afraid if she says how depressed she really is, she'll be transferred to a psych hospital. There's one in town. They get a lot of business from us. Every so often, an ambulance pulls up at the back door here and someone gets carted away. We always know why, even if one of the staff says it's an infection or a heart problem or pneumonia. The truth gets around here real fast. It's almost always a psych problem."

Lucy could understand that. In spite of Jeannine's encouraging words about the possibility of her walking again, she still felt depressed. Maybe she was just missing Dash.

"You got an appointment with Giardello yet?" Tony asked.

Lucy shook her head. "No one's said anything to me. Maybe they don't think I need one."

"They don't think that." Tony broke a piece of toast in half, dipping one half in the soupy yellow of an over-easy egg on his plate. When the toast was completely covered with egg, he took a huge bite. After chewing and swallowing noisily, he added, "They never think that. You'll have to see Giardello just like everyone else. When you do, remember what I told you. Don't complain or admit that you think you got a raw deal. Doesn't look good in your file. That's why Robin won't tell Giardello the truth."

Realizing that she had no intention of eating the food on her plate, Lucy pushed it aside. "Am I *acting* like I think I got a raw deal?"

"Yeah, you are. Are you going to eat your toast?" Lucy handed Tony the toast. Waving it at her, he added, "Giardello will say your feelings are only natural, that you have every right to them. But she'll still write it down in your file, and it won't look good, I'm telling you."

He sounded so certain. And Jude didn't argue with him, so Lucy assumed Tony was right. If she ever did have to see the psychiatrist, she'd be careful not to sound like she was filled with self-pity.

Knowing that if she waited until after her physical therapy session to hunt down Robin, she'd be too tired and sore, she took the elevator back up to the third floor to knock on Robin's door again.

Still no answer. Shouldn't Robin have finished with her shrink session by now? Maybe Jude was wrong this time, and Robin *had* told the truth. Maybe she'd confessed that she was so depressed, the doctor was making arrangements to send her to a psychiatric facility.

The possibility that the only girl she'd made friends with in this place so far might be leaving horrified Lucy. She tried to quiet her fears by telling herself that Robin hadn't been depressed that long. Yesterday afternoon she'd seemed totally normal. But then, Lucy reminded herself, she didn't really *know* Robin well enough to know what was "normal" for her, did she?

Then relief swept over her as Robin's voice called out from the other end of the hall, "Hey there, neighbor, looking for me?"

Lucy wheeled around. Robin looked better. She had color in her face again, and though her eyes were red-rimmed, she was smiling. "Hi! You okay?"

Robin's smile widened. "Never better. Starving, though. Had breakfast yet?"

"Didn't eat it. I'll go back down with you. I've got time before Tom attacks my limbs with a vengeance."

Jude had left the cafeteria, but Tony was still there and still eating. No wonder he's so overweight, Lucy thought unkindly.

He saw the look she gave him, and responded with his customary nonchalant shrug. "Yeah, I overeat. So what? It's the only interesting thing to do around here."

"Don't you have physical therapy sessions?" Lucy asked. "I thought everyone did."

"Nope. Not me. I gave up. What's the point? I told you, all I'm doing now is biding my time till the insurance runs out."

Lucy buttered fresh toast. "I didn't know people were allowed to give up on therapy." In spite of what she had said to Jeannine that morning, and as much as she knew she was going to hate, to dread, the therapy sessions, she didn't really see any point to being at Twin Willows if you weren't going to work at getting better.

"I told you, this isn't a prison." Tony drank from his milk glass, leaving a thick, white mustache above his upper lip. He wiped it away with a paper napkin. "They can't make you do anything you don't want."

"Don't you want to get better?"

Robin answered. "No, he doesn't. Tony doesn't want to get better." She fixed her eyes on Tony's round face, now beginning to flush with anger. "He thinks he should be punished for his accident. No one else did it, so he's going to do it himself, by never walking again. By not even trying. Isn't that right, Tony?"

"You've been spending too much time with that shrink," he said heatedly, pushing away from the table. "You sound just like her."

"Aha!" Robin cried, "so I was right, wasn't I? Dr. Giardello has told you the same thing. It's dumb, Tony, that's all, it's just dumb. You could walk again if you tried, and everyone here knows it."

Lucy hadn't known it. She felt a sharp pang of jealousy. Everyone already knew that Tony had the ability to get out of that wheelchair? She wished fiercely that everyone knew that about her, too. Even if they weren't ready to tell *her* that. She would love to believe that everyone at Twin Willows was positive Lucy St. Cloud could walk again. It would feel so good to know that was true.

She started to say that she agreed with Robin, that Tony was being very dumb about the whole thing.

But he was already halfway across the room, his plump shoulders hunched, his hands furiously spinning the chair's wheels.

Lucy thought she saw tears shining on his eyelashes as he sped away.

Chapter 17

Lucy's second physical therapy was much worse than the first. Fifteen minutes into it, she was in tears. "You're *hurting* me!" she cried out after a particularly brutal sequence of stretching exercises. "Why do you have to be so mean?"

"I'm not being mean, Lucy." Tom's voice remained calm, and he continued with his work unperturbed. "I'm helping you. If someone told you this work would be easy, they were lying to you. That's what *I* would call being mean."

"No one told me it would be easy." Lucy rubbed her side. "But they didn't tell me it would be this kind of torture, either. I have friends coming to see me tomorrow, and if you don't let up, I'll be too sore to even get out of bed."

He didn't let up. "The whole point," he said as he worked Lucy's atrophied muscles, "is that you *won't* be too sore to get out of bed, not if you cooperate with me. If you choose not to, I can't do anything about that."

Lucy suspected he was talking about Tony. She felt the need to defend him. "Maybe if you took it a little easier on people in the beginning," she said defiantly, "they'd hang in there longer. Maybe you scare them off."

"Am I scaring you?"

Yes, he was. He was making her dread the future, when the therapy could only get worse. But she wasn't about to admit that. He already thought she was a wimp. "No. I just want to be able to visit with my friends tomorrow without groaning in agony because I ache all over."

He did let up a little then, it seemed to her. His touch seemed a little lighter, the stretching a little less painful. And he never once mentioned the swimming pool.

Lucy was so grateful, she found herself thanking him at the end of the session, surprising herself.

He *was* trying to help, she knew that. Why shouldn't she thank him?

Robin was nowhere to be found after the session, and Tony and Jude weren't in their rooms, so Lucy spent the rest of the morning in the second-floor library. It was comfortably furnished with round tables and tweed overstuffed chairs, and the shelves were well-stocked. There were computers, but they were all in use. Lucy really missed hers. She couldn't wait to get back to her on-line chats.

Curious about Robin's condition, Lucy read everything she could find on spinal injuries. Although she didn't know the specifics of Robin's injury, nothing Lucy read made her optimistic.

So Tony had chosen not to fight to walk again, and Robin might not be able to no matter how hard she fought, and Jude was still struggling.

And, Lucy wondered despondently as she left the library, what are *my* chances?

After lunch, Robin offered to French-braid Lucy's hair for her. "If you like it, I'll do it again tomorrow before your friends come." She seemed less depressed. She'd been animated during conversation at lunch, and her color was high again.

Lucy was relieved. She didn't expect to be at Twin Willows very long, but while she was here, she really needed a female friend. And she was impressed, too. Robin had been in the depths just the day before. Maybe that shrink upstairs knew her stuff. Not that Lucy expected to need her services. And since no one on the staff had made an appointment for her with Dr. Giardello, that must mean they were in agreement that Lucy St. Cloud was not in need of psychiatric care. Tony and Jude had probably been yanking her chain when they told her it was required of every patient. Hassling the new girl, that's all that was.

Big relief. If there was one thing Lucy didn't feel like doing, it was crying on some stranger's shoulder. It didn't matter how nice the doctor was, or how competent at what she did. It would still feel too, too weird.

And it wouldn't change anything.

"That looks great," Jude commented at dinner when Lucy showed up with her dark hair in a thick, intricate braid. "Robin do that?"

"Yep. She's good isn't she?"

Robin beamed. Then, her mood switching instantly, she said soberly, "I guess I should be glad I can still use my hands, just like Tom is always telling me. Lots of spinal-injury patients can't." But she didn't sound glad, and she was silent all through dinner. Lucy noticed that she ate almost nothing. Robin was already thin, with no trace of the excess weight Tony had accumulated since his accident. Lucy thought, she really can't afford not to eat, and tried to persuade Robin to at least try the pumpkin pie, which was almost as good as her grandmother's. "That's real whipped cream, Robin."

"I hate pumpkin," was Robin's vehement answer. "It reminds me of Halloween, a holiday I loathe. Everyone dressed up in stupid costumes, and kids out running the streets begging for candy. It's disgusting!"

Ten minutes later, when Robin left alone, saying she had a new book she wanted to read, Jude shocked Lucy by telling her that Robin's accident had happened on Halloween weekend. He said that the motorcycle hadn't "just skidded," as Robin had told Lucy, but had slid on the slimy pulp of half a dozen smashed pumpkins on the highway, sending the bike on a collision course with the culvert.

"Nothing Robin's dad could do," Tony added knowingly. "That kind of mess is as slippery as slush. Anyway, that's why she acted like that just now. It's not really Halloween she hates. It's being reminded of the accident."

Lucy was horrified. "I would never have mentioned the pie if I'd known."

"She doesn't like to talk about it." Jude's eyes narrowed. "I don't remember you sharing the details of your accident, either, Lucy."

Vividly detailed scenes from That Night flashed in front of Lucy's eyes, as if someone had switched on a video — the cool mist falling, the trouble she'd had seeing the road, the lights of the tractor trailer coming at her in *her* lane, the trailer section of the big rig sliding around from behind and facing her like a giant wall, the horror of pumping frantically on her brakes, knowing even as she did so that it was futile, and then the nightmare of being trapped in a smashed car for such a long time, believing she might die there.

The images, returning so suddenly, so vividly, made her dizzy. "No," she said shakily, "I haven't shared them. And I'm not going to. I can't."

Jude nodded. "I know. None of us can. Except to Giardello. Have you seen her yet, Lucy?"

"No. I guess I don't have to. No one's said anything about it."

"They will," Tony said emphatically. Setting his pie plate aside with a sigh of satisfaction, he said in a fake aside to Jude, "Of course, maybe Lucy won't have to go, because she is, after all, going to walk again any minute now, unlike the rest of us. So she doesn't have the same problems we do." His voice rose, gathered strength, and his eyes moved to Lucy. "Like, for instance, our sudden loss of identity because we're not who we used to be and never will be again. Like, for instance, rage at either someone else or, in my case, myself, for wrecking my own life and ending someone else's, someone I cared very much about . . ."

Lucy paled and shrank back in her chair, needing to escape Tony's sudden and unexpected wrath. Was he mad because she had said she would walk again? Or because she had said she didn't need to see the shrink?

". . . Like, for instance, trying to deal with the indignity of not being able to put on our own shoes." A harsh, bitter laugh. "If we needed shoes, which, of course, we don't. And then there's —"

Lucy interrupted him. "I've felt all of those things! All of them! My accident was over two and a half months ago. I've had plenty of time to feel the same things you have." She pushed her chair backwards and threw her crumpled napkin on the table. Her heart was pounding in her chest so hard, she was sure the people seated at the table behind Tony, all of them staring at her now, could hear it. "But that doesn't mean I'm giving up, Tony. I'm not like you. I'm not a quitter!" Then, only because she really had finished her dinner and was ready to leave, she turned her chair and wheeled away, careful not to seem in a hurry. She wanted *no* one to think that Tony had chased her out of the room.

But from behind her came his angry shout, "Why don't you just get up and *walk* out, Lucy?"

Over the shocked whispering in the room, Lucy heard Jude telling Tony to shut up. She enjoyed a brief moment of satisfaction at his defense of her, only to have the feeling shattered in the next second by Jude's voice adding, "Hey, ease up on her, okay? Everyone thinks like Lucy when they first get here, you know that. You did, too. Like we can do anything, no problem, don't need any help, everything's gonna be fine. Still in denial. Some people get stuck there. But Lucy won't. She's too smart. And then there are the people, like you, Tony, who move on to the anger stage but get stuck there. You're not the best person to be giving Lucy advice."

The words were so utterly unexpected that Lucy's hands froze on the wheels of her chair. Jude thought she was still in denial? That wasn't true. She knew what she had to do. And she was doing it, wasn't she? Working with the therapist even though she didn't want to, admitting it was something she needed. As for the shrink, why should she say she needed one when she didn't? She was dealing with what had happened to her. Didn't Jude see that?

He had meant to defend her. Instead, he had hurt her.

It took every ounce of will and dignity Lucy possessed to begin wheeling again, her head high, her eyes so blinded by tears that she narrowly escaped ramming her chair into the door frame as she left the room.

Upstairs, her regret at reminding Robin of what must have been the most horrible night of her life stopped Lucy from knocking on the door of room 302. Besides, she had her own depression to deal with. She couldn't handle Robin's, too.

Tomorrow will be better, Lucy told herself as she entered her room. The weather outside had cleared, and although it was getting darker earlier now in the waning days of summer, there was still ample light beyond the open window. It brightened her room, casting warm shadows across the bare floor. Tomorrow Dash, Tia, Jenny, and Kendra would arrive, and they would all spend the whole day together. They would go to the mall, because in spite of what Tony had said, Dash could handle the wheelchair with one hand tied behind his back if necessary. Tomorrow would be fun. Maybe she'd even go into the mall, after all. Just to show Tony. And Jude.

She couldn't be depressed when her friends came. They'd never want to visit her again. If they asked her how she was doing, she would lie. Fine, she would say, I'm just fine. I will, she would tell them, be out of here in no time. I'll be home before you can say Twin Willows. I just might even walk all the way.

They wouldn't believe her, of course, but that was okay, because they'd lie, too. They'd say, Oh, that's great, Lucy, that's just the greatest! And all of them, herself included, would know everyone was faking. But that was okay. As long as no one said it aloud.

Lucy missed her mother and Elizabeth, even Tim more than she had expected. The only time she'd been away from home for any length of time was summer camp last year. But that had been different, because the whole time she was there, she knew exactly when she would be going home.

Lucy laughed harshly. As if *that* was the only difference!

Since her friends were coming this weekend, her family was waiting until the following weekend. She'd see them then. That would have to be good enough.

Robin, wearing a pretty pair of white shorty pajamas decorated with red hearts, arrived in the open doorway just as Lucy was unplaiting the French braid. "I'll do it again tomorrow if you want," Robin said as she wheeled into the room. Seeing the look on Lucy's face, she grinned. "You're wondering how I got into these pj's, aren't you?"

The grin showed Lucy that even with the scar on one cheek, Robin still looked a lot like Heather Locklear, only younger and with much shorter hair. Why couldn't Robin's father see that? And couldn't he see how Robin yearned to have him tell her that again, just as he had before the accident?

At least Robin's legs, though very thin and pale, weren't scarred. Lucy nodded. "I *was* wondering. I mean, I realized in the hospital that if I wore long T-shirts to bed, I could dress myself at night. But I could never handle pj's. Couldn't make my legs cooperate enough to get them on."

Robin's grin faded. "Lucy, it doesn't really matter what I wear to bed, because nightie, T-shirts or pj's, I can't dress myself."

Lucy frowned. "Why not? You can use your arms."

"My arms work. I just can't sit up long enough to get dressed. Ethel, the night attendant, helped me put these on."

Lucy's frown stayed in place. "I don't get it. You can, too, sit up. You do it all day long. You're sitting up right now."

"No, I'm not. Not without help." Without further explanation, Robin reached down and lifted her pajama top a few inches, revealing a thick, dark brown, leather strap fastened securely around her midriff.

Lucy let out a soft, shocked sound.

Robin dropped the pajama top. "Sorry. That was crude. It just seemed like the easiest way. There's another strap up higher. They fasten in the back and then onto my chair. It's a kind of harness, like people use on little kids to keep them safe in a mall, or on ponies or dogs." There was no bitterness in her voice. She spoke calmly and without emotion, sounding like a clerk imparting information from a ticket booth in a railway station or a theater. The fare is thirteen dollars and fifty cents; the feature begins in ten minutes; I'm wearing a harness. "I couldn't sit up for very long without it."

Lucy struggled to keep her emotions hidden. A harness? Like a pony or a dog? Why hadn't Jude *told* her? Unless . . . unless he didn't know. She felt stupid and, worse, completely incapable of saying a single intelligent, comforting word.

Seeing her struggle and guessing the reasons behind it, Robin said gently, "It's okay, Lucy. I'm used to it. I'm even grateful for it, because without it, I'd be stuck in bed all day, flat on my back." Her eyes moved to Lucy's bed, and Lucy knew she was remembering Holly. Holly, who couldn't sit up and whose lungs had filled with fluid, who had been taken from this place to a hospital and had never returned.

Lucy wanted to ask if Robin's condition was permanent, if the only way she would be able to sit up for the rest of her life would be with the help of the harness, which had to be uncomfortable, but she couldn't. She just couldn't.

The question must have been in her eyes, because Robin said, in that same gentle voice, "I don't know yet. Sometimes I think yes, sometimes I think no. It's when I'm thinking no that I have to see Dr. Giardello. All she'll tell me is maybe, but that's so much better than no, don't you think, Lucy? I can keep going on maybe for quite a long time."

When Lucy, still stricken, failed to comment, Robin said, "I'll come by early tomorrow, before my family gets here, to braid your hair. Don't get so excited about your friends coming that you can't sleep. You don't want to look like a hag. Neither do I, so I'm going to bed now. I'm really tired. Sometimes when I ring for an aide, it takes them a while, so I've figured out I should always ring early."

Though Lucy was pretty sure she had mastered the pulley arrangement over her bed and wouldn't need the help of an aide, she didn't go to bed right away when Robin left. She sat for a long time in her chair, without music, without turning on the light when darkness fell, without once glancing out the window. She sat alone in the darkened room, telling herself she should be excited because Dash was coming tomorrow.

But it was hard to let herself feel happy, after what she had just learned about Robin. That would have felt all wrong. Still, she knew better than to let herself feel pity for Robin. Robin would hate that.

The only emotion Lucy would allow herself was a deep, irrational rage at the cook for serving pumpkin pie at dinner.

If this reaction struck her as odd or unnatural as she wrestled with the pulley arrangement, won, and was finally lying prone on the bed, her back and legs aching, she couldn't afford to think that, either. Thinking that might lead to a reluctant but necessary visit to Dr. Giardello.

Lucy pushed the thought aside and, telling herself she had a big day tomorrow, willed herself into sleep.

Chapter 18

Lucy felt like she was going to jump right out of her skin, waiting for Dash and her friends to arrive on Saturday. Tia had said they would leave Poughkeepsie at eight that morning. Lucy expected them by ten o'clock, and was up early, dressed with Jeannine's help in jeans that completely hid her stockinged legs and a pink, mock-turtleneck, sleeveless top. Too excited to eat, she skipped breakfast, but when Robin came at nine o'clock to French-braid Lucy's hair, she brought steaming hot coffee and a fat, still-warm croissant slathered with butter and raspberry jam. Lucy insisted on eating it at the window, where she had a clear view of the circular driveway in front of the building and could watch for Dash's father's black Buick. Dash couldn't very well ride three people on the back of his motorcycle.

"Maybe they'll come in the back way," Robin teased.

"No, they won't. I told Tia to use the front entrance, so I could see when they got here."

And Lucy did recognize the first car that pulled into the visitor's parking lot directly across from the wide, front doors of the hospital. But it wasn't black, it wasn't a Buick, and Dash wasn't driving. The car was Tia's, a small, brown Datsun Tia had dubbed "Bear."

"That's Bear," Lucy said, leaning forward to see clearly. "I guess Dash couldn't get his dad's car. Tia drove."

Lucy and Robin watched through the window as Tia, in orange-striped shorts and top, emerged from the car. She was followed by Kendra, in a white sundress, and . . . and no one. Only the two girls got out of the car.

Frowning, Lucy said, "Dash and Jenny must have driven up separately. I wonder why."

But no black Buick parked behind Bear.

They continued watching out the window until Tia and Kendra appeared in the doorway and said, almost in one voice, "Hey, Lucy, look who's here!"

Without even saying hi, Lucy turned to ask, "Where is Dash? He promised."

"He had to work," Kendra answered. They moved into the room, hugged Lucy, and plopped down on the bed. Tia began talking immediately. "Aren't you glad to see us? You don't look glad. Man, this place is something else, isn't it? It's huge! I thought we'd never find your room. Is there a drink machine around here somewhere? I'm dying of thirst. Bear isn't air-conditioned, and it's hot enough out there to grill hot dogs on the sidewalk. Who's your friend?" referring to Robin.

Lucy guessed instantly why Tia was prattling on so. Because she didn't want to talk about Dash. And why was it, exactly, that Tia would rather talk about the building and the heat instead of Dash?

She already knew the answer. It made her sick, but she knew it. "This is Robin Papajohn. Robin, these are my friends, Kendra and Tia." When they had exchanged greetings, Lucy dove in. "Dash is with Jenny, isn't he? That's why neither one of them is here. And you don't want to tell me because you figure I've already had enough rotten stuff happen to me, so you're going to protect me by not telling me the truth. Thanks, but no thanks. Just tell me, Tia! I need to know."

Tia studied her long fingernails, but Kendra, after a guilty sidelong glance at Tia, said, "I think we should tell Lucy. Dash didn't have the guts to. And she's right, she should know."

Disgust lacing her words, Tia said, "Yeah, okay, he's with Jenny. They're together almost all the time now. It's disgusting. I thought he would tell you over the phone, but I guess he chickened out. Gutless wonder. I'm not speaking to either one of them. They never said a word when we were making plans to come up here to see you. Acted as if they had every intention of coming along. Until this morning, when Jenny called and said her mother was sick and she had to stay home. Two seconds later, Dash called and said he had to work. But when we drove by Jenny's house, her mother, looking like the poster child for good health, was cutting roses in her garden, and Dash's bike was parked in the side driveway."

Lucy felt sick. He had sounded so sincere on the telephone, had never even hinted that he might not be coming up for the weekend. Was he lying even then? Or had he and Jenny decided at the last minute that they couldn't hide the truth from Lucy if they were sitting in the same room with her? And hadn't been willing to take that chance?

"How long?" she demanded then. "How long has it been going on?"

Tia's heart-shaped face flushed. "Ever since the accident, I guess. Maybe even before. And we wanted to tell you, we did. But god, Lucy, you were having such a rough time, there never seemed to be a good time to tell you."

"Like there *is* such a thing," Lucy said bitterly. "What would be a good time to stick a knife in someone's back? Morning? Afternoon? Maybe right after a really good meal?"

"Jenny didn't mean it to happen," Kendra said softly. "I'm furious with her, too, but she's not a terrible person. She's just in love. With Dash. Always has been. You already knew that, Lucy."

"Right," Lucy said, nodding emphatically. Her cheeks were red with pain and anger, her eyes blazing. "What I *didn't* know was that the feeling was mutual."

"It wasn't," Kendra insisted. "Not until ..."

"Until I ended up in here." Another angry nod. "I know. I *get* it. Absence makes the heart grow fonder ... of somebody *else*. In this case, someone with two good legs." Lucy was shocked as well as hurt. He had sounded as loving as ever on the phone. Not a hint, not a clue. What kind of guy would betray someone fighting to walk again in a rehab hospital? Was that who Dash was? Why hadn't she seen it?

But she'd always known that he needed a lot of attention ... from females. And now she wasn't there to give it to him. Jenny was. End of story.

They were both disgusting. Jenny *and* Dash. She would never forgive either of them. "I hate them both," she said aloud.

"Good," Tia said. "Sounds healthy to me.

Now let's go shopping. Kendra and I can handle your chair. Piece of cake. And you *are* going into the mall, Lucy. We're not leaving you out in the car to obsess about two people who aren't worth the nail polish on my pinkie finger."

"Tia!"

"Stuff it, Kendra. Let's go."

At the mall, Lucy picked out a somber navy-blue cardigan with large, plain, white buttons marching up the front.

"Oh Lucy, that's awful!" Kendra protested. She held up a soft peacock-blue turtleneck. "You'd look prettier in this one."

As if anyone cared how she looked. Dash certainly didn't. "I need something I can slip in and out of faster than a turtleneck. I'll take this one. It's on sale."

Tia said drily as they left the store, "Don't let me forget to snap a picture of you in that lovely garment, Lucy. Your friends back home will think your mom made a mistake and sent you to a retirement home instead of rehab."

Lucy ignored her.

Even if Dash hadn't abandoned her at the last minute, disappointing her so painfully, Lucy still would have been unsettled by how difficult it had been to make the short trip from Twin Willows to the mall. Tia and Kendra had wrestled with the intricacies of the wheelchair, finally conquering it, climbing into the car hot and sweaty and breathless. They'd had to go through the whole routine again when they reached the mall, just five minutes away, and then they'd had to struggle to get Lucy from the front seat of the car into the chair, something she hadn't had time to practice yet. Jeannine was sturdy and strong and hadn't had any trouble lifting Lucy from the bed to the chair before she learned to do it herself. But Jeannine had had more room and no open car door in her way, swinging back and forth as Tia and Kendra struggled to get Lucy into the chair. And Jeannine never had to do battle with the wheelchair.

Then there were the stares once they got inside. Lucy didn't mind the stares of children. That seemed natural enough. A wheelchair wasn't a sight they saw every day. She'd expected as much from children. It was the adults who got to her. Shouldn't they know better? She especially hated it when a parent wrenched on a child's hand, whispering harshly, "Don't stare, it's rude!" You could tell by the look on the child's face that he wasn't sure exactly what it was he'd done wrong.

She bought the ugly sweater and she talked with her friends about what was going on back home, and about what it was like at Twin Willows, and she even laughed a couple of times, surprising herself. But all the while, every strained, painful minute that they were in the mall, somewhere in the back of Lucy's mind a voice whispered cruelly, "Dash didn't come, he didn't, he's with Jenny, he's never coming, he said he would but he didn't and he won't and that's over, that's over, that's over . . ."

By the time they left the mall and repeated once again the torturous business with Lucy and her chair, the voice was taunting, "Well, what did you expect? You know Dash. Did you really think he'd wait for you? You could be in rehab for months and months, like Robin and Tony. Dash would have to be positively self-sacrificing to wait that long. And let's face it, Lucy, 'self-sacrificing' won't be one of the things they write under Dash's name in the yearbook when he graduates. And don't pretend you didn't already know that, Lucy. Because you did."

Yeah. Yeah, she did know that. But it had never mattered. Because she hadn't needed Dash to do any sacrificing for her. Not until now.

Before Kendra and Tia went back to their motel to freshen up and change, they offered to take Lucy out to dinner at a nice restaurant in town. "We've been saving up for it," Kendra had said proudly.

But the thought of enduring more battles

with the chair to get to and from the hospital and restaurant led Lucy to say, "Oh, you know what, guys? I'm really beat. How about if we have dinner here? The food's not bad, honest." She laughed. "In fact, if I don't watch myself, by the time I'm discharged, I'll be the size of Syracuse. My mom will have to hire a moving van to get me home." Both girls still looked doubtful, so Lucy added, "Besides, I have a couple of friends I want you to meet."

They agreed then, and left. Lucy was fairly certain they were relieved. If Dash had been here, there would have been no problem. He would have been able to lift both the chair and Lucy with little effort.

But Dash wasn't here.

Still, he did call. Five minutes after Kendra and Tia returned to the motel to change their clothes. Lucy's jaw dropped when she answered the phone and heard the familiar voice.

"Lucy? Lucy, is that you?" When she said it was, all he said was, "I'm . . . I'm sorry." Then he stopped talking.

Lucy knew what he was waiting for. He was waiting for her to say, "Oh, that's okay. No problem. I can take a vicious stab in the back as well as anyone. You are still a fabulous human being. I wish you and Jenny the best of luck."

That wasn't what she said. What she said

was, "Hey, lowlife, how's it going?" Her voice was as icy as a January morning.

"Lucy, come on, don't be like that. I meant to come up there, honest. I just got tied up."

"To railroad tracks, I hope."

He laughed uncertainly.

"Just my luck no train came along, or you wouldn't be ruining my evening with this lame phone call now."

A pause. Then, "Tia told you. I knew she would." In that gee-I'm-just-a-guy-and-can't-help-these-things voice that Lucy had always hated, he added, "We didn't mean for it to happen, Lucy. I mean, I wouldn't hurt you for anything in the world. Neither would Jen."

Wrong. To get her hands on Dash, Jen would. She *had*. It was a done deal.

"Especially not *now*," Dash added, "when you're already having a rough time."

Big mistake. "Don't you dare patronize me!" Lucy shouted into the telephone, not caring who on the third floor might hear her. "Like what you and Jen have done wouldn't matter if I could walk? If I hadn't had the accident? Listen, Jen could stand on your shoulders and I'd still be ten feet taller than the two of you together, wheelchair or no wheelchair! I can at least *try* to walk again. You can't *try* to be faithful, because you don't know the meaning of the word."

"Hey, chill! Can't we talk about this in a mature, reasonable, intelligent way?"

Lucy thought for a minute. Then she said heartily, "Sure! Sure, you bet, Dash! Why not?"

She heard the beginning of a sigh of relief. She cut it off in mid-sigh. "I *maturely* think that between the two of you, you don't have the morals of a blade of grass. I *reasonably* believe that the two of you deserve each other. Who else would have you? And I *intelligently* choose never to speak to either one of you again as long as I live!"

The sound of the receiver slamming into its wall cradle was almost as satisfying to Lucy as the thought of the shocked look on Dash's handsome face. He had *really* expected her to forgive him, just as she'd always forgiven the flirting in the past. She had heard it in his voice.

Shocker. Let him live with it.

"The same thing happened to me," Robin said quietly when she arrived in Lucy's room to wait for Tia and Kendra before going down to dinner. Lucy was sitting at the window again. With trembling hands, she had unbraided her hair and was in the process of carelessly pinning it up on the back of her head with a pair of plain, brown barrettes. She wasn't even using a mirror. Who cared?

"The boyfriend thing, I mean." Robin joined Lucy at the window. "I heard you yelling into the phone." She lay her close-cropped head back against her chair and mused, "His name was Ernie. Ernie Damico. Cute. Really cute. I met him in New York. He wasn't a dancer. Music was his thing. There was a music school on the fourth floor of our building. We met in the elevator. And it was like we clicked right away, know what I mean?"

"Yeah, I guess." If there was one thing Lucy didn't feel like listening to just then, it was the story of someone's soured romance. Her insides were still shaking violently from the encounter with Dash. But Robin hadn't talked much about herself yet and probably needed to, and it seemed selfish to interrupt.

"He dropped me the minute he found out I wasn't going to be dancing for a while. I mean, it wasn't like we were having this great romance or anything. But I liked him, and it scared me. I figured that was the way it would always be, if I never got out of this chair. Boys wouldn't be interested. And I wasn't even sixteen yet."

Although Lucy was listening, she was also peering out the window, watching for Tia and Kendra. "Jude likes you," she said. "It's written all over him."

"I like him, too. But I'm not interested in romance now. Not in here. All I want to do is get better. And" — sighing heavily — "that doesn't seem to be happening. I just feel sometimes like I'm never going to make any progress, and I'll never again be who I was before. And I liked who I was before."

Me, too, Lucy thought. She turned away from the window to look at Robin. "You're still the same person you were before the bike skidded."

Robin lifted her head then. She looked shocked. "Oh, no, Lucy, don't make that mistake. Lots of people say that, and I know they mean well. They say, You're still the same person inside. But I'm not. That's not true at all. Of any of us in here. How could it be? Who I was inside had a lot to do with what I could do. I can't do most of those things anymore, so I'm a different me now. No," she added emphatically, her mouth set in a grim line, "I am *not* the same person inside. And Lucy, neither are you."

Chapter 19

Tia and Kendra hit it off well with Jude and Tony, as Lucy had suspected they would. There was only one bad moment when Kendra, after laughing at some wisecrack of Tony's, said in awe, "I think it's amazing that you guys can joke about being in here. I mean, I know I couldn't, if I were suddenly crippled."

The word hit them like a slap in the face. An ugly silence descended upon their table.

Kendra realized her mistake immediately. "Oh, jeez, I didn't mean to say that. I mean, I don't think of any of you that way, I'm sorry, I just meant —" Understanding that she was just making things worse, she stopped in mid-sentence. Lowering her eyes to her plate, she sat in miserable silence.

"Look, it's okay," Jude said finally. "The word crops up once in a while. Forget it. We can't always expect people to be politically correct."

"I know better," Kendra said quietly, her gaze still downcast. "I'm sorry. I should have been more careful."

"I know the feeling," Jude said with a rueful, disarming grin. "I've said that a lot since I got here. Shoulda been more careful when I dove off that board."

Robin laughed. Then Tony did, too, at Jude's willingness to laugh at himself. Kendra smiled gratefully at Jude, and the moment passed.

But Lucy knew the word Kendra had thoughtlessly used would haunt them all later, when they were lying in bed in a building so quiet they couldn't help hearing themselves think.

After a long and sleepless night, Lucy knew she looked like roadkill the following morning. Her eyes were red and puffy, her face drawn. She didn't care.

Kendra pretended not to notice, saying a bright and cheerful hi as she came into Lucy's room.

Tia was not so cautious. "Oh don't tell me you were bawling over those two!" she cried in disgust. "Like they're worth it!" She pulled three coffee cups and a trio of bagels from the white paper bag she was carrying. "Here, eat this. It's onion, your favorite. You'll feel better. Men are pond scum. Food is the real joy in life. Never let a man take away your appetite."

"Easy for you to talk," Lucy grumbled, though she accepted the bagel and the hot coffee. "You wear a size four. You've never weighed more than one hundred pounds in your life. Weren't you listening when I said I was worried about becoming grotesquely overweight in this place?"

"The people here are supposed to keep that from happening." Tia, in black capri pants and a lacy white peasant blouse, plopped down on Lucy's unmade bed. "If you come out of here wearing a size twenty-two, you can sue. You'll win the lawsuit, you'll be rich for life, and then you won't need Dash or anyone else to take care of you."

Lucy's eyes narrowed. Tia had just touched on one of her deepest fears: not being able to care for herself. "And if I don't sue, and I'm not wealthy, I *will* need someone to take care of me forever? Is that what you're saying, Tia?"

Exasperated, Tia's voice rose. "Will you cut it out? *I'm* not the one who's afraid you won't walk again. That's *you*. Don't get us confused, Lucy." More quietly, she added, "I know you're hurting. I know how you feel about Dash, even if I never did understand it. But you've got more important things to think about now, like getting out of this place, and you shouldn't be distracted by romance, anyway. Although" —

her dark eyes twinkled — "that Jude is really cute."

"He's Robin's. At least, I think he might be."

"Whatever. Listen, I've planned a picnic."

"*We've* planned a picnic," Kendra corrected. "We didn't even need permission. Tony told us last night that on weekends the cooks make up picnic baskets for anyone who wants to eat outside on the lawn. It's a gorgeous day, so that's what we're going to do. Your friends here are coming, too. Robin and Jude and Tony, even though Tony complained that he hates devilled eggs." She laughed. "He said eggs should only be eaten at breakfast and should always have a side order of bacon or sausage."

In spite of the heartache of the night before, Lucy did have a good time that day. Because they never left campus, there was no sweaty struggle with the wheelchair, and everyone but Robin was in a good mood. She spent the morning with her parents. When they'd gone, she joined the picnic. She never said what was bothering her, but she ate very little in spite of the ample supply of picnic food, which turned out to be very good. She was quiet most of the day.

"She's not exactly a barrel of laughs, is she?" Tia commented later, back in Lucy's room. It was time for good-byes, and all three girls were stalling. "Robin, I mean."

"Well, would you be," Lucy asked defensively, "in her position?" She said nothing about Robin's harness. That seemed far too private to share without Robin's permission. "Sometimes she's happier. I guess something's bothering her, but she hasn't said what it is. It's more than just being in here, I think, although just being in here is more than enough to depress anyone."

Kendra, the romantic, proposed, "Maybe she's nuts about Jude and sorry that he'll be leaving soon. Or she's afraid that he doesn't feel the same way she does."

Lucy didn't think that was it. "Anyone with eyes can see that he does. I think it's something else. She's probably scared that she doesn't have much of a future. Everyone in here must feel that way most of the time."

Tia's eyes filled with concern. "You don't, do you, Lucy? I mean, your mom said you would almost certainly walk again, if you do what they tell you to in here."

Lucy laughed. "It's the 'almost' that gives me some rotten moments, Tia. An 'almost' can scare the heck out of you, if you let it."

"Then don't let it."

They finally said their good-byes. Because Lucy's family was planning to visit the following weekend, Tia said they would plan on the weekend after that.

But Lucy thought, school starts soon. The faint smell of autumn was already in the air, and it made Lucy heartsick that she wasn't out there, getting ready for senior year with everyone else. She wouldn't be at Dash's side, as she'd been last year. People would see him on campus with Jenny, and in no time at all, they'd be saying, "Dash and Jenny" instead of "Dash and Lucy." People would forget that it ever had been Dash and Lucy. They'd forget her.

Kendra and Tia would be busy. There'd be shopping trips to buy just the right jeans, just the right shoes, a few fall sweaters, there'd be haircuts to get and notebooks to buy, and Tia and Kendra might get so caught up in all of it that a trip all the way to Twin Willows would be hard to fit in. If that happened, Lucy would just have to understand, that was all. If the situation were reversed, and Tia or Kendra were in this place and Lucy were on the outside, all excited about senior year, how many trips would *she* make to Twin Willows?

The question was a disturbing one, and she thought about it a lot after the girls had gone. Just how unselfish *was* she? Not that it mattered, because she *was* the one in here. Still, it troubled her. Though it seemed years ago now, it wasn't that long ago that Elizabeth had accused her of being selfish. How much have I changed since then? Lucy wondered, watching from the window as Kendra and Tia climbed into Bear three floors below. Robin said we do change when this kind of thing happens, that we change on the inside as well as on the outside. But she didn't say if the inside changes were good ones or bad ones.

"Your friends are nice," Robin said, wheeling into the room to sit beside Lucy at the window. "Really nice. You're lucky."

It occurred to Lucy then that although Robin's family was apparently faithful about visiting, Robin had never mentioned any friends. Bear disappeared into the fading twilight. If Robin hadn't been sitting beside her, Lucy would have felt newly abandoned. "What about your friends? Do they visit?"

Robin averted her face, so that the jagged scar faded into the purple shadows of twilight. "Not anymore. They did at first, but when Ernie dumped me, I sort of fell into a depression. I wasn't very good company when my friends visited." Sadness thickened her voice. "I used to be a lot of fun. Really, I was. The life of the party, in some ways. But after I came here, visiting me was probably a lot like paying a condolence call. You know . . . it's not much fun, and you don't want to go, but you know you should. After a while, though, everyone except my family stopped coming."

"Can't you call your friends and tell them you're feeling better now?"

Robin turned to look at Lucy. "Oh, but that wouldn't be true, Lucy. I hardly ever feel better."

Startled, Lucy asked, "But Dr. Giardello . . . I thought . . ."

"She helps. But it doesn't really change anything, like I said before."

"Jude would help, if you'd let him."

"Jude's nice. But he'll be leaving soon. And I won't."

Lucy went to bed thoroughly depressed.

All that week, she renewed her efforts in physical therapy. She wasn't going to be like Tony, angry and sarcastic, and she wasn't going to be like Robin, who seemed to have so little hope. The sooner she got out of this place, the better. The work was exhausting and painful, but Tom was encouraging and supportive. The pool, once Lucy got over the pain of revealing her scarred legs, which no one paid the slightest bit of attention to, was soothing and refreshing and helped a lot. She began to feel more hopeful than she'd felt since That Night.

Dash didn't call. But she hadn't expected him to, and decided she wouldn't talk to him even if he did call. Not yet, anyway. She was still too angry.

Her mother, Liz, and Tim visited on the weekend. Sara explained that Mitchell Dwyer was negotiating with the insurance company but said that if they weren't willing to settle, the matter would have to go to court. Tim and Lucy talked mostly about computers, Lucy and Elizabeth about the wedding.

"Your color is really good," Lucy's mother said, and Tim and Elizabeth nodded agreement.

No one asked her if she was walking yet.

The following weekend, just as Lucy had suspected, Tia and Kendra begged off, sounding regretful but saying their mothers were taking them into New York City for school shopping. Lucy was doubly disappointed, because she had intended to share with them her progress. Her legs were getting stronger. She could feel it, and she could see that they were beginning to take on some shape again, though not much. Her progress report would have to wait.

Saturday night, she was sitting in her room with Robin, watching a boring television show, when Tony called from the open doorway, "Hey, you guys, how come you're sitting in the dark?" When Lucy turned to look, he hoisted a fat, squat bottle of purple liquid high in the air. "Grape juice. All I could get. The cooks here aren't gourmet enough to stew their chicken in wine. It'll have to do. C'mon, let's go to the roof."

Lucy hesitated. "It's almost time for lights-out, Tony. And it'll be dark on the roof. I have enough trouble negotiating this chair in the daylight."

Tony's eyebrows arched. "You're not planning on ever going out in that thing at night when you get back home?" Then, "Oh, that's right, I forgot, you're not *taking* that thing home with you. You're leaving it behind and walking out on two good legs. Sorry. My mistake." Dismissing Lucy, who responded to his comments with an offended glare, Tony directed his attention at Robin. "Robin, how about you? You up for a small soiree in the heights? Say yes. You look like you could use a little pick-me-up. It's not champagne, but it *is* made out of grapes, right?"

Robin wheeled over to the doorway. "You've taken some pills, haven't you, Tony? You're never in this good a mood unless you've taken something. Did you steal them from some other patient or beg them from a nurse?"

"Giardello thought I seemed depressed. She put me on antidepressants. Prescribed by a doctor, perfectly legal, perfectly acceptable, so quit worrying."

Lucy had to admit Tony did seem to be in better spirits than normal. "Did you ask Jude, too?" Maybe if Robin and Jude spent enough time together, Robin would see how much he cared about her. It might give her some hope. She could use it.

"He's already up there. Waiting for us. So get a move on, okay?"

The idea of wheeling around on the roof, so high above the ground, made Lucy nervous. She wasn't a pigeon. But she didn't feel the least bit sleepy, and maybe a party would help her forget Dash and Jenny's treachery. If she stayed alone in her room, she'd think about nothing else, and she'd descend into the pits. Where she didn't want to be.

"I'm coming, too," she called as Tony and Robin began wheeling toward the elevator. It went all the way to the top of the building, exiting directly onto the roof. "Wait for me!"

Chapter 20

The impromptu roof party began pleasantly enough, even though it was already drizzling when they emerged from the elevator into the oppressively humid night. Lucy thought she heard the grumble of distant thunder. It was so completely dark on the roof, she wouldn't have known Jude was there if he hadn't called out, "It's about time! I thought you guys had changed your minds." She could barely see to steer, and had visions of herself rolling her chair right off the edge of the roof and tumbling all the way to the ground, until Tony turned on the flashlight he had brought to light their way.

"It's going to pour," Robin announced. But she made her way to Jude, who was holding four plastic champagne glasses on his lap. "Where did you dig up those? Nobody drinks champagne around here."

Jude had retreated to his wheelchair, and he

looked tired. Lucy understood why. Maneuvering that steel walker all day had to be a drag.

"Found them in the supply closet. I think they're left over from New Year's Eve. Staff party. There was a dead fly in one, but I washed it out."

"Thanks for sharing," Robin said dryly, taking one of the glasses. "We'd better drink up fast. Ethel's on attendant duty tonight. She's tougher than Jeannine. If I get drenched, she'll have a fit when she comes to help me get into bed. It's not like I can get into dry clothes by myself."

"I'd help," Lucy offered. But she cast an anxious glance toward the ominous sky overhead. If she got soaked and chilled, she'd probably catch a nasty cold. The doctors at the hospital had warned her that she should guard against infection of any kind. Wasn't a head cold a kind of infection? She needed another medical complication like she needed ice skates.

Once they were settled, their chairs grouped around a table made from an overturned cable spool, they had trouble carrying on a conversation. Each was in a different mood. Tony was bouyed by the mood-elevating pills, Robin exhausted from the effort of sitting upright all day visiting with her family, Jude annoyed because he'd been parked on the roof alone for thirty minutes waiting for the others, and Lucy downcast because she'd had no visitors that day.

"Can I start sketching you tomorrow?" Jude asked Lucy suddenly. "It'll take your mind off your problems, I promise."

"I don't feel like posing. I feel ugly and icky and gross. Let Robin pose for you."

"I already have about a trillion sketches of Robin. They're great, but I need a new subject. Come on, Lucy, it'll be fun. It's something different, right? Aren't you just about bored out of your skull in here?" He sounded as if he was.

She was, too. Or was she just sad and lonely? It was hard to tell the difference. She really missed her on-line chats on the computer. People to talk to. People who couldn't see her wheelchair, wouldn't know the truth unless she told them. Which she wouldn't. "Oh, all right, I'll pose. But not for very long. Can I read while you sketch?"

"Sure. As long as you lift your head when I yell at you. I have no mad desire to sketch the top of your head." Thunder boomed again, this time sounding closer. When Lucy glanced off to her left, she saw a silvery streak of lightning zigzag across the sky. She found herself wishing it wouldn't rain. She was comfortable. Okay, so it wasn't a dance at school, but it was nice sitting up here in the sticky darkness, sipping grape juice with three people who were in the same mess she was. Even if Tony and Jude didn't understand her, Robin probably did. They were both in wheelchairs, they'd both been dumped by guys, and their friends were all busy elsewhere, living normal lives.

The nicest part of the roof party was, when Tony switched off the flashlight, the wheelchairs disappeared into the darkness. Lucy was able, for a little while, to pretend they were just four ordinary, normal, average teenagers sitting around talking. Until her legs started throbbing. That and a sudden, sharp crack of thunder brought her back to reality.

A moment later, the black clouds overhead split open and a strong, steady rain began. Laughing, they all made a break for the door. When Lucy tried to follow, her chair refused to obey. Peering downward into the darkness, she discovered that she had parked on a wide crack in the surface of the rooftop. Her left wheel was now firmly lodged in the crevice. She pushed harder, but to no avail.

The others were already inside the elevator, waiting for her. "I'm stuck!" she shouted as chilly rain poured down upon her. "My wheel —"

"Push harder!" Tony urged. The booming of the thunder and the snap-crackle-and-pop of the lightning intensified. Jude shouted, "You've gotta get off the roof, Lucy! You're a prime target for lightning out there. Hurry up!"

Now there's something I really need, Lucy thought angrily as she struggled with her chair in the pelting rain. I need to be struck by lightning. Thunder cracked sharply above her, and she recoiled in fear at every streak of lightning that lit up the sky. Water dripped from her hair and nose, her clothes were quickly soaked through, and she knew without checking that the ugly beige stockings covering her legs had to be wet, too.

She continued to try desperately to wrench the chair free, but made no progress.

Thoroughly miserable, disgusted, and frightened, Lucy lifted her head and let out an anguished, helpless cry, directing it toward the thunderous sky. The sound of her voice rang out across the rooftop, but was quickly swallowed up by the storm.

Lost in her misery, Lucy was unaware that Jude had appeared in front of her to begin tugging and yanking on the wheels of her chair until she felt movement beneath her. It wasn't much — the stuck wheel had only jiggled a tiny bit — but it was enough to snap her out of her helpless rage.

"Can you lift yourself up, just a little?" Jude shouted over the constant boom of thunder. He was soaked through, his white T-shirt looking like a wrinkled second skin. "Take some of the weight off the chair? That would help."

"I'll try!" Lucy shouted back. She had not stood up on her own since the accident. Even the stern taskmaster Tom hadn't asked that of her yet. Wednesday morning, in anticipation of weekend visitors, she had made a hesitant effort to plant both her feet firmly on the floor when she was sitting upright on her bed, and had nearly fainted from the resulting pain in her legs. If she fainted now, Jude would never be able to get her dead weight over to the elevator.

I won't faint, Lucy vowed, and gripping the arms of her wheelchair firmly with both hands, she raised herself up from the seat. By using only her arms and upper chest, she was able, for just a few seconds, to keep most of her weight off the seat of her chair. But she was breathing heavily from the effort, and her head began to swim. The danger of passing out terrified her.

Jude's suggestion worked. As Lucy hoisted her weight off the chair's seat, Jude yanked on the chair, and the wheel came up out of its crevice. He pulled again, and as Lucy fell backward, the chair rolled forward just enough to keep it from slipping back into the deep crack.

"Go!" Jude shouted, pushing the chair forward another inch or two. "Go!"

Lucy went, slapping at the wheels wildly, hunching her already drenched head and shoulders against the storm. She glanced backward only once to make sure Jude was right behind her.

Chapter 21

For the next four days, Lucy concentrated on physical therapy, in spite of a sore and scratchy throat and a bad case of the sniffles. But by Thursday, she was unable to get out of bed. Her temperature skyrocketed, and Jeannine sent for a doctor. Lucy was sick for three weeks. She spent the first week in the infirmary, then was transferred by ambulance to a local hospital, where she lay in bed for two solid weeks, fighting pneumonia. Her mother and Liz came, but Tia and Kendra weren't allowed. It was a miserable round of more needles, more medication, a hazy period of slipping in and out of reality, and being cared for by more strangers.

During those moments when awareness hit her, Lucy thought with terror of Holly Buford. She, too, had had pneumonia. And she hadn't left the hospital alive.

"It's that *place* that's making me sick!" she croaked to her mother when her fever finally began to descend. "I was never sick at home!"

Her mother patted her hand and said, "The worst is over now, Lucy. You're going to be okay."

But Lucy wasn't so sure. The pneumonia — or some other terrible infection — could happen again. Any time. When she least expected it. If it did, she wanted to be surrounded by her family and friends. She was *not* going to die two hours from home in a rehabilitation hospital. Like Holly Buford.

But what really convinced her was what had happened to her legs during her illness. When the fever was completely gone and Lucy, as weak as a newborn kitten, sat up in bed and tossed the blanket aside, she felt sick again. Her legs looked as limp as they had when she first entered Twin Willows. Three weeks of lying in bed had undone all of her painful, difficult therapy. Gone, all of her hard work! Gone. Wasted effort.

It was too much for Lucy. When she returned to the rehab hospital, the first thing she did was call her mother. "I want to come home. Now! I'm not giving up. I promise I'll do my exercises at home. I will. But I'll get better faster there, Mom. I hate it here, and I almost died. It could happen again. Just come and get me tomorrow, okay? I can't stand it here another day."

Sara argued. Gave it her best shot. But Lucy was adamant. Short of threatening to leave on her own if she had to, which even she realized was ridiculous, she never let up for a second.

Sara finally gave in, insisting that after Lucy left Twin Willows, she would have to continue some form of rehab. "You can't just give up. I won't let you."

"I'm not giving up. I will walk again, I promise. But that's not going to happen in here. I'll work twice as hard at home."

Then her mother dealt Lucy a bitter blow. "Lucy, you haven't forgotten there's no wheelchair access to this building? I've been looking for a suitable place for us, but they're not that easy to find. We haven't received any insurance settlement yet, so I can't afford to stop working to stay home and take care of you. It looks like we're going to have to go to court. That could take a while." Her voice softened. "I was hoping by the time you left rehab, you might not need the wheelchair access. But if you leave now . . ." More briskly, she added, "You'll have to go to your grandparents'."

Lucy jerked backward, holding the telephone away from her, staring at it in dismay. No! *That* wasn't what she wanted. Her grandparents lived out in the country. She didn't want to be forty-five minutes away from home, from her friends. "Mom, the apartment building has an elevator. All I have to do is get into the elevator in my chair and get out on our floor. I do it here all the time."

"Lucy, the building also has twelve wide, stone steps leading up to the entrance. How on earth would you manage those? And I don't even know if I could get you in and out of the car to take you anywhere. And what if you get another infection? Honey, I'm sorry, but if you insist on leaving rehab, you will have to go to Grandma's. There just isn't any other choice."

Lucy debated with herself. Her grandparents' home might be out in the country, but it was still a lot closer to home than Twin Willows. Besides, her grandparents doted on her. They'd be a lot easier on her than Tom.

She returned to the telephone. "Okay, I'll go there. For a little while, until you can find a place that's accessible. But," Lucy added hastily, "you'll probably never have to do that, because I know all of my exercises by heart and I'm going to work really, really hard, Mom. Pretty soon, I won't even need the stupid wheelchair. Then I can come home for real."

"There's no equipment at your grandparents' house. I'll have to see about getting some. You can't work without equipment. And," Sara was thinking aloud now, "maybe I can find someone to work with you. There might be therapists who will go to a patient's home, like a personal trainer. I'll ask around." Giving it one more try, Lucy's mother asked, "Are you absolutely certain you're not making a mistake, Lucy?"

The only thing Lucy was absolutely certain about was that she had to leave Twin Willows. The panic she'd felt here, first when she'd arrived, then later on the roof when she got stuck, and then when she got pneumonia, all of that panic was still with her. She'd never be able to forget it if she had to stay here. She said as much.

"All right then. You can expect your grandfather tomorrow. I'm against it, but I can see that you've made up your mind. You're almost eighteen. I guess I can't force you to stay there."

Lucy went to bed at Twin Willows light of heart for the first time since she'd arrived. Her head filled with wonderful pictures. She even dared to include Dash in some of them. Together, the way they used to be. Her anger toward him had dissipated along with the high fever. She missed him. If he came to see her now, she'd forgive him for his treachery.

"But that's not the only reason I'm leaving,"

Lucy told Robin the next morning at breakfast. "I'd never make such a major decision because of a guy, not even Dash."

"Yeah, right." Robin hadn't eaten a thing, and sipped her juice without enthusiasm. "I can tell."

"I'm serious. I'm just not getting better here, that's all. Some people do, and some people don't. Like that girl who had my room before, that Holly. You said she didn't get better, right? Maybe if she'd left sooner —"

Robin interrupted. "She was in bad shape when she got here. You weren't, Lucy. And you could get back the strength you lost while you were sick in no time, if you just worked at it. Tom would help." Robin sat lost in thought for a few minutes. Then her expression darkened. "You're a lot better off than me. It makes me mad that you don't see that."

Lucy *did* see it. But it wasn't enough. As for being "better off," she'd be even more so when she left this place.

"I thought you were going to *walk* out of here," Tony remarked when he heard that Lucy was leaving. "Looks to me like you're going to ride out, in a chair, just like me the second my insurance runs out."

Lucy was too excited to take offense. "I'm not changing my game plan, Tony. I'm just changing the location of the playing field, that's all. I'll get better faster at my grandparents' house. Fresh, country air, lots of sunshine, tons of pampering . . ." She said this last lightly, letting them know she was kidding.

But Jude, who had just joined them at the breakfast table, nodded and said seriously, "If pampering is what you want, Lucy, you're not going to get it here. Might as well leave, I guess."

Lucy did flush, then. Jude made her sound like a spoiled brat. A label she hated. "If I hadn't been sick," she said defensively, "I wouldn't be leaving. But it scared me. I don't want to die in here."

"But you didn't. Die."

"I thought I was going to. And the doctors weren't sure, either." Lucy could see that they didn't get it. They didn't understand. That made her angry. "I think I should get a little credit from you guys for making a sensible, mature decision on my own, taking charge of my life this way."

Tony hooted in derision. "Oh, you bet. It's my guess the doctors here are sitting around a conference table upstairs right this minute, your discharge papers spread out in front of them, all of them applauding you for being sensible and mature." More seriously, he added, "You should have at least talked to Giardello before you made up your mind. She's pretty good at straightening people out."

Then why aren't you doing physical therapy? Lucy thought. But because she was leaving that day and didn't want to leave angry, she sat it out. She pretended to listen while Robin and Jude tried to persuade her to stay, with Tony interjecting snide little comments from time to time. But she wasn't hearing a word. She was thinking of how lovely it would be to lie on a bench in her grandparents' garden this time of year, surrounded by fresh air and flowers and open spaces, listening to the peaceful gurgle of the creek that flowed through their backyard. And she was thinking of how terrific it would feel when Dash was sitting beside her on that bench, holding her hands and apologizing until his face was as purple as the grapes on her grandfather's vines. She would forgive him, of course. She loved him, so she would forgive him. But . . . not right away.

She would forgive Jenny, too. Like Kendra said, Jenny was in love. She couldn't help what she'd done. Besides, who knew better than Lucy that Dash Cameron could charm the fish right out of the sea? She should never have been so angry with Jenny.

Lucy ignored the voices of two doctors, including Dr. Giardello, who came into her room later that day in an attempt to persuade her to stay. When they had gone, shaking their heads in frustration, Tom stomped into her room, clearly disgusted with her, and told her in no uncertain terms what he thought of her decision to leave "just when we were beginning to make progress."

Lucy tuned him out.

She did the same to the voice of Jeannine, who sputtered the whole time she was packing Lucy's clothes. "I can't believe you're doing this. You *were* making progress. It just wasn't fast enough to suit you. What is your mother thinking, letting you leave therapy now?" She went on and on and on, until the last T-shirt had been folded and placed inside the black tweed suitcase. When she straightened up, Jeannine looked at Lucy with regretful eyes. "This is a big mistake, Lucy, and I think you know it. But we can't keep you here against your will. I hope when you think things through, you'll be back."

Never, Lucy thought vehemently. Aloud, she said, "Thanks for packing my stuff, Jeannine. And thanks for all your help while I was here. I hope you know how much I appreciated it."

Jeannine only nodded curtly. But she did wheel Lucy, her suitcase and purse on her lap, downstairs when her grandparents arrived.

Robin and Tony and Jude were waiting at the entrance, where her grandfather had parked his car. Lucy's grandmother held the back door open.

"I wish I thought you knew what you were doing," Robin told Lucy as they reached across their chairs to hug good-bye. "Tony thinks you'll be back. If you do come back, I'll probably still be here."

She sounded so sad, Lucy gave her another hug. "I do know what I'm doing. And when I'm out of this disgusting chair, I'll come and visit you. On my own. I promise."

Tony relented at the last minute, grinning at Lucy and saying, "I just figured out why you're leaving early. It's to cheer me up, isn't it? You know I'd look like a fool if you walked out after I'd told everyone you never would. Awfully generous of you, Lucy. I didn't know you cared that much."

But Lucy was grateful for the sudden change in his attitude. Tony was a good sport. She returned the grin. "I knew you'd figure it out. Such a keen, investigative mind. You really should think about becoming a private eye, Tony. Or an international spy."

His grin widened. "Yep. James Bond on wheels. That's a new twist. Why not?"

Jude, leaning on his walker behind Robin's wheelchair, said only, "Good luck, Lucy."

She heard his unspoken, You'll need it, but gave him a good-bye wave, anyway.

Then she was lying on the backseat of the station wagon, lifting herself up just enough to watch out the rear window as Twin Willows and the trio waving good-bye at the front entrance grew smaller and smaller. They finally disappeared from view.

They were out on the main highway when her grandmother said from the front seat, "You know we're always glad to have you, Lucy. But your mother is very concerned. She seems to feel you might be making a mistake. I hope she's wrong."

Me, too, Lucy responded silently, uneasiness rearing its ugly head for the first time since she'd made her decision. Everyone was so dead set against her leaving. Everyone! What if she was wrong?

No. She wasn't wrong. She had to leave. Being around Robin and Tony, constantly being reminded that she might be just like them for her whole life, was just too hard. She could do the therapy at her grandparents'. Not right away, of course. When she got her strength back. She had no more energy after that long, debilitating fever. But after some rest and recuperation, then she'd tackle therapy again. And show them all that she'd made the right decision.

Just as soon as she felt better.

She was relieved that she experienced no panic at being in a car.

That seemed like a good sign. She *had* made the right decision.

No matter what anyone else thought.

Part Three

Part Three

Chapter 22

Whatever small hope Lucy had clung to regarding a reunion with a penitent Dash began to fade when she had been at her grandparents' house a week. Her room on the first floor, complete with her own phone, computer with modem, and color television, was lovely. But there was no sign of Dash. He didn't even call.

Lucy complained to Tia by telephone a week later. "I thought he would at least call."

"Well, excuse me for being blunt, Lucy, but Ken and I tried to explain to you while you were still in that place that Dash has moved on to other things, other things being your ex-friend and mine, Jennifer Cooper. May I just remind you that you vowed never to speak to either of them again? Why the sudden change of heart? Have you decided we were lying to you, or are you as much in denial about Dash as you are about needing Twin Willows?"

Tia had been horrified when Lucy called to tell her she was now living with her grandparents. "You're *what*? You left rehab? Are you nuts? Lucy, what's *wrong* with you?"

It had taken all of Lucy's powers of persuasion to convince Tia that she could get well on her own. Not that Tia was actually convinced. But she eventually stopped arguing, saying in defeat, "Talking to you about this is getting me nowhere."

Still, unlike Dash, Tia had been to visit and had called faithfully every day, sometimes twice in one day, guessing that with nothing to do but watch television and play at the computer, Lucy would be bored out of her skull. Which she was. She had always loved visiting her grandparents, but this was different from just visiting. It felt so weird to be out of rehab but not living at home as she'd pictured. Her grandfather was at work all day, running his bookstore, her grandmother busy with an active social life, although she never left the house without first making sure Lucy had everything she needed. A cold blanket of loneliness had settled over Lucy within the first few days away from Twin Willows. What was she doing *here*? And, more important, where was Dash?

What scared Lucy was, if she was being stupid about Dash, maybe she was also being stupid about her chances of ever walking again. In her mind, the two things went together. Because when she thought about walking again, she thought about walking hand in hand with Dash. When she thought about dancing again, she felt Dash's arms around her. It was hard to separate the pain of not walking from the pain of not having him.

Sometimes she couldn't remember which had come first, the accident or the loss of Dash. Then she would remember why the accident had happened, and she would hate Dash and Jenny, and that would help for a little while. But her anger never lasted. She was perfectly willing to forgive him, if he would just come back to her.

In the meantime, Lucy's mother had seen to the installation of several pieces of rental exercise equipment, positioned in the sunroom of the two-story, white frame house. Sara was also trying to find a physical therapist willing to make house calls to work with Lucy. Lucy wasn't in any rush. The pneumonia had drained her. She was still very, very tired.

Until she was ready, she spent most of her time at the computer, visiting several different chat rooms. Heeding her mothers' warnings, she always used a code name, just in case she inadvertently met some lunatic. Her favorite code name was "Swifty." She found it ironic, since she was currently anything *but* swift.

She'd been at her grandparents' less than a week when she encountered someone new on the Internet. She had ventured into a chat room for amateur photographers. She had been there before, but this time there was only one other person there. He struck up a conversation with her immediately.

Hi there. Superguy here. What kind of camera do you use?

Superguy? Lucy laughed. He *wished*. Pentax 1000, she typed.

That's old. Got to load it by hand. Bummer.

No problem there. Her hands still worked. If she had to load it with her feet, she'd be in trouble. But he didn't need to know that. I love it. Gives me great pics. She had taken no pictures since the accident. Didn't even know where her camera was.

What do you look like?

The question, put so abruptly when they'd been talking about cameras, startled Lucy. And she didn't know how to answer. Oh, just your average seventeen-year-old girl, nothing spectacular, nothing stunning. Of course, the wheelchair sometimes stunned people, but that was their problem. The thing was, he couldn't *see* her. She could make herself look any way she wanted to. She typed a quick, totally fictitious description of herself — short, thin, blond, blue eyes, leaving out one tiny little detail — her legs. Then she asked the same question of him.

Six feet two. Blond hair, brown eyes. Some people tell me I look like Keanu Reeves. But his hair and eyes are dark.

Lucy liked Keanu Reeves. He was very, very cute. She owned a video of the movie *Speed* and had watched it half a dozen times.

Are you really a superguy? Faster than a freight train? Can you leap tall buildings in a single bound? Do you dress in a phone booth?

He answered, Yes to the first, no to the last.

Then, How old are you, Swifty?

Swifty. What a misnomer. Still, she had become pretty speedy in her wheelchair. Practice makes perfect. Lucy typed, Eighteen. That was as honest as she intended to get. She had no intention of giving anyone on the Net her real name, address, or telephone number. Not even someone who might look like Keanu Reeves.

Sports? Hobbies? he asked.

What the heck. Didn't she want to be the "old Lucy" more than anything? This was her chance.

Track, swimming, baseball, tennis. And I consider dancing a sport. I'm very good at it. Her nose must be growing a foot, like Pinocchio's. But she was starting to feel like the old Lucy again. She felt lighter, happier, more interesting. The way she used to be.

Great. Me, too. You sound exciting. Let's go dancing. But first, Swifty, tell me more.

Lucy "talked" to Superguy for over an hour. Most of what she wrote was a pack of lies, though only months ago, it wouldn't have been. It did occur to Lucy once or twice that if it was this easy for her to lie, the same was true for him. But what difference did it make? This wasn't reality. It was . . . a game. She was never going to meet Superguy in person. So why not just have fun? For a change.

It wasn't a crime to have fun. She was disappointed when other people entered the chat room and joined in the conversation. But Superguy said he'd talk to her again. She meant it when she answered that she'd look forward to it.

Even though they were back in school, Kendra and Tia came often, and called every night. On the third weekend after Lucy had left rehab, they drove up on a Saturday afternoon. Lucy was bored and restless, tired of dumb old television and its stupid talk shows, even tired of "talking" with Superguy on the computer, though he seemed interesting and fun. Still, he wasn't real. He wasn't here. Just messages typed into a machine, that's all he was. She hadn't heard a word from Dash, and her spirits were at an all-time low.

"What a great place to exercise!" Kendra declared as she glanced around the bright, square room at the rear of the house, facing the lush, beautifully landscaped backyard. The walls were painted white, but the sunshine streaming in through floor-to-ceiling windows cast a buttery glow over the room, and blue sky could be seen through the glass ceiling overhead. "It's almost like being outdoors. Maybe you were right, Lucy. You'll probably get better faster here than at Twin Willows. That place was so gloomy!"

"If she doesn't snap out of the black funk she's in over Dash and start using this equipment," Tia said grimly, taking a seat on the stationary bicycle. "She's not going to get better at all." Addressing Lucy, she added, "You haven't used any of this stuff even once, have you?"

The two girls had arrived in the middle of the sultry, sunny afternoon to find Lucy sitting in her wheelchair on the front porch, reading a fashion magazine. She had insisted on showing them the equipment immediately, intending to drive home the message that she really did intend to work here. Tia's skepticism made her mad.

"I can't use any of this on my own," Lucy snapped. The first few times Bear had arrived, Lucy had hoped fervently that a tall, lanky, athletic body would unfold itself from the backseat and step out into the dusty driveway. But as the visits continued and no Dash appeared, that hope had begun to die a painful death.

This time, when the two girls climbed out of the car unescorted, Lucy had tossed her magazine to the porch floor in disgust and faced the truth. Dash was *not* coming to see her. He wasn't going to call her. He just wasn't interested anymore. He didn't want a girl in a wheelchair.

Fool, fool, fool, Lucy berated herself. How could I be so stupid? Maybe that crack on the skull when my head hit the steering wheel unhinged something in my brain. Didn't Tia try to tell me? Didn't Kendra? Why didn't I listen? Fool!

"I can't work out by myself," she repeated. "I have to have a therapist. Mom's trying to find one. She found one guy, but when she told him I'd left Twin Willows without being officially discharged by the doctors, he said that since I clearly wasn't interested in getting help, I didn't need his. He sounded like a jerk. Awfully judgmental, if you ask me, so I'm glad he turned us down. I bet I'd hate him."

"Are you getting any exercise?" Tia asked, beginning to pedal on the stationary bike. "I mean, every time we come out here, you're either lying down or just sitting in your chair or pounding away at your computer. Aren't you doing any of the routines they taught you at Twin Willows? There must be some things you can do on your own."

Lucy fought against the envy caused by Tia's effortless pedaling. Such a simple thing, pedaling a stationary bicycle. Yet it would be next to impossible for *her*. Like climbing an ice-covered mountain in her bare feet. She dreaded the moment when she would be forced to make her stiff, useless legs push against those pedals, making them go around and around and around. "On my own? No," she answered Tia, knowing that wasn't exactly true. The bedtime exercises were designed to be done without aid. "Why, does it show?" She glanced down at the waistline of her jeans. She didn't see any ugly bulges. "My grandmother bakes the greatest pies on this earth. I guess she must bake one every other day. Strawberry-rhubarb is my favorite, so she makes that the most often. I try to resist, but —"

"I wasn't talking about your weight." Tia climbed down from the bike and joined Kendra on the white wicker loveseat cushioned with vivid red-and-yellow flowered pillows. "I was talking about using your legs. You've been out of rehab three weeks now. If you're not careful, by the time your mom finds a therapist, your legs will be so stiff, it'll take a blast of dynamite to get them moving again."

"Tia! Don't scare Lucy like that," Kendra scolded. "It's not her fault her mom hasn't found anyone yet."

Tia shrugged. "I didn't say it was. Lucy, can't Ken and I help you do something? You said you remembered all of the exercises from Twin Willows. We could put you through your paces, couldn't we?" And Kendra added, "Yeah, Lucy, we'd like to help."

Lucy thought about it. She did remember the painful movements Tom had put her through. Every single one of them. How could she forget them? And while they didn't have all of the proper equipment here in the sunroom, the three basic pieces they did have were enough to get her started.

But she didn't want to. She was too tired, too bummed. On such a hot and sultry early-autumn afternoon, when the waves of heat shimmering up from the concrete retaining wall in the backyard gave her a headache, when the sun streaming in through the long, wide windows assaulted her eyes, when the slightest movement of her arms, wrists, hands seemed to take far too much energy, the thought of exercising seemed unbearable.

For one thing, Tia was right about the stiffness. Mornings, when Lucy awoke, she had no trouble sitting up by herself. She no longer needed an attendant or a pulley for that. But swinging her legs over the edge of the bed to scoot over and slide into the chair was agony. With every passing day, it became more difficult. And each morning, the pain of moving stiffened joints and muscles was more intense. That scared her. Scared her enough that she had tried, the past few evenings, to do the bedtime exercises Jeannine had showed her. They were very simple, mostly leg raises and gentle knee bends. She hadn't been able to do them.

She had tried. She'd been able to do them in the hospital. But now, only three weeks later, it took no more than a few difficult seconds before her legs hurt too much.

The stiffness terrified her. Somewhere, behind a tiny door in the far reaches of Lucy's mind, the thought lurked that she had made a terrible mistake leaving rehab. Each time the sickening thought tried to scurry out into the open, she swatted it back behind the door again. But she wasn't sure how long she could keep doing that. Sooner or later, it was probably going to triumph. She didn't know what she would do when that happened. Right now, it was all she could do to face the fact that she'd been an idiot about Dash. She couldn't afford to face any nasty truths about her decision to abandon rehab and retreat to her grandparents' house, where she did nothing more monumental than eat and sit or lie around all day. She could at least be using the computer to research her condition, find out what the medical experts had to say about her chances of walking again. But she hadn't done that, either. All she did was play games and talk to Superguy.

"Thanks for the offer," she said easily, "that's a great idea. But not today. I pulled a muscle getting into my chair this morning. Exercising will have to wait a day or two. But we'll do it then, okay?"

She could tell by the expression on Tia's face that Tia thought the cows in Mr. Bouldin's pasture just up the road would sprout wings before Lucy St. Cloud asked for help in exercising her stiffened limbs.

All Kendra said was, "Great, Lucy." Then, "Do you think there's any of that strawberry-rhubarb pie left?"

To prove that she wasn't completely helpless and that visiting her wasn't going to be as boring and miserable as Robin had said *her* friends' visits were, Lucy wheeled away to the kitchen to obtain refreshments for her guests.

Chapter 23

Loneliness and depression sent Lucy to the computer often. I never asked how old you are, Superguy.

He typed, I turned nineteen last month.

An older man. Cool. Tia would freak. Where do you go to college?

No college. My family owns a bunch of companies. My grandfather left me a hefty trust fund, so I'm independently wealthy. But my old man makes me work. Says it's good for my character. I work in one of his companies.

He was rich? Maybe, and maybe I'm Madonna, Lucy thought cynically. But you never knew. Maybe he was. Didn't make any difference to her, one way or the other.

How about you, Swifty? College? Or still in high school?

Vassar. Freshman. Not such a huge lie. If she ever learned to walk again, she *would* go to Vassar.

Meet me. In person. This weekend. We'll go dancing.

Oboy. Here it was. Sorry. No personal meetings. My policy.

He typed, Policy? You're kidding, right? Policy is for governments.

She could *not* meet him. Then think of me as a government. No personal meetings. Sorry.

She changed the subject by telling him about Elizabeth's upcoming wedding.

He interrupted: A wedding? Just an excuse to get presents. You probably have them all over the house.

Lucy laughed. Not yet. Too early. But Elizabeth shops almost every day. Silverware and dishes and linens, stuff like that. She's excited about moving into her own house.

He wrote: Speaking of houses, where in Poughkeepsie do you live?

Lucy stared at the screen. She hadn't told him where she lived. Oh, jeez, she'd said

"Vassar." He knew where the college *was*. She'd have to be more careful. She wasn't giving him her address or her phone number, no way.

Gotta go. See you, she typed hastily. He'd be mad that she'd left so abruptly, but he needed to understand there would be *no* personal meeting. That would ruin everything. She'd like to see him, though. Just to see if he really did look like Keanu Reeves.

Lucy called Twin Willows half a dozen times, wanting to speak to Robin or Jude, even Tony. It surprised her that she missed all of them, but she did. They at least understood how it felt to be stuck in a wheelchair. Tia and Kendra wanted to, tried to, but couldn't. One Saturday afternoon, with Lucy parked on the stone bench, Kendra had playfully hopped into the empty wheelchair and spun it around on the cement walkway a few times. "This is kind of fun!" she had cried thoughtlessly, and then, seeing the look on Lucy's face, added with chagrin, "I mean, just for a few minutes. Sorry, Lucy."

Robin would have understood how Lucy felt then.

But when she phoned the rehab hospital, the three always seemed to be in therapy or outside. She hadn't talked to any of them once. She frequently found herself wondering if Robin still needed the dreadful harness, if Tony's insurance had run out yet, if Jude was finally free of his walker and would be discharged soon. And if Robin would miss him when he left, or if she was still thinking about the guy who had dumped her.

The way I obsessed over Dash, Lucy would think grimly. But I'm over that now, I *am*.

Nevertheless, her grandmother asked at breakfast one morning, "Lucy, you're not crying yourself to sleep every night, are you? Your eyes look a little red."

"Allergies," Lucy replied blithely. "Pollen. I'm not used to the country anymore, Grandma. It'll go away when I've been here a while."

She didn't *want* to be there a while. She wanted to go home.

But after that, she forced herself to push back the tears that threatened late at night because she was scared. She had made absolutely no progress since she left Twin Willows. Her legs were getting stiffer with every passing day. They hurt all the time. Her mother called two or three times every day to see how she was, and the frustration in her voice at not having found a therapist willing to work with Lucy increased with every call.

Worried, Lucy tried again to do the simple exercises Jeannine had taught her. She waited until her grandparents were out of the house, so that if she screamed, there would be no one to hear.

She did scream.

The first solitary session lasted no more than two or three minutes. That was as long as she could stand the simple movements. But the second day, she forced herself to endure the pain for an eternally long five minutes, keeping her eyes on the clock beside her bed the entire time. She allowed herself the luxury of crying out as loudly as she wanted to, and that helped. On the third day, she disappointed herself by lasting only four minutes before she could no longer bear it, and on the fourth day she gave up after two, telling herself it was much too beautiful a day to be inside lying on her bed when she could be enjoying fresh air and sunshine.

"It'll be good for me," she muttered to herself as she wheeled through the sunroom's French doors to the backyard. "Sunshine, fresh air, whatever." She was able to slide from the chair to the stone bench, and once she was reclining there, her legs covered with a lightweight plaid blanket, she tilted her head back and let the sun warm her face. The fragrance of her grandmother's rose garden, on Lucy's left, filled the air around her, and the lazy gurgle of the creek behind her lulled her into an almost-peaceful doze.

"You asleep?" a deep voice asked, startling her.

Lucy's eyes flew open, her heart fluttering wildly because the voice was a young male voice and could be . . . could be . . .

But it wasn't Dash standing in front of her. The boy who was smiling down at her was shorter than Dash, not much taller than Lucy. He was wearing cutoffs and had a white T-shirt wrapped around his waist, his thoroughly bronzed shoulders and chest bare, glistening with sweat. His hair, light brown where the sun hadn't bleached it blond, strayed across his forehead. He wasn't gorgeous, like Dash, but he had a nice face, a warm, friendly smile, and intelligent hazel eyes. He was carrying a shovel in one hand and in the other a pair of scissors. Lucy recognized them as pruning shears. Her grandmother used them when she picked a bouquet of roses for the dining room table.

What was this person doing with her grandmother's pruning shears?

"I didn't wake you, did I?" he asked. Pocketing the scissors and extending a hand, he added, "Andrew Loftis. Andy. I do some of the outside grunge work around here. We haven't met, have we?"

Lucy sat up and shook the hand. She clutched the blanket tightly around her legs. She wasn't wearing the stockings today. They were too uncomfortable in this heat. She would die if he caught a glimpse of the bared ugliness beneath the blanket. "Lucy St. Cloud. The granddaughter. My grandfather never mentioned hiring anyone."

"I've worked here every summer since I was thirteen. Had to take a couple of weeks off this year. My own grandfather was sick. He lives in Albany. We just got back." He glanced around the yard. "Doesn't look too bad, though." His gaze returned to Lucy. "You been helping out?"

She shook her head. Hardly. "No, I . . . I've been sick. My mom works full time, so we decided I should come here until I was" — she almost said "back on my feet again" — "better." If he thought she might have been helping in the garden, he couldn't know anything about her, which meant her grandfather hadn't talked to him, not about her legs, anyway. Good. This friendly, interesting-looking guy didn't need to know that the chances of her "helping out" with *anything* were remote. If he knew she couldn't walk, he'd probably turn around and beat a hasty retreat. Like Dash. And if Superguy knew the truth about her, that would be the end of *that* relationship, too.

Of course the stupid wheelchair was sitting right there, next to her bench. How was she supposed to explain that? "Car wreck." There, let him think the wheelchair was because she was recovering from an accident. That wasn't exactly a lie. It wasn't the whole truth, either, but how honest did you have to be with someone you'd just met? Not *that* honest.

"So I guess you're okay now?" he asked. "I mean, I know your grandparents pretty well. They wouldn't leave you alone out here if you were still sick, right?"

"I'm . . . lots better. But I'm going to hang out here a while longer. School hasn't started yet, so . . ." Like she would be going back to school. Although Seneca was wheelchair-accessible, Lucy had no intention of being the object of a zillion stares every single day of her junior year. She had already begun talking to her mother about a private tutor, and although Sara hadn't yet agreed, Lucy could tell she was weakening.

Andrew . . . Andy . . . asked her where she went to school and told her he had already graduated, not from Seneca but from a high school in a nearby community. He was about to enter his sophomore year at Vassar.

An older man. Like Superguy. Only she couldn't very well lie about her age to this guy, because her grandparents might just contradict her. Might as well be honest.

"That's probably where I'll go, too," Lucy said nonchalantly. Why not act like there was nothing wrong with her legs? Why not let herself believe, just for a little while, that she was Suzie Average High School Girl talking to a cute guy she'd just met? How could it hurt? She hadn't really lied and said her legs were fine. So if . . . when . . . he found out the truth, because of course he would if he was going to be working around here, he couldn't accuse her of lying. Not actually lying. "When I graduate, I mean." Duh. She couldn't very well go to Vassar *before* she graduated. Jerk. She hadn't talked to an interesting boy in so long, she'd forgotten how to do it.

He dropped the shovel and lowered himself into a crouch. She found that having his face at eye level was very disconcerting. Then he asked her what she planned to do after college. What should have been a perfectly normal question so stunned Lucy, she couldn't answer. She had stopped thinking about her future. It seemed too bleak to even consider. All she thought about now was getting from one day to the next without falling out of her wheelchair or letting anyone glimpse her scarred legs. After college? She didn't even know if she would ever get to college. She certainly wasn't going in a wheelchair, she knew that much.

The perfume of the roses suddenly seemed overpowering, the sunshine painfully bright. "I don't really know yet," she answered. "Haven't made up my mind." She reached out and pulled the wheelchair over to the bench. Thanks to Jeannine's tutoring, she knew how to get from the bench into the chair without actually revealing that she couldn't walk. The smile that she pasted on her face was designed to say, I could get up and stand if I wanted to and then sit down in this chair like a normal person, but I choose not to. I choose to slide into the seat this way. It was suddenly very important to Lucy that he see her as a person who had choices.

"Maybe you'd like to go out sometime with my girlfriend and me," he said as she wheeled away.

Well, of course he had a girlfriend. Why wouldn't he? He was nice-looking and friendly and seemed okay. Probably faithful as a puppy dog, Lucy thought. "I don't go out," she called over her shoulder. "But thanks, anyway." She wondered as she left how long it would be before he understood that she was someone without a lot of choices, after all.

Lucy decided to forget about Andrew Loftis. What was the point of even pursuing a friendship? The only thing she could do with him was sit on the back lawn and talk. She couldn't go to the movies with him and his girlfriend, because they'd have to park her wheelchair in the aisle, and he'd be embarrassed. She couldn't go for walks with them on the country roads, or biking, and she certainly couldn't go dancing.

She'd just stay in her room. And if her mother did find a therapist who'd come to the house, Lucy would insist that the blinds in the sunroom be drawn completely before they began work. If Andrew ... Andy ... showed up to do yard work, he wouldn't see her painstaking efforts to become mobile again.

Passing a full-length mirror in the hall, Lucy gasped. Look at yourself! she commanded, stopping the chair to turn it so that her reflection stared straight back at her. You haven't done a thing with your hair in weeks. Your complexion looks like you've just spent six weeks in solitary confinement, and every ounce of makeup you own lies untouched in the top drawer of your dresser. Why are you planning on hiding in your room from this guy? Talk about unnecessary! He was just being polite when he asked if you'd like to go out with him and his girlfriend. He didn't mean it. Probably knew you'd say no. Forget him. Stick with Superguy, so easy to "talk" to because he can't see you. He's safe. Safer than anyone.

Disgusted with the way she looked, Lucy whirled away from the mirror and back to her room, where she slid into bed and burrowed beneath the covers to sleep the rest of the afternoon away.

But that night, when Tia called, she couldn't resist saying, "I met this guy today —"

"A guy? Where?"

"In the backyard, of course, Tia, where else? He's my grandfather's yardman, but he's already got a girlfriend, so don't get all excited. And don't get any ideas about him dumping her for me because first of all, I look like compost, and second, I don't play the same games Jenny Cooper does. He asked me if I wanted to go out with the two of them, and I said no. Three's a crowd."

"You should go, Lucy. You need to get out of that house."

I need to exercise, too, Lucy thought, but I'm not doing that, either. If I had a Things I Should Be Doing list, it would stretch from here to New York City. "Yeah, well, maybe I'll think about it. He seems nice."

But she knew she wouldn't.

Chapter 24

Hi Swifty. Where you been? You sick?

If he only knew. No, not sick. Busy, busy, busy.

Don't you ever relax?

Amazing how hard it was to relax when all you were doing was sitting or lying around all day. But he didn't know that. I have lots of activities. Getting ready for school and for Elizabeth's wedding.

He wrote: She still shopping till she drops?

Lucy laughed. Yep. My mom says she should wait until she sees what she gets for wedding presents. But Liz is impatient.

Swifty, meet me this weekend. We'll go to a park, take our cameras, have a picnic. I'll bring

cookies and bananas and tuna sand-
wiches.

All of her favorites. He'd been paying attention when they'd talked about foods they liked
and disliked. Broccoli, she remembered, he
hated. They listened to each other. Lucy didn't
want to give that up. But he kept pressing her
for a meeting, and that couldn't happen.

Sorry. Love to, but going to the
city this weekend with mom. Shopping for school wardrobe.

He answered: Sounds like fun.
You'll look great in anything you
buy. I have to meet you in person.
Forget your dumb rule. Save the
next weekend for me, okay?

Lucy sighed. Who else listened to her the
way he did? She would love to meet him. But of
course she couldn't. Without promising to save
a weekend for him, she made an excuse and
signed off.

She'd bought some time. She still had him to
talk to when she was so lonely she felt like
climbing the walls — if she could climb — and
he still didn't know the truth. If he ever found
out, she'd lose him . . . like she'd lost Dash.

In the meantime, she'd decided to stop
avoiding Andy Loftis. For one thing, she saw
him out in the yard almost every day. Her
grandfather said Andy was trying to get as

much done as possible before school began. For another, since he already had a girlfriend, she didn't have to give a thought to how her hair looked or whether or not he liked her. They could just be friends. Friends were not so easy to come by when you stayed in your grandparents' house all day.

She felt bad that she hadn't told him about her legs. That wasn't a very good way to begin a friendship. She'd wait a while, see if he seemed like the type to be repulsed by the news. If she decided that he was, she wouldn't tell him at all. She'd just retreat to the house and forget about him.

When she did go back outside, she was careful to arrive on her stone bench early enough to avoid any chance of Andy watching her maneuver her way out of the chair. Although the sun was hidden behind clouds, it was hot and sticky in the backyard. Lucy knew the blanket hiding her legs was a mistake. She'd sweat a lot. But she had left the stockings off again, and put on shorts. So there were her scarred legs under the blanket, as bare as the day she was born. Pale and useless. The "zippers" were gone now, but Lucy could still see traces of them if she looked hard enough. Usually, she didn't. She couldn't stand to. Even if Andy didn't show up, the blanket was essential, because Lucy couldn't bear to look at the ugly things herself.

Andy did show up. By the time he arrived, Lucy had finished six chapters of a very long book. Her legs were sweating because of the blanket. She was reaching down, desperate to toss it aside for just a few minutes, when she heard his truck drive up. Her hands flew away from the blanket.

He seemed glad to see her sitting there. It probably wasn't much fun for him, working out here all alone throughout the summer. Dash would have hated it. No one to talk to . . . and no one to flirt with. Even someone parked on a bench would be better than no one. She might not be able to walk, but she could talk.

But conversation wasn't so easy, Lucy discovered, when you were trying to hide something. So many things Andy talked about forced her, if not to tell outright lies, to dance around the truth until her head ached. He said he lived not far away and liked to bike along the country roads. She said, "Me, too," meaning that was something she'd done a lot on previous visits to her grandparents'. She did *not* use the past tense, and when he suggested they ride together sometime when she was "feeling better," she nodded and said, "That sounds like fun." It did sound like fun. It just didn't sound like something she'd be doing any time soon. When he asked her if she liked to dance, she answered yes with enthusiasm, almost forgetting at that moment that dancing, too, was off-limits. She kept trying to steer the conversation toward impersonal things like what he did for her grandparents and what he was studying at Vassar, but he kept redirecting questions toward her, obviously intent on getting to know her better.

He sat on the lawn in front of her and seemed relaxed, but it was all very painful and awkward for Lucy. He was nice, and she knew she shouldn't be lying to him. Not only because it was wrong, but because she knew she'd be found out soon enough. Then he'd be disgusted with her for not being honest with him.

But she kept the blanket firmly wrapped around her legs as they talked.

She was relieved when he pulled himself to his feet, brushing off his shorts, and said, "Enough yakking. Your grandad isn't paying me to sit here jawing." He grinned. "That'd be cool, wouldn't it? I'd take that job in a second."

"Yeah," Lucy said, returning the grin, "so would I."

"Can I get you anything before I throw myself into manual labor? A cold drink?"

"No, thanks. I can get it myself if I get thirsty." She didn't want him thinking he had to take care of her. *That* wasn't what he'd been hired for, either.

She waited until he was working on the

other side of the house before slipping off the bench and retreating to her room. She was glad that she had, because during her awkward maneuvering, an edge of the blanket became caught under one of her wheels, pulling the covering completely free of her legs. She yanked it back up immediately, but she was grateful Andy wasn't around. She could just imagine the look on his face if he'd seen.

They talked every day. Lucy didn't even mind that they talked about his girlfriend, Nan Barone, a lot. It was just nice having someone to keep her company. And although Andy didn't usually work on Sundays, that Sunday he dropped by, bringing a book he thought Lucy might like. He was on his way to the library in town, but said he'd be back later to finish up some work on the gutters.

The cellular telephone in Lucy's lap, provided by her grandparents, shrilled. It was her mother, excited with the news that she had, at last, found a physical therapist willing to work with Lucy. "He'll start tomorrow morning, first thing. His name is Ted Noonan. You'll be ready when he gets there, right? I haven't actually met him yet, but he comes highly recommended. He'll be there at eight."

Lucy groaned aloud. She hadn't been up before ten in weeks. Some mornings it was eleven o'clock before she could face the pain of getting herself out of bed and into the chair. "Mom! Eight? That's practically the middle of the night!"

Her mother laughed. "Honey, most people are up and showered and dressed and on their way to work by eight o'clock."

"I don't work, Mother." And getting up at eight o'clock would make her day an impossibly long one. She could barely get through the shorter ones as it was. "Tell him eleven, okay? Let him schedule someone else earlier."

Her mother's tone sharpened. "Lucy, I won't tell him any such thing. It's taken me forever to find this guy. None of the other therapists were willing to drive all the way out there. I was on the phone more than thirty minutes persuading Mr. Noonan to do it. No way am I calling back and asking him to change your time. Eight o'clock, Lucy. Be up, and be ready." Before she hung up, she added, "And I think I may have found a place for us. It's small, but it's one-story and wheelchair-accessible. I'll let you know when I've taken a look at it."

When Tia and Kendra arrived late that afternoon, they were far more excited about the new therapist than Lucy. They saw it as a beginning, a step in the right direction, a way of getting Lucy back on her feet at last.

She saw it as a beginning, too . . . the beginning of more pain. It was hard to believe it would do any good. Her legs were so stiff now, if this Ted Noonan person yanked on them too hard, they'd probably snap in two like twigs.

And if her mother thought this therapist was so hot, why was she looking for a wheelchair-accessible house?

She doesn't think it'll work any more than I do, Lucy told herself darkly when she lowered the cell phone. She doesn't expect me to walk again. She's just pretending. Like mother, like daughter.

When Tia and Kendra arrived, Lucy didn't ask them about Dash. But when they were standing by the car, ready to leave, Kendra, her cheeks reddening, asked slowly and reluctantly, "I guess you wouldn't want Jenny to come visit you, would you?"

Lucy stiffened in her chair.

"Kendra . . ." Tia said warningly.

But Kendra persevered. "It's just that I saw her yesterday, at Burger Bar, and she asked me about you. She knows you probably hate her, but I think she misses you a lot, Lucy. I could tell she wanted to come with us today." Kendra's voice weakened a bit, the last of her courage melting in the face of Lucy's cold, hard, stare. "Don't you miss her at all?"

"No." A lie. Lucy did. When she had pretended that Dash might come back to her, she'd been willing to forgive Jenny. But Dash hadn't come back to her. So why should she forgive either one of them? During those rare moments when she could push away the image of Jenny walking hand in hand with Dash or worse yet, wrapped in his arms, she was able to remember how much fun she and Jenny had had together — before That Night. How close they had been. How Jenny had been there for her when her father died.

"What would we talk about, Kendra? Jenny and I?" Her voice grew harsh, bitter. "Would we talk about the way Dash kisses? What a terrific dancer he is? How he's almost certain to take the state championship in the mile next spring? What it feels like to wear his athletic jacket on cold nights?"

"You could talk about what fun you've had, you and Jenny, before all of this happened," Kendra said softly.

Lucy went white.

"Get in the car, Ken!" Tia ordered. "Now!"

They left in a flurry of dust, Tia driving too fast because she was angry with Kendra.

Lucy, tired and headachey and hot, hoped they wouldn't argue on the way home. Kendra was no match for Tia's sharp tongue.

It hadn't been the greatest Sunday Lucy had ever had.

And she couldn't very well tell herself that tomorrow would be better.

Because tomorrow, practically at the crack of dawn, the new yanker would arrive.

Let the games begin, Lucy thought ruefully as she pulled the screen door open and wheeled into the house. Maybe I just won't get out of bed at all tomorrow. I'll tell Grandma I'm deathly ill and she'll have to send Mr. Ted Noonan on his way.

That sounded like a good plan. Lucy brightened a little as she wheeled into the sunroom, intending to read for a while before her grandparents arrived home from antique shopping and started dinner. She would read the book Andy had loaned her.

She wasn't prepared for the sight of him, up on a ladder just outside the sunroom, facing her, his arms reaching up toward the roof. Lucy smiled, pleased. He must have arrived while she was coming into the house. Maybe he would stay for dinner. That would improve her mood.

It took her a moment to realize that something was wrong. Andy wasn't just reaching. His face was contorted, and his arms were waving, at first as if he were shooing a mosquito, then more wildly, as if there were many mosquitos.

Only they weren't mosquitos. Wheeling closer to the window, Lucy realized with a stab of shock that what he was batting at, now frantically, were bees. Many, many bees. Hundreds of bees, flying angrily around his unprotected face and head. Although the sunroom windows were all closed, Lucy could almost hear the frantic buzzing coming from what had quickly become a yellow cloud surrounding Andy.

Bees could be deadly, especially when there were so many. She'd been warned about them the very first time she'd come to this house.

"Get down!" she shouted at Andy. "Get down off the ladder! Run!"

But he had panicked, and probably couldn't see very well, and all he could do was continue to bat his arms about him, struggling at the same time to maintain his balance on the rungs.

He's going to fall, Lucy thought, and he's up very high.

She had to get outside and help him.

Chapter 25

Lucy's wheeled herself outside and around the house to the backyard, but it seemed to take forever. She could hear Andy shouting for help. She shouted back that she was on her way. When she rounded the corner, she could see two things immediately. The first was that the bees were gone. The second was that, although the threat to him had vanished, Andy was still on the ladder. He was holding his right hand against his left, bare upper arm, and the expression on his face was pained.

"I've been stung," he called down from his perch.

Lucy knew what to do. Pull the stinger out if it was still there, and apply half a raw onion to the puncture. She hoped her grandmother had an onion in the house. "Come on down. We'll fix it up," she called back.

But there was something wrong with the

way Andy was coming down the ladder. Lithe and strong, he should have scrambled down it like a monkey. Instead, he was moving very slowly, one rung at a time, and he kept shaking his head as if to clear it.

Lucy rolled her chair to just below the ladder. "Andy? What's the matter?" The bee sting couldn't have upset him that much. She'd had several. They hurt a lot, but they weren't scary. "Andy?"

He had managed to make it to the third rung from the bottom. When he turned his face to her, she was shocked by its appearance. It was completely drained of color, but his lips were bluish, and she could see that he was having trouble breathing. "Allergic," he whispered, and pointed with a shaky arm toward a small white box lying at an angle on the slanted ramp Lucy's grandfather had built for her chair. "Kit. Get it, Lucy. Hurry! Run!"

Lucy gasped. He was allergic to bee stings? That could kill him!

"Run, Lucy! Get me the kit! Hurry!"

She turned the chair, intent on heading for the ramp. Andy clutched the ladder rungs with his gloved hands and breathed, "No, not the chair . . . take too long . . . you have to run . . . I need it now . . ." Out of breath, he lowered his head and rested it against the ladder.

Lucy wanted to run more than she had ever wanted anything in her life, except perhaps to stay alive on the night of the accident. She wanted to toss the plaid blanket aside, jump out of her chair, and race across the lawn to the porch to grab the kit and save Andy.

But she couldn't do any of that.

She had never felt so helpless in her life.

Still, she had to do something. There wasn't even time to summon help on her cell phone. But she couldn't sit by uselessly while he died right there on the ladder.

Taking a deep breath and shouting, "Hold on, just hold on, Andy!" she wheeled furiously toward the porch and the white kit that would save him. But her chair got hung up on a slight rise in the ground, and she had to back up and start again. Then she had to wheel around a pile of grass and shrub clippings. The whole time she was trying desperately to navigate, it seemed to her that every time she glanced up at her destination, someone had moved the ramp and its precious kit farther away from her. She was hot and dizzy and her arms ached and the feeling of frustration inside made her want to scream. And all the while, she was aware of Andy, struggling for breath on the ladder.

She had almost reached her goal when her

grandparents pulled up in the driveway. Her grandfather assessed the situation immediately. He jumped from the truck, ran to the back porch, snatched up the kit and was at Andy's side in seconds, helping him down the ladder and then administering the injection that would save him.

Lucy watched with conflicting emotions: heartfelt gratitude that her grandparents had arrived in time, chagrin because of her own helplessness, and envy at the swiftness with which her grandfather was able to act.

The shot worked almost instantly. Just to be on the safe side, her grandfather took Andy to the nearest emergency medical clinic, but they were back within the hour. Andy's color had returned, and his breathing seemed perfectly normal by then.

"It's happened before," Lucy's grandfather explained as Andy sat on the lawn, then lay down, as if he needed to fully relax after his scare. "Andy is allergic. He was stung the first week he worked for me, that first summer. That time, we took him in to the hospital in town. But the doc there said he could learn to take care of it himself, and he did. Carries his own kit now." Lucy's grandfather, tall and lean and with just a few streaks of silver at his temples, shook his head. "Should carry it *on* him.

Leaving it on the porch isn't going to do him any good."

"I tried really hard to get it for him," Lucy said. Tears of frustration and humiliation stung her eyes. "But my chair —"

"Never mind," her grandmother said, patting Lucy's shoulder. "Everything's all right now. It wasn't your fault."

But when they went to unload the truck and take the groceries into the house, Lucy saw the questioning look in Andy's eyes. He was lying on the grass at her feet, his head supported by his folded denim jacket. He asked slowly, "You can't get out of your chair even in an emergency?"

Lucy knew she had no choice. She had to tell him the truth now. If only she'd done it in the beginning. Now, he'd hate her. And why not? Maybe if he'd known there was no one in the house who could walk, he wouldn't have left that kit on the ramp. He'd have had it with him.

"I really was in an accident," she began slowly. "That was the truth."

When she had finished talking, there was a long silence. Andy listened quietly as she spoke, not interrupting even once. But Lucy had been watching the way his expression changed. It went from disbelief to shock to sadness (for her, she knew), and then, as she finished her story, his eyes had the same questioning look they'd had when she began speaking. He thought for a few moments, then looked up at her to ask, "Well, you're not just going to *leave* it like this, are you? I mean, you're not paralyzed. So that means you can learn to walk again, doesn't it? How come you're not in rehab somewhere?"

Lucy flushed. "I was. But it . . . it wasn't the right place for me. And our apartment building isn't wheelchair-accessible, so I had to come here instead of going home."

Andy glanced around the backyard. "Well, it's nice here. Not a bad place to recuperate. But . . . but how are you going to learn to walk again? Your grandmother waits on you hand and foot, I've seen her. That's nice, too, for you. But I don't see how it helps."

Lucy said a silent prayer of thanks for her mother's earlier phone call. It made it possible for her to tell Andy, "Oh, that's all taken care of. My mom found a physical therapist who's willing to come out here to work with me. We start tomorrow." And whatever reservations she'd had about therapy evaporated completely in the face of her terrible frustration over not being able to rescue Andy. What if she were home alone with Tim and something terrible happened? She wouldn't be able to save her younger brother, any more than she'd been able to get that kit for Andy.

She had to at least try to walk again.

"Well, that's good." Andy nodded his approval. In his scramble down the ladder, his sunglasses had fallen off. He reached out now to retrieve them. When they were settled into place, Lucy could no longer see his eyes. So she couldn't read his expression as he said, "If you haven't waited too long." But she suspected, from the tone of his voice, that the eyes were probably disapproving.

She knew she deserved the reprimand, if only for not telling him the truth in the first place. "Look, I'm really sorry about the kit. I mean, that I wasn't fast enough to get it to you. If my grandparents hadn't come home when they did —"

"But they did," he interrupted, climbing to his feet. "Anyway, I shouldn't have left it on the porch. Not your fault. Forget it."

Oh, no, that she wouldn't do. She wasn't going to forget this afternoon, not for a long time. When the therapy got especially rough and everything in her cried out for an end to the exercises, she'd remember the sight of Andy up there on that ladder, struggling to breathe. She'd remember how hard she had tried to reach that kit in her wheelchair, and how she hadn't been able to. "Run!" he had shouted at her, not knowing how impossible that was for her. He had expected her to save him, and she'd let him down. That, she would not forget. Ever.

"I'm not working this week," he told her then. "Your grandfather gave me the week off. I have to go into town and register for school. But I'll see you when I get back. Good luck with the therapy, Lucy." And to her surprise, he bent and kissed her softly on the cheek. She decided as she watched him walk over to his truck that he had probably kissed her to show that he had forgiven her. Nice of him.

But she didn't believe him when he said he'd see her again. She was pretty sure that the next time he was on her grandfather's property, bees wouldn't be the only thing Andy would be avoiding. If he had any brains, he'd steer clear of her, too.

She sat in the chair for a long time after he'd gone. The heat had intensified as the afternoon wore on, and she could feel sweat trickling down between her shoulder blades. Her room, with its window air-conditioner, would be much cooler. Still, Lucy stayed where she was, lost in thought. Her grandmother came to check on her, was assured that Lucy was fine, and went back inside to prepare dinner. Lucy continued to sit, her hands in her lap, going over and over the events of the afternoon. What she remembered most about it was the terrible feeling of helplessness when she couldn't jump from the wheelchair and run to grab that kit for Andy. Sinking in a bog of quicksand couldn't feel much worse.

She *had* legs. They were still there, beneath the blanket.

Lucy inhaled deeply, and exhaled. Then she reached out and flipped the blanket aside. There they were. Useless. Ugly. But they were still firmly attached to her hips, still hers, and they weren't paralyzed. Not like Robin's legs, or Tony's. Hers still moved . . . or would, with some help. Maybe.

Testing, Lucy lifted her right leg, just a little. Even that small movement hurt.

She lifted the leg another fraction of an inch higher. The pain was more intense, but she found that by taking deep breaths, she could stand it. Still, it was an enormous relief to drop the leg and let it settle back into the footrest again.

She waited a few minutes, taking deep breaths, then performed the same mini-movement with the left leg.

All in all, she spent no more than two or three minutes challenging herself. Then, exhausted, she focused on tomorrow morning's therapy session. She would hate it . . . every second of it. She couldn't kid herself about that.

But she still had her legs. It was time to learn to use them again.

If, as Andy had suggested, she hadn't waited too long.

Chapter 26

Ted Noonan, the physical therapist Lucy's mother had hired, was, like Andy, of average height. But his shoulders and chest were massive, his legs as sturdy as tree trunks. He was about the same age as Lucy's mother, and not bad-looking. His sandy hair was thinning, but his face was free of lines and wrinkles, and he had piercing blue eyes. Lucy had the uneasy feeling she wasn't going to be getting away with much with this guy. "Ex-Marine," Sara said in an aside shortly after the two had arrived at the country house on Monday morning. "He knows what he's doing, Lucy. Don't give him a hard time, okay?"

Lucy, awake and dressed in gray sweats, her hair carelessly piled on top of her head, wasn't wild about the way Ted smiled at her mother. Not the same way he smiled at her grandparents. The smile he gave them said, How do you do? I'm pleased to meet you. The smile he aimed at Sara said, I know a fine-looking woman when I see one.

Gross.

"This guy is single, isn't he?" Lucy asked Sara in the foyer while Ted got acquainted with her grandparents in the breakfast room over juice and coffee.

Sara actually blushed. "I didn't ask him if he was married. Why would I?"

"He's not, mom. I can tell. I'm not blind. He looks at you like he's shopping and he just saw something he wants."

Lucy's mother laughed self-consciously. "Don't be ridiculous, Lucy."

"You'd better set him straight right now, Mom. Before he gets any ideas. You can't be getting romantic with the guy who's going to be torturing me five days a week. I hate him before we've even started. I'll hate him more after our first session. So just forget it, okay? You can't like someone I hate."

Although Lucy wasn't kidding, Sara smiled as she adjusted the jacket of her beige suit. "You won't hate him if he helps you walk again. And dance again, maybe even run someday. You'll be crazy about him. We all will be."

Unimpressed, Lucy said, "That wouldn't be love, Mother. That would be gratitude. I would never mix them up, and you'd better not, either." Ted Noonan wasn't her mother's type. He didn't look anything like Lucy's father. And, she discovered when she followed Sara into the breakfast room, he was a very different kind of person. Her father had been a lot of fun, the life of the party, always cracking jokes and laughing. Noonan seemed far more serious, involved now in a deep discussion with Lucy's grandfather about taxes. Nope, not her mother's type at all.

So why did Sara seem to be hanging on every word the guy uttered? As if she'd never in her life heard anything so wise and witty and wonderful.

It had never occurred to Lucy that her mother, who was only forty-two and had been widowed for sixteen months, might be lonely.

It didn't occur to her now.

Noonan was a stern taskmaster, far more demanding, Lucy quickly discovered, than Tom had been. While he worked, he kept up a steady, disapproving commentary on the condition of Lucy's legs. He had a great deal to say about that. None of it was good. As the painful "yanking" began, Lucy heard muttered words like "atrophy" and "flaccid" and phrases like "waste of time" and "lack of facilities." She knew that last phrase meant they didn't have all the equipment they needed. That made her mad, on her mother's behalf. Sara wasn't rich, and they still hadn't received the insurance settlement. She had done the best she could. Besides, Lucy could barely use the stuff they did have. Anything more complicated, meaning more difficult, would have been a total waste of money.

But after the first few minutes she was too busy concentrating on not crying out to really listen to what Noonan was saying. She needed desperately to scream, but refused to give him the satisfaction. He pushed and he pulled and he yanked and it didn't matter how gentle he was (and he *was* gentle, which amazed her) because even the slightest touch to her legs hurt.

After only thirty minutes, he lowered the leg he'd been working on and stood back from the table. "That's enough for today." He regarded her with stern eyes. "We could do some damage here if we overwork you the first time. I'm not at all happy with the condition of those legs. Your mother tried to explain to me why you copped out on rehab, but I didn't get it. You feel like taking a shot at helping me understand?"

No, Lucy didn't. She didn't care if he understood. And he wouldn't, anyway, she was sure of that. This guy had probably never quit at anything in his life. Shoulders back, barrel chest out, spine stiff as a lightning rod, ready at every minute to meet any challenge that came his way. What could he possibly know about "copping out"? About why sometimes you just had to do that. And what did he know about pain? Probably zilch.

"I don't want to stop now," she told him. That was an outright lie. She most definitely did want to stop. But she had already wasted so much time, and she could feel the precious seconds flying by. She kept seeing Andy standing, dazed, on that ladder, unable to get down, unable to get help, and getting none from her. "I want to work some more. I don't think my mother expected you to spend only half an hour with me."

Noonan handed her a clean towel, though she hadn't worked up enough of a sweat to need one. "Your mother expects me to know what's right for you. Quitting now is what's right. Tomorrow, we'll add another five minutes, and another five the day after that. Just be as ready for that as you are to keep working now, okay?"

Lucy hated him. She had him pegged. Control freak, that's what he was. Everything had to be the way *he* wanted it, when he wanted it, how he wanted it. She hated that type. "Do you have kids?" she asked as he helped her sit up. She was sure he was single, but figured he was probably divorced. What woman could stand him for more than five minutes?

To her surprise, he smiled at her. It transformed his face completely, took away the hard edges, made him look almost human. "No. So you can forget about feeling sorry for them. That *is* what you were thinking, right?"

The smile weakened Lucy's defenses. Tyrants weren't supposed to smile. Since there didn't seem to be any point in a denial, she asked instead, "You're not married?"

"Nope. I was engaged once, but she found someone she liked better. And she hated fishing, which I happen to like a lot, so it's probably just as well."

Lucy's mother liked fishing. She'd done a lot of it with Lucy's father. Sometimes their fishing trips lasted all weekend, after they'd dropped Elizabeth, Lucy, and Tim off at their grandparents. She hoped Noonan hadn't mentioned his love of fishing to Sara. She didn't want them bonding, not even over something as dumb as fishing.

Lucy studied him with a cool, measured gaze. "You're pretty old not to be married. My dad was in his twenties when he married my mother." And then, because she needed to, she added, "They were crazy about each other."

He returned her gaze. "I know. Your mother talks about him a lot."

"She does?" He didn't sound like he minded that so much. Most guys would.

"Yep. Did you know I knew your dad?"

274

"No." She'd never seen him at their house. She'd remember.

"A long time ago. In college. I was a year behind Luke. In your mom's class. She was the prettiest girl on campus."

"She still would be," Lucy said loyally.

"True. I didn't know either of them that well. They were pretty popular, and I wasn't."

Lucy believed that. "Your mom wants what's best for you, Lucy," Noonan added. "You should, too."

That made her mad. Hadn't she said she was willing to keep working? He was the one who'd copped out this time. "You don't have to tell me anything about my mother," she said, her voice cool again. "I know her a lot better than you do."

"Sorry. You're right. See you tomorrow." And without helping her down from the padded table, he turned and left the room, his muscled legs in khaki shorts striding across the room so confidently, Lucy felt like throwing something after him.

When her grandmother asked her how the session went, she answered, "Great. Just great. The man's a genius."

Because it was raining, and because she knew Andy had the week off, Lucy spent the rest of the day in her room, reading and sleeping. She didn't go to the computer. Too hard to concentrate on making conversation when she was so scared. What scared her was that those brief thirty minutes had pretty much wiped her out. How was she going to handle an additional five minutes tomorrow?

It wasn't as horrific as she'd thought. Noonan used the same gentle touch of the day before, and didn't rush Lucy. Just before they finished, he said while raising her left leg to a ninety-degree angle, "I know it hurts. I'm sorry."

She appreciated that, but thought, If he says, "No pain, no gain," I *will* scream.

He didn't. What he said instead was, "I'm thinking of asking your mother out to dinner. Would that freak you out?"

She hated it when adults used expressions that were far too young for them. "Freak me out? No one says that anymore. I can't even remember what that means." A fib. Of course she knew what it meant. "Are you asking me if it would make me mad?"

His face reddened, and she knew she'd hit her mark. She was instantly ashamed, and to make up for her meanness, said quickly, "Why would it make me mad? My mother eats, just like everyone else. But she'll probably say no. She's very busy. That's why I'm not living at home. Partly why, anyway. Go ahead and ask her."

"Thanks," he said dryly. "I'll do that."

When Lucy called the house that night to talk to her mother, Elizabeth answered. "Of course she said yes, Lucy. Why wouldn't she? She hasn't had a single date since Daddy died, and I think Ted Noonan is cute."

Cute? He was forty years old! Forty–year-old men were not cute. Handsome, maybe. Her father had been handsome. Noonan wasn't. He wasn't ugly or anything, and when he smiled, he was almost good-looking. But only almost. "Well, tell Mom to call me when she gets home. I need to ask her something."

"Ask me. I might know the answer." Elizabeth laughed. "I is a college graduate, after all."

"She told me about a house she was planning to look at. One with wheelchair access. Do you know if she's seen it yet?"

"Yeah, she has. It needs a lot of work. Some elderly woman lived there, and nothing has been done to the house for about twenty-five years. But Mom's still thinking about it."

"Good. Because I want to come home." And see Dash, Lucy thought, then quickly banished the thought. Why would she want to see Dash when he obviously wasn't interested in seeing her? "And I can't as long as home is still the apartment." Wistfully, she added, "I guess you've probably decorated it by now, right? The apartment?"

"Nope. I started to, but Mom said we should wait and see if we'd be staying here."

Meaning, Lucy interpreted, wait and see if Lucy would ever walk again. Because if she did, they could stay in the nice, new apartment and wouldn't have to pack up again so soon after moving in, wouldn't need to lug all their boxes and bags and suitcases and furniture and the lovely things Elizabeth had bought for her own new home, to some grimy, decrepit old shack because of Lucy.

"How's the therapy going?" Elizabeth asked. "Don't forget, the wedding is in December. Tell Mr. Noonan it's crucial that you're on your feet by then."

Lucy said the therapy was "going fine." A wave of homesickness hit her like a blow to the chest. She said she had to go to the bathroom, and hung up.

It took her a few minutes to realize that it wasn't "home" she missed. It wasn't the apartment. They hadn't been in it long enough before the accident for her to miss it. It wasn't a *place* she was missing. It was her old life. Her life the way it used to be before That Night. She hadn't even realized how great that life was until she didn't have it anymore. She missed the Lucy she used to be.

She shouldn't call the way she felt "homesickness." She should call it "old*me*sickness." Because that was what it was.

Chapter 27

When Elizabeth had hung up, Lucy called Twin Willows, hoping for good news about Jude, Robin, or Tony. If Jude had been discharged because he'd made stunning progress after she left, that would give her the incentive she needed to work her buns off for Noonan tomorrow morning. Or if Robin was free of the harness now, or if Tony's condition had, through some amazing feat of medical technology, improved at all, Lucy would know there was hope, and would be eager to approach the sunroom tomorrow morning.

But there was no good news from the rehab hospital. Although Lucy asked to speak to Robin Papajohn, it was Jude who came to the phone. They were, he said, all the same. "Robin's giving everyone a hard time, but it's because she's depressed. I'm in braces now, up and around without my walker. She says she's glad, but I know it's hard on her when she's not making any progress herself. And I think she misses you, Lucy." Then he asked, "So, how are *you*? We've all been wondering. Are you getting physical therapy?"

Lucy was relieved to be able to tell him yes. After what he was going through with Robin, she'd have felt like a horrible coward telling him she was making absolutely no effort to walk again. Especially since, no matter how hard Robin was willing to work, she would never be as lucky as Lucy.

Lucky? Lucy was stunned. When since the accident had she ever thought of herself as lucky? Never. But compared to Robin, she was.

She told Jude about Noonan, calling him the "ex-Marine drill sergeant," then asked, "And Tony? How's Tony?"

"Tony's gone. His insurance ran out, so he had to leave our happy home here. He's living with a cousin in Rhode Island."

"A cousin? Not with his parents?"

"They said they thought Tony would be happier not coming back to his hometown, where everyone knows about the accident. The girl who was killed was really popular, and I guess some people haven't forgiven Tony. Tony figured even his own parents couldn't deal with having him there. But I've talked to him a couple of times after he left, and he seems to really like it at his cousin's. They have a pool, and he's in it a lot. And he's planning on going to school. He knows his way around computers pretty well, and there's a tech school where he lives that's wheelchair-accessible. He's going for a degree. He says, and he's right, you don't need legs to work on computers."

"That's great!" It *was* great. When Lucy left Twin Willows, Tony's future had seemed to be the furthest thing from his mind. He had never talked about it, and hadn't seemed to be planning for one. "I'm glad for him. I guess it's better that he went there than to his hometown."

Jude agreed.

"So, when are you leaving, Jude? If you're in braces, you must be just about ready, right?"

"Well, I still can't dance, but then," he added, laughing, "I wasn't much of a dancer before, either." His tone more serious, he said, "Technically, I could leave now. But I'd like a little more practice on these things, and besides, I want to wait until Robin feels better. I can't just desert her."

He wasn't anything like Robin's old boyfriend. "She's lucky to have you on her side, Jude. Tell her I said hi, okay? I'll try to call again soon."

When they had hung up, Lucy's emotions were in turmoil. She was happy for Tony. The news about him had given her an idea. She, too, knew her way around computers. There were a lot of things she could do with computer knowledge. Maybe she could run a business from her home one day.

Her own days fell into a pattern of sameness. Up early every morning, dressing in comfortable clothing in preparation for therapy, carelessly tossing her hair behind her ears and fastening it with clips to keep it out of the way. She worked her way up slowly to forty minutes, then forty-five, finally to a full hour of rigorous, painful exercises with stern taskmaster Ted Noonan. Ted wanted more time than that, but Lucy couldn't handle it. As it was, the sessions wiped her out so thoroughly, she spent most of the rest of the day in her room, reading or sleeping. She didn't even have enough energy to go to the computer, though she thought about Superguy often. He'd be wondering where she was.

Many evenings, Tia and Kendra drove out to see Lucy, bringing her magazines, books, and gossip. They were both upset to learn that Lucy's mother had given in and hired a tutor for her, which meant she wouldn't be returning to school with them. Lucy was impatient with them, wanting to return to her bed. She found that she had less and less to talk about with Tia and Kendra. They were "out there," living a life, and she wasn't.

But she could see how disappointed they were that she wasn't coming back to school. She tried to cheer them up by saying, "Maybe by January, I'll be out of this chair and back at Seneca with you guys, just like before."

"It won't be like before," Tia pointed out. "Dash will be walking through the halls with Jenny, not you," she added bluntly. "Are you sure that's not the reason you begged your mom for a tutor? Because you can't bear the thought of seeing them together?"

"No, that's *not* why, Tia. I'm over that." Liar. "I just don't want to have to steer this stupid chair up and down the halls at Seneca High. And my legs are already getting stronger, Ted said so. So I think maybe by December I'll be able to walk down the aisle at Elizabeth's wedding. Then I'll come back to school after the holidays."

"But it's senior year, Lucy," Kendra said sadly. "I can't believe you're going to miss the whole first half!"

Lucy held up a hand and counted on her fingers. "September, October, November, December. That's not the whole first half, Ken. That's only four months. I'll have five whole months of senior year. That's better than nothing, which," she added grimly, "is what I thought I was going to have the night that tractor-trailer came at me."

Kendra shuddered. "Yeah, you're right, I guess. But we'll miss you like crazy. Maybe if you work extra-hard with Mr. Noonan, you could come back even before January. By the way, I saw him and your mom having dinner at the Village Teahouse last night. They look so cute together."

"Cute? Please don't call my mom cute. She's a grown-up. She's very attractive. Pretty, even. She is not cute. Neither is he."

"They are when they're together," Tia insisted. "I saw them, too, yesterday afternoon. They were biking through the park downtown. Your mom was laughing at something he'd said. She almost fell off her bike."

Lucy drew her lips together in a thin, straight line. Her mother and Ted Noonan? Gross. "He never says anything that hilarious to me. And he never laughs at my jokes. I just figured he was born without a sense of humor. Laugh-challenged, that's my take on Noonan. Are you trying to say that I've read him wrong and it's really my jokes that stink?"

"Yes, Lucy, your jokes stink," Tia said with a grin.

"Maybe," Kendra offered, "he's just concentrating so hard on helping you get better, he doesn't really hear your wisecracks."

"Or maybe he just plain hates me." As much as Lucy loathed the idea of her mother liking

Ted Noonan, she kept thinking of what Tia had said — that Lucy's mother had been laughing so hard she almost fell off her bike. How long had it been since her mother had laughed like that? A long, long time.

Kendra also told Lucy that the house her mother was planning to buy was "a real dump."

"It belonged to some lady who was too old to work on the house. It even has a wheelchair ramp, because she couldn't get around. The ramp is why your mom is buying it, I guess. But boy, does it need work! My mom thinks your mom is throwing money away."

"Kendra," Tia said dryly, "depress Lucy some more, why don't you? I'm glad you're not running for Queen of Tact. You'd lose. Lucy, don't worry about it. Your mom and Elizabeth and Tim will have that place in great shape in no time. It's cute, really. It just needs fixing up a little, that's all. Ted Noonan will probably help, too."

Lucy wasn't worried about the house itself. It wasn't part of her reality. When she thought about going home, it was the apartment she pictured, not some old lady's house. What did worry her was the wheelchair ramp. How long was she going to need that?

It rained during the night, a cool, steady shower that broke the heat and provided a clear-skied, sunny, cool Friday afternoon.

Lucy's grandmother urged her to take advantage of the lovely day, but Noonan had been especially demanding that morning, and she was exhausted. "Maybe later," she promised, wheeling straight to her room.

She had just awakened from a deep, grateful sleep when a knock sounded on her door. Thinking it was one of her grandparents, Lucy called drowsily, "It's open!"

To her amazement, Andy entered the room, strode straight to her bed and scooped her up into his arms. "You," he said as Lucy stared up at him with her mouth agape, "are going outside. No argument. You're as pale and wan as a heroine in a Victorian novel. But this is not Victorian England, Lucy, and twentieth-century America likes its heroines pink-cheeked and healthy. So out you go!"

He didn't even take her chair.

When she was situated on the stone bench and Andy had taken a seat on the lawn in front of her, Lucy was painfully conscious of her sleep-tangled hair and lack of makeup. "You've got a lot of nerve," she said irritably, wishing she had changed out of her gray sweats after therapy. They weren't wrinkled. It took a lot to wrinkle sweats. But they weren't especially attractive, either. "I'm tired."

"You're not tired. You're oxygen-deprived."

"There's plenty of oxygen in my room."

"That's stale oxygen. This is fresh oxygen, which is what you need."

"Oxygen doesn't get stale." If he was still angry with her for not telling him the truth about her condition, it didn't show in his face. "You'd better watch out," she warned, "there are bees in that grass." She didn't see the white kit anywhere.

Andy laughed. "Nan would say it would serve me right if I got stung, if I'm stupid enough to intrude on bee territory."

Nan. The girlfriend. Lucy had forgotten.

Andy began talking then, about Nan, making her sound like the greatest thing since the compact disk.

As he talked, Lucy stopped listening. She was wondering, with a painful ache in her chest, if Dash had ever talked about *her* in that same way, with so much love and affection in his voice.

She didn't think so.

Because if he had, he couldn't have left her for someone else.

Chapter 28

"You have to rejoin the real world." Andy's stern admonition snapped Lucy back to awareness. "It's good that you're working so hard on your therapy, but you're not having any fun, Lucy. You sleep too much and when you're not sleeping you're hiding out in front of your computer. You're supposed to be having fun. You're seventeen."

"I'm almost seventeen."

Andy laughed. "So the fun stops at eighteen? It didn't for me."

Lucy didn't laugh. She didn't remind him that *he* hadn't had a close encounter with a tractor-trailer. It seemed pointless.

"Nan and I want you to come to a concert with us tonight. It's outdoors. No problem with your chair. It's a local group, no one you've ever heard of, but we like them. I think you will, too."

The "Nan and I" stung a little. Lucy had been part of a pair, not too long ago. She missed that.

She loved all kinds of music. But the thought of wheeling into a throng of music lovers sprawled on blankets on a lawn, all of them staring at her with curious or pitying eyes, made her feel sick. "Can't. I . . . I have a million things to do tonight."

Andy laughed again. "Oh, right." He stood up. "Pick you up at seven-thirty. Be ready, Lucy. If you're not on the porch, I'm coming in to get you. I've got to go pick up Nan now. You sit here for a while and think about how good that music is going to sound."

He was leaving? "How am I supposed to get back into the house? You're the one who brought me out here!"

"Your grandfather will take you in when you're ready. You haven't had enough fresh air yet. See you at seven-thirty."

"I'm *not* going!" she called after him as he rounded a corner of the house. "I'm *not*!"

But she did. And it was . . . interesting. People *did* stare as Lucy, with Andy and Nan behind her, wheeled into the crowd already situated on lawn chairs and blankets. But they didn't stare for long, and if they whispered about the "poor girl in the wheelchair," Lucy didn't hear them. Tia and Kendra had dates elsewhere that night, but Lucy ran into friends she hadn't seen since she left for rehab. Everyone seemed glad to see her. If some of them seemed at a loss for words after the initial, enthusiastic greeting, Lucy told herself it was because they weren't used to seeing her the way she was. She was different now. They didn't know how to deal with that. Join the club, she told them silently.

The music, loud and upbeat, was great, the air balmy, the sky starlit. Nan, a cute, plump, blond, was friendly and seemed determined not to treat Lucy like an invalid. When Lucy wanted lemonade, Nan pointed to a stand on the other side of the park and said casually, "It's only fifty cents. Quite a bargain, right? Get me one, too, okay?" handing Lucy two quarters. Lucy had expected Andy to go get the drink for her, and was appalled at the easy way Nan assumed Lucy could weave her way through the crowd by herself.

How was she supposed to wheel her chair and carry two cups of lemonade at the same time?

Reading the question in Lucy's face, Nan said in that same casual tone of voice, "They'll give you a little cardboard tray to sit on your lap to hold the cups."

Lucy was both astonished and annoyed. But she began to feel something else, as well. Something that she hadn't felt in a very long time. Someone other than Ted Noonan actually expected her to do something for herself. Noonan was just doing his job. He got paid to expect Lucy to do certain things. But Nan didn't. She had no stake at all in whether or not Lucy St. Cloud could do for herself. Yet she was not only taking it for granted that Lucy could wheel her way across the park and come back with refreshments, she was taking it for granted that Lucy would be willing to do it. As if . . . as if Lucy were just anyone . . . any healthy, normal person who wouldn't balk at being asked to go fetch a little lemonade.

As much as Lucy dreaded wheeling her chair back through the crowd to the lemonade stand, she was even more reluctant to disappoint Nan, to say, "Oh, no, you're wrong about me, I can't do that. I just can't!" She dreaded the look on Nan's face if she said that. Disappointment. Annoyance. Maybe even disgust. Andy would probably feel the same way, and Lucy would see it in *his* face, too.

"I do *not* want to do this," Lucy complained, but she was already turning her chair around, aiming it toward the lemonade stand.

"I know," Nan said softly. Then, "Make sure they put ice in it, okay? And don't spill any, 'cause for fifty cents they don't give you that much to begin with."

Don't spill any? Lucy was fuming as she steered carefully around the music lovers sprawled on blankets and sitting in lawn chairs. Don't *spill* any? Nan could walk to the lemonade stand and back twice in the time it would take Lucy.

But she made it. She had spilled no more than a few drops from one cup. A sly smile on her lips, that was the cup she handed to Nan. Okay, so Nan had been right. Lucy *could* do a thing or two. It hadn't been easy. She was sweating, her arms ached, and her legs hurt from jostling the chair over an uneven, grassy terrain. But she'd done it, and survived. Just the same, Nan shouldn't be bossing people around. So Lucy got the full cup.

A knowing grin creased Nan's features as she took the cup. But all she said was, "I guess we're even now, right?"

Lucy laughed.

She began going out more frequently with Andy and Nan. It was tricky. Sometimes it was very difficult maneuvering her chair, and there were places she simply couldn't go. The beach was out. Sand would have been impossible to negotiate. Stairs, too, were out of the question. Then there was the usher at one of the theaters who refused to allow Lucy's wheelchair to be parked in the aisle, pompously calling it "a fire hazard." They had to sit in the last row at the rear of the theater, her chair parked behind the pillars.

But there were accessible spots that were great fun. More open-air concerts. Restaurants with plenty of navigating room, where Lucy enjoyed her first cheeseburger since the accident. Malls with elevators. Once she learned to cope with the stares and the questions of children, Lucy relaxed and began to enjoy herself. She even reached the point where she could joke about being "a third wheel . . . I mean, wheels, plural."

Sometimes Tia and Kendra went along. Tia liked Nan. "She doesn't baby you, Lucy."

But I *want* to be babied, Lucy thought instinctively, then quickly realized that wasn't true. Not anymore. Not since the concert. She liked the way it felt to do things again. Because the laundry room at her grandparents' house was on the first floor, just off the kitchen, she had begun doing her own laundry, amazed at how useful that made her feel. She set the table every evening for dinner, a simple task as long as her grandmother got the plates down from the cupboard and placed them on the kitchen counter where Lucy could reach them from her chair. She was able to prune and water the potted flowers on the back porch, dust the furniture and the books in the lower bookshelves, and unload the dishwasher, though she couldn't reach the cupboards to put the dishes away.

There were still many, many things she couldn't do, and that was painfully frustrating. But she was also working very hard with Ted Noonan, and she was more optimistic than she had been since the accident.

In the last week before school began, she reached the point in her therapy where she could, with the help of a thick, padded shoulder harness that hung from a ceiling hook Ted had installed, pull herself up out of the chair and into an upright position. She could hardly call it "standing," since her feet weren't touching the floor that first time. The harness, its thick, black loops fastened under her arms and over her shoulders, supported her. It felt weird to be hanging upright from the ceiling, like a fixture or a fan. "I feel like a marionette," she told Ted the first time she tried the arrangement. "Look at the way my legs are dangling. Can't you lower me so I can put my feet on the floor?" He did so. But, the moment Lucy's feet touched the hardwood, she nearly fainted from the pain. Ted had to quickly yank her upward again.

They tried it again and again, and each time the pain was too intense to continue. Her optimism shattered, Lucy wept in bitter disappointment. "I'm never going to be able to stand up!" she shouted angrily after another aborted attempt. "Just shoot me now! I don't want to spend the rest of my life in that stupid wheelchair. I'm not brave enough. I'm *not*!"

"Yeah, you are," Ted said lazily, though he did try to comfort her by patting a shoulder. She was lying on the exercise table, her hands covering her eyes as she wept. "I admit, I didn't think you had it in you when I first walked into this house. But you've worked harder than any patient I've ever had, Lucy, and your legs are much stronger now." He flexed her left leg, bending it at the knee. "See there? Look at the muscle tone. That's a far cry from the way it was when we started. You see that, right?"

Lucy nodded. "But I also see that they still look like I'm wearing wrinkled stockings, and I also see that I can't put my weight on them, and I also see that they hurt all the time, and it's been months since the accident. Months!"

"Plastic surgery will take care of the way they look. Your mom has already talked to one of the doctors at Vassar about it. They're ready when you are. As for the pain, I'm no doctor myself, but I think that'll go away in time, too, once your legs are completely healed. If not, you'll just have to take aspirin, the way chronic arthritis patients do. There are worse things, Lucy."

He hadn't mentioned her third complaint — that she still couldn't put her weight on her legs without feeling faint. "And walking?" Lucy asked, removing her hands from her eyes and brushing tears from her cheeks. "What about that? Is that going to happen or isn't it?"

Ted shrugged. "Don't know. Like I said, I'm no doctor. We just have to keep trying, that's all. I'm game if you are. I think your family's just relieved that you haven't had anymore infections. The pneumonia really scared them."

Lucy knew he was seeing a lot of her mother. Tia and Kendra were happy to share any sightings they had of the happy couple. They were always disappointed when Lucy didn't share their enthusiasm.

But now, she thought maybe Ted wasn't so bad. He could have told her she was a vain, silly, shallow creature for caring how her legs looked, and he hadn't done that. And he never, ever lied to her about the way things were. Her grandparents did, sometimes, and she knew it was because they loved her and wanted her to feel better. Sometimes it even helped, for a little while. But most of the time Lucy wanted, needed, to be able to handle the truth. And Ted gave her that.

"Would it be so terrible," he asked now, "if it turned out that you couldn't walk again? I know your mom's worried that you might not be able to handle that, but I think you could, and I've told her so. How about it, Lucy? You must spend a lot of time thinking about it. How does it make you feel?"

The question startled and angered Lucy. Mostly, it startled her. She hadn't talked about her feelings in a long time. When people asked her how she felt, they meant physically, not emotionally, and she answered accordingly. She didn't even tell Tia and Kendra how she really felt about things, because she knew it would depress them, maybe even scare them. They'd been really relieved when she'd started going out in the evening at Andy's urging. They didn't want to think of her as depressed. So she'd stopped sharing her bad, scared moods with them. And her night terrors. But Ted Noonan wasn't a shrink. He wasn't Dr. Giardello at Twin Willows. Like he said, he wasn't even a doctor. If she was going to tell anyone what she was feeling, it wouldn't be him. Besides, he'd just tell her mother, and then her mother would be depressed.

"I don't think about it," she answered cooly, pulling herself upright by gripping the sides of the table with her hands. "Because I *am* going to walk again. I have to, for Elizabeth's wedding." For just one scary second, she was afraid that Noonan, with his usual honesty, would blurt out, "But that's only four months away!"

He didn't. He nodded and said, "Okay, then,

let's get back to work." If he was disappointed or hurt that she hadn't confided her true feelings, it didn't show in his face. His expression was impassive as he once again hooked her into the shoulder harness and urged her to try putting some of her weight on her legs when her feet touched the floor.

This time, she managed to remain standing nearly a minute before the pain became too much. Ted was jubilant.

But all Lucy could think was, What good will a minute do me? I can't even brush my teeth in one short minute.

She left the therapy session discouraged, her heart heavy. Loneliness sent her to the computer.

Hi Superguy.

Where you been? Missed you. Been looking for you. he answered.

She'd missed him, too. But it was getting difficult to carry on a conversation with him. There was so much he didn't know about her. So much he *did* know that wasn't true. She had to be so careful. Every time she was tempted to tell him the truth, confess everything, she reminded herself that only in her chats with him could she be the old Lucy. She needed that.

Just really busy. How about you? Lucy replied.

I get really cranky when I don't talk to you. Busy with the wedding plans? Superguy replied.

Oh. She'd forgotten she'd told him about Elizabeth's wedding. Very. Very busy.

Give me your phone number. I remember, no personal meeting. But I want to hear your voice.

She'd been warned about this, too. If she gave him her phone number, he could get her address, and might show up in person. She could just imagine the look on his face when he saw the wheelchair. Liar! his eyes would accuse. Then he'd turn around and run. Fast. Away from her.

But she did want to hear his voice.

Where do you live? she typed. She couldn't have a long-distance call on her grandparents' phone bill.

Ohio, he typed. The Buckeye state.

Long distance. Not good. Lucy debated with herself. If she gave him her phone number, what were the chances that he would suddenly show up on her doorstep? From Ohio was too far to drive just to see a girl, wasn't it? And he had said he understood about no personal meetings. It would be so great to talk to him on the phone, hear what he sounded like. And if he was willing to call her, pay the phone charges himself...

She gave him her grandparents' telephone number. But, she typed quickly, can you call during the day? After one o'clock? Ted would be gone by then. She could talk to Superguy in the privacy of her own room. Her grandparents would just assume it was a friend from town.

He said he could call whenever she wanted.

Telling him she had a date and "had to run," Lucy wrote, Talk to you soon, Superguy.

He wrote, Count on it.

She hoped she wasn't making a big, fat mistake. But when they moved into the new place, she wouldn't need to talk to him anymore, because she'd be back with family and friends. She wouldn't give him that new number.

He called the very next day. They talked for over an hour. They seemed to like all the same things, and he seemed interested enough in Elizabeth's wedding that he didn't cut Lucy off when she talked about it.

They talked every day for a week, always after one o'clock in the afternoon. When he asked Why aren't you in school? she wrote back, I only have morning classes. That might not be true in high school, but she knew it could be in college, because Elizabeth had worked her way through college by attending classes in the morning and working afternoons.

Lucy's telephone conversations with Superguy did a lot to ease her loneliness. And it was wonderful to spend that time being "the old Lucy."

At the end of that week, on a bright, sunny, Saturday morning, Lucy's mother arrived to tell her that the new house was ready, and she could, at last, come home.

Part Four

Part Four

Chapter 29

Watching from the sunroom window as Andy and her grandfather loaded the exercise equipment into her grandparents' pickup truck, Lucy's excitement at going home dimmed a little. She felt like a vagabond, wandering from place to place. First the hospital, then Twin Willows, then her grandparents' home, now on to a new and foreign place where she wouldn't feel any more at home than she had at rehab. Kendra had said the new house was "a dump." Lucy had never lived in a dump before. Even the apartment had been new and nice.

It's because of me, she thought despondently, because of my accident that we have to live in a horrible place. Tim will hate me. Elizabeth won't, because she's too nice, and she'll be moving out in December, anyway. But Tim just finished making new friends at the apartment complex, and now Mom's moving him again and he'll have to start all over. Because of me. Sooner or later, he'll get mad at me about something stupid and scream, "I hate you, Lucy! It's your fault we had to move to this old wreck of a house!" And she wouldn't blame him.

But the new place wasn't that bad. She knew it must have been when her mother bought it, because Kendra wouldn't make up something like that. But now the outside was freshly painted blue and white. Her mother told her Ted, Andy, Tim, Tia, and Kendra, had held a "painting party." "The house isn't that big," Sara said, "so it didn't take them that long. Do you like it?"

Lucy did. It was almost cute, just as Tia had said. The small, square lawn needed mowing and there was no front porch, just a wooden ramp leading to a platform and a glass front door. But the shutters had been painted a glossy black, there were potted red geraniums standing guard at the front door, and a brand-new shiny red mailbox hung on the wall beside the door.

The inside wasn't too bad, either. The house was small and compact, but very open, with a wide center hall. The rooms opened one to another, providing ample space for Lucy's wheelchair. The walls in the halls had been painted a creamy white and Elizabeth, Lucy guessed, had applied enough finishing touches to give the house a homey, welcoming look. The linoleum in the kitchen was old and faded, and the cupboards needed painting, but Sara said they would get to those things when they had time. "We decided to work on your room first."

Lucy's room was small, but very pretty. The walls had been papered in a rose-and-white stripe, while everything else — new bedspread, pillow shams, and curtains — were a crisp, pristine white. Her computer was in place on its desk and someone, probably Elizabeth, had provided Lucy with a new pencil cup, paper clip holder, and memo board covered with the same wallpaper that hung on her walls. A wide, deep window filled most of one wall, allowing in bright sunshine, making the small, pretty space welcoming. Pennants from Seneca High and framed photos of Lucy and her friends, brought from her room in the apartment, were displayed on the other walls and on the top of the white dresser. A white vase filled with flowers the same shade of rose as the wallpaper stripes sat on the white nightstand. Bookshelves framed the wide window, and Lucy's ancient stuffed animals served as bookends on each shelf.

"It's nice. I like it. Thanks, Mom." Lucy meant it. Judging from the faded yellow walls, ancient green draperies, and worn avocado rug in the living room, a lot of hard work had gone into updating her room. "It's really pretty."

"We had to put the exercise equipment in the dining room," Sara said. "We don't have time to entertain, anyway, so why do we need a dining room? There's a table in the kitchen where we'll eat our meals."

The problem with the dining room, Lucy discovered to her dismay, was that there was no door on the wide entry from the living room. The entire dining room could be seen from the front ramp, through the living room wall of windows. She didn't want the whole world watching her endure her therapy, and said so.

Her mother understood, and promised, "We'll hang a curtain over the entrance to the dining room. After the wedding, we'll move the equipment into Elizabeth's room. Right now, it's crammed with boxes and shopping bags. Looks like a department store. All of that will go when she goes, and there will be plenty of room for your therapy."

It wasn't a bad house, and the neighborhood seemed nice enough, though Tim complained that there were "too many old people." But he had already made two friends, who didn't stare at Lucy's wheelchair. Maybe he'd warned them earlier. The three of them spent most of the afternoon setting up Lucy's computer.

The house still needed a lot of work, and it bothered her that she wouldn't be able to help much. That first day, she did what she could, unpacking boxes and setting their contents on the kitchen table, making it easier for someone else to put the things away. It didn't seem like much, but her mother said, "Every little bit helps, Lucy."

Ted Noonan dropped in, and Tia and Kendra. Andy and Nan came shortly after two and spent the afternoon unpacking boxes. A few of the neighbors brought casseroles and didn't ask Lucy what had happened to her, which meant they'd already been clued in. Lucy was grateful. There were people in and out of the house all day. Neither Dash nor Jenny showed up, but Lucy hadn't expected them to. Hoped, maybe, just a little, but not expected. She wouldn't know what to say to them, anyway, and wouldn't want to create a nasty scene with so many people around.

Lucy didn't mind the noise and confusion. After feeling alone for so long, she liked having a full house. By the time she slipped beneath the sheets for the first night in her new room, she was exhausted. But she did feel like she had "come home," which surprised her. This little house had never been her home. Maybe she felt the way she did because her family had worked so hard to create a nice place for her to return to, or maybe it was because they had seemed so glad to have her back.

She didn't even mind that twice that day, she'd "caught" Ted Noonan with a familiar arm around her mother, Sara smiling up at him. It hadn't even bothered her that he seemed so at home in this house. He was going to be coming here every day to help her. Why shouldn't he feel at home?

She was almost asleep when the phone rang. When she answered, an unfamiliar male voice said, "Hi, Lucy. Bet you didn't expect to hear from me so soon, did you? How come you didn't give me your new number? I got it from your grandmother at the number you gave me. She sounded a little confused when I asked for Swifty, but then she figured out that I was a friend of yours. I like your real name. It's nice. Lucy St. Cloud. Pretty. Mine is Carl, by the way. Carl Swenson."

Superguy. In the excitement of the day, Lucy had forgotten that she'd given him her grandparents' telephone number. She hadn't planned to give him the new one. But she'd forgotten to tell her grandmother not to give it out. She didn't like it that he knew her name. Her grandmother always answered the phone, "St. Cloud residence." So he'd had her last name right away. And it wouldn't have been that difficult for Superguy to get the name "Lucy" out of her grandmother.

And now he had this new phone number. She hadn't planned to continue her conversations with him once she was home. The worst part was, it was her own fault.

She tried to put him off by telling him she was too tired to talk.

Instead of saying good-bye and hanging up, he told her he wanted to see her new house. "I don't mind making the trip. I want to meet you, and I want to be able to picture where you live. You say when, and I'll be there."

Like *that* was going to happen. "This isn't a good time. With the move and the wedding plans, we're really going nuts here. Maybe later, okay?"

Although he didn't sound happy about it, he didn't push, and promised to call her the following night.

If Lucy hadn't been so exhausted, she might have lain awake for hours, wondering what she was going to do about Superguy. Carl Swenson. Whatever. But she was too tired, and was asleep in minutes.

In the morning, she put her worries about him aside while she unpacked. Elizabeth came in to help, and after they had worked for a while, Lucy said abruptly, "I can't wear that peach dress in your wedding. It's too short." And she showed her sister her legs.

Elizabeth didn't even pale. "No problem," she said airily. "I've already ordered a longer version. To the ankle. That okay?" So she had already known about Lucy's legs. Their mother had probably told her.

With the new, longer dress already in the works, Lucy figured she had no choice. She had to do the very best she could to walk by December.

She tried. She gave Ted Noonan the best she had to offer, and when he wasn't there, she went into the dining room alone to exercise. Sara still hadn't got around to hanging a curtain in the doorway that faced the front entrance, but Lucy told herself that people were at work and at school during the day. It wasn't as if there'd be a steady parade of passersby to look at Lucy St. Cloud, in ugly gray sweats, bending and stretching and trying like mad to put her full weight on her legs. Which she still couldn't do.

When the phone rang around two o'clock, Lucy let it ring. She turned off the answering machine, unwilling to be distracted by an argument with Superguy about coming to see her. All she wanted to do now was work on her legs.

They were getting stronger every day. And she knew she looked healthier. All that exercise had improved her color. She was learning to do more things on her own, too. Ted had installed, with Andy's help, a lower-than-normal sink in the bathroom so Lucy could lean over it to wash her own hair. He had also rigged up a seat in the bathtub and a pulley overhead, which Lucy hadn't quite got the hang of yet. Elizabeth and Sara still had to help her. But she'd master it. She would.

Her tutor came every day. Mrs. Welsh was a retired teacher who spoke quietly but firmly, and politely ignored Lucy's condition. It felt weird to be "in class" alone, but Lucy was determined to graduate as scheduled, and did the work diligently. Tia and Kendra, back in school now, kept her updated on gossip, though they never once mentioned Dash or Jenny. And Lucy didn't ask. Couldn't ask. Didn't want to know.

She was deep into the middle of a solitary workout one late-September afternoon when the doorbell rang.

Darn! First of all, she didn't want to be interrupted because she had just this minute figured out how to place all of her weight on one foot while keeping the other off the floor by holding onto a chair. Second, anyone at the glass door had a full, clear view of her, which could *not* be a pretty sight.

The bell shrilled again. No one else was

home. Tim was at school, Sara and Elizabeth at work. Noonan and Mrs. Welsh had already left for the day.

Sighing with annoyance, Lucy plopped into her wheelchair, brushed runaway bangs out of her eyes, and wheeled to the door to yank it open. A salesperson probably. She'd get rid of him or her, fast.

The young man standing on the ramp's level platform was so tall, Lucy had to crane her neck to look up at him. He was wearing a navy blue suit, white shirt, and hideous tie striped in bright gold, purple, and scarlet. He looked older than her by a few years, and had a lean face with brown eyes behind wire-rimmed glasses. "Hi," he said informally. "I'm Donovan Ives. My father is your lawyer. Mitchell Dwyer's partner? Dwyer, Sloan, and Ives? I've been sent over here to ask you a few questions. Your mom said it would be okay, as long as I came after three, when your tutor and therapist had gone for the day."

"You're not Mr. Ives's son."

A dark eyebrow arched. "I'm not? He disowned me and forgot to break the news to me?"

Lucy had opened the door no more than a few inches. She kept it that way. "I've met Donovan Ives. A long time ago, at a Fourth of July picnic." Four years ago, to be exact. She was thirteen then, and just discovering that boys weren't so bad. The lawyer's son she'd been introduced to at the picnic was fifteen years old, short, skinny, had zits and a crew cut, which made him look as if he'd been scalped. She had quickly dismissed him as a nerd. Nice smile, she remembered now, but still a nerd. She hadn't seen him since. No way could this tall, confident-looking guy on her doorstep be Donovan Ives.

Seeing the skepticism in her eyes, her visitor fished around in an inside jacket pocket and brought out a picture ID, which he held up in front of her. The name on the license clearly read IVES, DONOVAN JOSEPH. And then he smiled, and there was no mistaking that smile. She still remembered it.

Amazing what four short years could do for a person. But then, look at how she'd changed in just a few short months. Only hers weren't such positive changes. The changes in him were better. Much better.

"You're too young to be a lawyer." But she opened the door a bit wider.

"I never said I was a lawyer. Not yet. I'm a freshman at Marist. But I work for my dad part time. Can I come in? This suit is hot, and the tie is killing me."

It was Lucy's turn to raise an eyebrow. "Yeah, me too. It would kill anyone with decent eyesight."

He laughed. Her estimation of his looks, which she had placed at about a seven — dark, thick hair, good bones, nice eyes — slid up a notch to an eight. "I'm color-blind," he explained. "Usually, my parents pick out my ties, but they weren't home when I left. My older brother gave me this one as a gag last Christmas. Didn't even know I had it on until just now. Is it really hideous?"

"Yes." Lucy smiled.

He laughed again. Lucy was painfully aware of how she must look. Why hadn't she worn the new pink sweats Elizabeth had bought her? She hadn't shampooed her hair yet, either. A waste of time when she was going to be working out. She had planned to do it later. Served her right for putting things off. But who knew an "eight" with a great smile was about to ring her doorbell?

"Well, can I come in or do I have to stand out here like a door-to-door salesman?"

Lucy moved her wheelchair aside to let him in.

Chapter 30

They sat opposite each other in the living room, Lucy in her chair, Donovan Ives on the new blue tweed sofa from the apartment, which Lucy realized with chagrin clashed horribly with the dingy yellow walls. Then she remembered that he was color-blind, and she relaxed. "I don't know if I can help much," she began. "I don't remember the accident very clearly."

He reached up to loosen the garish tie. "That's okay. I'm not taking a formal deposition or anything like that. You'll do that in my dad's office. But there were a couple of things he wanted me to find out." He pulled a notebook from a pocket and, pen poised at the ready, asked, "Okay, first question. How fast do you think you were going that night?"

Lucy answered all of his questions as honestly as she could. He wrote steadily, his head down. She took some satisfaction out of noticing that he had a lot more hair than Dash did, and then chastised herself for being juvenile. If he was an eight, the way *she* looked right now made her about a minus-twelve. He was here on business. Besides, like Andy, who wasn't as cute as this guy, he probably already had a girlfriend. She wasn't going to make that mistake again.

It's not me, it's just my hormones raging, she told herself, and settled back in her chair.

"Last and most important question," he said then, lifting his head. "It's a two-parter." He adjusted his glasses, pushing them firmly into place on what Lucy thought was a really great nose. Strong and straight, no bumps, not even a freckle. "The first part of my question is, What are you doing Saturday night?"

"Excuse me?" She must have heard him wrong. Her hormones had heard him wrong. He must have said, What were you doing *that* night? meaning the night of the crash.

Before she could tell him what she'd been doing that night, he repeated, "I said, are you busy Saturday night?"

It wasn't sinking in. Lucy wouldn't let it. "Saturday night?"

He grinned. "That would be the night after Friday night. The one that comes right before Sunday."

He couldn't possibly be asking her out. Then what *was* he doing? Alarm bells went off in Lucy's head. He had said he was in college. A freshman at Marist. Did Marist college have fraternities? She'd heard stories about fraternity hazings. Pranks and practical jokes. Was that what this was? A see-if-you-can-get-a-date-with-the-girl-in-the-wheelchair challenge?

Well, Mr. Fraternity had come to the wrong house. Lucy answered tartly, "Saturday night? Well, let's see, I was hoping for snow so I could brush up on my skiing. But since it's still in the seventies outside, I guess I'll have to settle for practicing my tap dancing instead."

The grin disappeared. "You don't think I'm serious? Why not? Couldn't be because of the wheelchair, could it?"

"No, it couldn't." Lucy hesitated, then asked, "I was wondering which fraternity you were pledging."

"None. No time right now, between classes and my job and basketball practice. Maybe later." He frowned. "Why? What's that got to do with what I asked you? Look, it's a simple question. Yes or no answer. Make it no, you're not busy. Then I can get on to the second part, which is, how about dinner and a movie Saturday night? That's the night after Friday, remember?"

He wasn't pledging a fraternity? This wasn't part of some stupid hazing ritual? "You're asking me out? To dinner?"

He shook his head in exasperation. "Yeah, Lucy, you know, food, waiters, a candle or two on the table, cloth napkins. Wherever you want. I'm partial to Italian myself but hey, food is food."

She tapped on the chair's wheels. "You have no clue what a pain this thing is."

"If the chair is a drag for you, we'll just leave it here." He flexed a muscle. "I think I can tote someone who weighs, what, about one fourteen?"

The thought of being carried into a restaurant like a small child repulsed Lucy. But she wanted to say yes. She wanted very much to say yes. Stalling, she said instead, "You don't even know me. You don't know anything about me except that I was in an accident."

"Yeah, I do." He leaned forward, waving the notebook at her. "Your mom likes to talk about you. In my dad's office. She made you sound so interesting, I took some notes." Reading from a page, he rattled off, "Computer literate, amateur photographer, loves to sing and dance, B minus student, popular —"

"Stop it!" Lucy cried.

Her shout silenced him.

"That was before," she said, more quietly.

He closed the notebook and asked dryly, "Does that mean you're not computer literate anymore?"

Lucy had to laugh. She couldn't help it. "Well, yeah, I still am. I spend a lot of time on the Net now. But that other stuff you said . . . I don't do those so much anymore."

"You can take pictures from your chair. You could sing. Dancing, I admit, may be out for now, but I'd guess you're still a B minus student. So, you haven't changed all *that* much, am I right? Anyway, I saw you exercising when I first got here, so you're working on dancing again. Your mom acts like she's optimistic, too."

Then why did she buy a wheelchair-accessible house? Lucy retorted silently.

"So what time should I pick you up?" Donovan Ives asked, standing up. "Seven o'clock?"

She was *not* going out with him. All she knew about him was that he was their lawyer's son, he had a great smile, and he wasn't too shabby-looking. But he had no clue about what it would take to get her to and from a restaurant or to and from a movie, and she didn't know *him* well enough to guess how he'd react to the hassle. What if he got disgusted and dumped her somewhere? If he was a jerk, that could happen. If he wasn't a jerk, he might still hate the hassle and then he'd regret pushing so hard for the date in the first place.

All she could do was save him from himself by turning him down. Anyway, this would not be a good time to have their lawyer feeling awkward with them because his son regretted the day he'd walked into the St. Cloud household and opened his big mouth. She had no choice here. Although his brown eyes behind the glasses were puppy-dog warm and that grin reminded Lucy that she was still a seventeen-year-old girl, she just had to say no.

"Okay," she heard a voice saying, "seven o'clock is good." The voice sounded suspiciously like her own, but of course it couldn't be. She had already made up her mind to say no.

"Great! Maybe I'll give you a call tonight, make sure you don't change your mind." Grin. "You might forget how completely charismatic and charming I was."

There was as much chance of that happening as there was of Lucy walking him to the door.

That *had* **been** her voice accepting the date.

When he had gone, she was conscious of feeling something she hadn't felt in a very long time. Excitement. Anticipation. She was actually looking forward to something, something a lot more interesting than going to the movies with Andy and Nan. Maybe she'd buy a new blouse, get her hair cut.... Too bad Robin wasn't here to work her magic.

Lucy thought of Superguy, and flushed guiltily. She had promised to call him. But she was running out of excuses about not meeting him in person. Besides, she'd just spent over an hour talking to a real human being. The need to talk to someone she'd never actually met had diminished. For now, anyway.

As she wheeled to her room, Lucy's heart was lighter than it had been for a very long time.

Until she parked in front of the mirror in the hall and caught a glimpse of herself. It was awful. Stringy hair matted down from the exertion of exercising. No makeup, not an ounce, and her skin was pale from being indoors far too much. Dingy gray sweats.

She stared, disheartened, into the glass, thinking, Why on earth would someone who looks like Donovan Ives ask out someone who looks like me? Even if I could dance, I'd still look repulsive.

She got it then. It hit her like a hammer between the eyes. How could she be so stupid?

Donovan Ives was the son of their lawyer. Mr. Ives was not only their lawyer, he was, like Mitchell Dwyer, a friend of the family. That's why they'd all been together at the Fourth of July picnic four years ago. Donovan had said her mother talked about her a lot in the law office. Lucy could imagine the conversation. Her mother saying, "Poor Lucy. She hardly ever gets out of the house, and when she does, it's never a real date. She used to date all the time. But now . . ." And Mr. Ives, a true gentleman, saying, "Oh, Donovan will ask her out, won't you, son?"

Lucy blanched in horror, envisioning Donovan, probably sitting at a desk, lifting his head to ask, "Who, me?" But if he was a good son — or if he just wanted to keep his job — he'd do what his father asked.

Lucy hid her face in her hands. She was on fire with shame and embarrassment. How *could* they? How could her mother and Mr. Ives do this to her? To Donovan?

Worse, how could *she* have been stupid enough to say yes?

Lucy whirled and went straight to the telephone in her room. With trembling hands, she looked in the directory for the correct number. The message she left on the answering machine was short, almost brutal. "Forget Saturday night. Can't make it. My mistake. Sorry."

She was pleased that her voice was steady and unemotional. And that she had restrained herself from adding, "I don't need pity dates!"

It was a good thing her mother wasn't home. If she was, the house would be ringing with angry shouting.

Lucy had advanced in her therapy to the point where she could hoist herself from her chair onto the special seat in the bathtub. To calm her fury, she took a very long, hot shower. It didn't help, but her hair, freshly shampooed and ponytailed wet, felt better. She put on a clean, red terrycloth robe, and was on her way to the kitchen for a cup of hot tea when the doorbell rang.

Now what?

She could see him standing outside the door the minute she wheeled into the hall. The stiff, upright way he was standing told her he was angry. Which probably meant he'd got her message.

What was his problem? What part of "Forget Saturday night" did a college freshman not understand? He should be thanking her.

He continued to ring the bell insistently. Lucy gave up and answered the door. He had changed his clothes, dressed now in jeans and a white long-sleeved shirt, open at the throat, sleeves rolled to the elbow. But it wasn't only his clothes that were different. The eyes, such a warm brown earlier, were dark and cold.

Before Lucy could say, "What are you doing here?" he strode past her and advanced into the living room, where he turned to face her.

Lucy sat mute at the door, staring at him, waiting to hear what, if anything, he had to say.

What he had to say was, "Do you really think that being in that chair gives you special privileges? Your legs may keep you from walking, but they sure don't stop you from stomping all over someone's feelings, do they?"

Chapter 31

Lucy stayed where she was, beside the open front door. He'd be leaving in a minute, anyway. "Excuse me?"

"If you've changed your mind about going out with me, that's fine," he said angrily. "I can deal with that. I haven't forgotten what it's like to be turned down. No problem. But you didn't have to be so rude about it. Answer my question. *Do* you think being in that chair gives you special privileges?"

No one had been so angry with Lucy in a very long time. Maybe Tia when she found the cache of pills. But that was different. Tia, at least, had understood. This guy didn't look like he was about to understand anything.

Lucy knew, then, that she'd jumped to the wrong conclusion. If Mr. Ives had browbeaten his son into asking her out, Donovan wouldn't be so angry now. She'd been way off base. How to explain that? "I . . . I thought —"

"You thought what?"

She didn't want to tell him the truth. It was too embarrassing. But she couldn't think of a lie that would work. That she'd had a better offer for Saturday night? Not likely. In a subdued voice, she said, "I thought my mother and your dad cooked this up. That they talked you into asking me out. It made me mad." She left the doorway then, wheeling on into the room to face him, tilting her head up at him to say, "I'm sorry. I *was* rude. I just —"

"You thought I wouldn't be asking you out unless someone forced me to? Why? Because of that chair?"

And the way I looked this afternoon, Lucy thought but didn't say. It sounded too shallow. Maybe he was one of those rare ones who didn't judge people by appearances. Had to be, or he wouldn't be here now. "It's not just that," she answered. "But I'm sorry I hurt your feelings."

He sank down on the couch and leaned toward her, his hands on his knees. "Look, Lucy," he said earnestly, "I do remember meeting you at that picnic. I thought you were the prettiest girl I'd ever seen." He smiled then. "I still do. But I could tell by the look on your face that what you saw was a total geek standing in front of you. Guys know things like that. It hurt. I knew it was true, but it still hurt."

Lucy felt the need to defend herself. "I was only thirteen, Donovan."

"And I was fifteen. And sensitive. Too sensitive, probably."

"You're not a geek now." Understatement. Tia would be impressed.

He shrugged. "Maybe not. But I haven't forgotten what that felt like. I hope I never do, because I plan to be a defense attorney and represent people no one else cares about. People who've been written off for one reason or another. So I need to remember how that feels. Sometimes it comes back to me in a nasty little rush, like when I got your message. You were dismissing me again, just like you did at the picnic. And not very politely, either."

Lucy felt her cheeks flushing. "I said I was sorry. And I am."

"Okay, I guess I get it. But my father doesn't pick my dates for me, Lucy. And as much as I like your mother, I don't know her well enough to let her play matchmaker for me." He shook his head. "You thought I'd let my dad set me up? His idea of a good time is an exciting game of bridge. I don't play bridge."

With a straight face, Lucy said, "I do. It's great fun."

Donovan's jaw dropped. "You're kidding!"

She laughed. "Yeah, I am. The only card game I know is Old Maid. And my brother always wins."

He laughed, too, then, the last bit of anger gone from his face. The eyes were warm again. "So, are we set for Saturday night?"

"I guess." To make up for her mistake and her rudeness, she added impulsively, "You could stay for dinner tonight if you want. I'm cooking. Spaghetti. No meatballs, just meat sauce, but it's pretty good. Garlic bread and a salad."

He stayed.

She was relieved that he didn't just sit at the kitchen table and stare at her as she wheeled from stove to refrigerator to sink and back again. He collected pots and kettles for her, chopped vegetables, and buttered the garlic bread, talking all the while about different subjects: music, movies, his classes at Marist. Lucy found herself relaxing. She had a hard time reaching the back burners on the stove from her chair, and wasn't insulted when he took the kettle of water from sink to stove for her. It was nice having someone to help.

They were getting along fine when the phone rang. Lucy plucked the red receiver off the wall and heard Superguy's voice. He sounded very angry. He was shouting so loudly, she was sure Donovan could hear it. She wheeled her chair as far out of the kitchen as the cord would stretch, aware of Donovan's curious eyes on her.

"I can't talk now," she said, her voice purposely low. "Later."

Ignoring that, Swenson asked, "Where have you been? I've been calling and calling! You're not trying to avoid me, are you, Lucy? I've decided to come see you this weekend. Meet me at the mall closest to your house, in the food court. They have one. I checked. Seven o'clock, Saturday night. If you're not there, I'll come to your house."

He was coming *here*? No, he couldn't. "How do you know where I live?"

"Real estate transactions. You can find them if you know where to look. Your grandmother said your mom bought the house, so I did some digging. Twenty-seven Laurel Lane, right?"

That *was* their new address. Lucy's knuckles whitened on the phone cord. He was coming *here*? She had counted on him not being dumb enough to make such a long trip just to see her. Maybe that made *her* the dumb one.

She had a date with Donovan Saturday night. Nothing on earth would make her break that. And who did this guy think he was, coming to see her when she'd said no personal meetings?

This was all her fault. She had started it by

giving him her grandparents' telephone number. From that, he'd found out her real name and her new number. Now he even knew where she *lived*.

"I'm busy Saturday night," Lucy whispered into the phone, painfully conscious of Donovan waiting in the kitchen.

"*Next* Saturday, then. And I won't take no for an answer a second time, Lucy. I *have* to see you."

On the computer, he hadn't seemed real. Just letters typed on a screen. But he seemed very real now.

"I'll be out of town for a while on business, but I'll call you a week from Friday night and confirm. *Take* my call, Lucy. Don't leave me hanging." And he hung up abruptly.

She sat with the phone in her hands for several minutes, hoping Donovan hadn't heard enough of the exchange to guess that she was upset. Amazing how much trouble she could get into without ever leaving her house. Dumb, dumb, dumb!

She had no idea how to handle this problem with Super . . . with Carl Swenson from Ohio. And she had less than two weeks to come up with something brilliant.

But when she returned to the kitchen, Donovan looked so at home there, sitting at the table shredding lettuce with capable hands as if he'd been doing it at that same table for years, she pushed all thoughts of Superguy out of her head and went to help. She wasn't going to spoil what could be the best evening she'd had in a long time by thinking about how dumb she'd been.

It *was* one of the best evenings she'd had in a long time. When her mother arrived home from work, she barely hid her glee at finding a good-looking guy in the kitchen with Lucy. Because of her visits to the law office, she knew Donovan, and seemed to like him. Ted Noonan showed up for dinner, and Andy and Nan arrived during dessert. No one seemed to have any trouble making conversation.

The best moment for Lucy came when Tia and Kendra arrived shortly after seven. Lucy met them at the door, saying airily, "Oh, c'mon in, I want you guys to meet Donovan Ives."

"Who's Donovan Ives?" Tia peered around the corner to look into the kitchen. When she withdrew her head, she said, "He looks too intellectual to be your type. But maybe you've wised up. And he *is* cute. I repeat, who is he?"

"Our lawyer's son." Lucy grinned. "We're going out Saturday night. Dinner and a movie."

They would have shrieked then, if Donovan hadn't been in the next room. Tia dragged Lucy into her room and made her give a play-by-play account of her first meeting with him. She left out the part about thinking her mother had arranged the date, also the rude message she'd left on his machine.

"It's about time," Tia said when Lucy had finished. "You'll have a blast." She grinned wickedly. "Let me know what movie you're seeing. I'll put a bug in Jen's ear that she's just got to see it and the best time to go is Saturday night. I'd kill to see the look on Dash's face if he walked into a movie theater with her and saw you sitting with a cute guy. A cute, *older* guy. Wouldn't that just be great?"

Lucy's eyes darkened. "It would be a whole lot greater if *I* were walking into the theater, too."

"Uh-oh, self-pity alarm!" Tia cried. "Don't start that, not when you're feeling so up. C'mon" — tugging on Lucy's chair — "let's go check this guy out. I have to give the Perez stamp of approval — which, may I remind you, I never gave Dash? And look how *that* turned out!"

Lucy didn't want to think about Dash. She didn't want to think about Superguy, either, but when she passed the phone in the kitchen, she felt a guilty pang. She should have told Tia and Kendra about him. This was something she wasn't going to be able to figure out on her own. Maybe three heads together could come up with a solution. If not, she could be in trouble.

Chapter 32

But it wasn't Tia whom Lucy talked to first about Superguy. It was Robin.

Their phone conversation was the first they'd had since Lucy left Twin Willows and it went on for two hours. They had a lot of catching up to do. Robin said they heard from Tony regularly. "He hasn't signed up for physical therapy, though. I don't think he's going to. It's such a waste. But he *is* going to school." Jude had been discharged, but returned faithfully every weekend to visit Robin. Lucy could tell she was happy about that. The best news was that Robin's upper body strength had improved to the point where she no longer wore the harness. "I can sit up alone now." She laughed. "And I can hug Jude."

That made it easier to tell Robin about Donovan Ives, although Lucy was careful to add hastily, "I hardly know him, but we *are* going out Saturday night." She then went on to say, "But I have a problem with this other guy." She really needed to confide in someone. Why not Robin? "I met him on the Internet. His code name is Superguy, but his real name is Carl Swenson, and he's from Ohio. I thought I was so safe talking to him on the computer, even on the phone, because I figured he'd never come all the way to Poughkeepsie, but he says he *is* coming. I should never have given him a phone number. That's how he found out everything else. He knows where I live. I don't want to meet him, but he's coming here, and if I don't meet him at the mall, he'll come to the house."

She was grateful that Robin didn't say, as Tia surely would have, "Oh, Lucy, how could you be so stupid?" Instead, Robin said, "I think you should go take a look at him. Check him out."

"You *do*?"

"Yeah. When he gets there. Take someone with you to the mall and hide where he can't see you but you can see him. He doesn't have a picture of you, does he?"

"No."

"Good. Then he can't recognize you even if he does catch you scoping him out. But . . . how will you know him?"

"I guess he'll give me a clue when he calls to set it up."

Robin thought for a minute. "Okay, so you'll

be able to pick him out. Just go there, take a look. If he's revolting, go back home without saying hello. If he looks interesting, maybe you should introduce yourself. You don't know if this thing with the lawyer's son is going to go anywhere, right? Might as well hedge your bets, Lucy. That's what my brother Crew always says. And you did say you liked Superguy a lot at first."

"I thought we had a lot in common. Now, I'm not so sure. I just don't get why he's so mad all of a sudden."

"Maybe he's one of those guys we've all heard about, the ones who use the Net like fishermen, only to catch people, not fish. And he's mad that you're not jumping into his net. But go take a look at him, anyway. You never know." But just before they hung up, Robin warned, "Be careful, okay? And call me after you've got a good look at this guy." She laughed again. "If he's cute, maybe *I'll* give the Net a shot."

In spite of Robin's unsettling warning, Lucy was glad she'd called. So much good news, and she felt better for having talked to someone about Superguy, even though Robin hadn't solved her dilemma. The thing was, she didn't have to think about it until a week from Friday. She'd come up with a solution by then.

Donovan had thanked her for "a great time"

when he left the house shortly after ten o'clock on Monday night. And if she hadn't known that he meant it then, she knew it for sure when he showed up at her house every night that week. At first, he brought papers, saying they were close to a settlement with the insurance company. That was good news. Lucy had been dreading testifying in court, in front of a bunch of people. But by Wednesday evening, Donovan dropped all pretense of being there on business. When she opened the door, he held out his hands and said with a grin, "Look, they're empty. No excuses this time. I'm just here to see you. Deal with it."

Lucy dealt.

Dealing with Donovan wasn't the problem. A lack of privacy was the problem. The house was small, and seemed always to be full of people. Lucy's mother and sister were home most evenings, going over wedding plans and sorting out their purchases from shopping trips to New York City. Tim and his friends were usually in his room, riveted to the computer screen, and Ted was there every evening, engaging Donovan in conversation about sports. It seemed to Lucy that if avid sports lovers weren't actually engaging in sports, they were talking about them. It was irritating. Donovan had come to see *her*, not Ted. Andy and Nan dropped in on Wednesday and Thursday nights and stayed until quite late, and Tia and Kendra were there every evening.

Lucy was torn about the lack of privacy. Sometimes, having all those people around made her feel safe. She didn't *want* to be alone with Donovan. She was so attracted to him, she just might fall right into his arms. That would not be good. She wasn't ready for that. Other times, she thought she'd go nuts if she didn't get at least five whole minutes alone with him. That was how she was feeling when Donovan left on Wednesday night.

She wheeled out onto the front platform with him, closing the door behind her. Everyone else was deep in conversation in the kitchen about Seneca's football team. Their loud words faded as she firmly shut the door. The sudden silence, except for occasional street sounds, was a relief.

It was cool and clear outside, with the crisp, tangy smell of autumn in the air. Donovan smiled down at her and said, "I guess I'm going to have to wait until Saturday night to get you alone." He paused, and then suggested, "We could go for a drive, Lucy. My car's right out front. I just filled the tank yesterday."

Lucy was tempted. But he'd have to wrestle with her chair Saturday night, as it was. If he found out tonight what that was like, he might cancel their Saturday date.

No, he wouldn't. He wasn't like that. At least, he didn't seem to be. He really was nice. And he laughed at every single one of her jokes, even the really lame ones. She loved the way he threw his head back when he laughed, loved the way a thick lock of dark hair fell across his forehead. Sometimes she was tempted to reach out and push it back into place. But she didn't. Because she couldn't forget how wrong she'd been about Dash.

And she wasn't getting involved with *any* guy while she was in this stupid chair. Maybe that was silly, because other people like her fell in love, got married, even had families. But she couldn't help how she felt.

"Can't go for a ride. It's late. I've been working on my therapy really hard this week, and I'm beat. December is coming up so fast. It scares me the way time is flying by. Liz is counting on me, and some days I feel like I haven't made that much progress." She had hoped to be in braces by Thanksgiving, but here it was late September already, and her legs still hurt almost all the time. But they *were* getting much stronger. And she could see the muscles developing.

"Ted says you're making great progress."

"He does? He never tells me that."

"Doesn't want you to get overconfident, probably."

"No chance of *that*." Maybe she had been once upon a time. She saw herself striding through the halls at Seneca, head high, smiling at everyone, her camera on one shoulder, backpack filled with computer disks swinging behind her. She had thought then that she had just about everything she wanted. Well, she *did* . . . *then*. Not now. "And it wouldn't kill Ted to say I was doing okay, once in a while. It might help."

"Would it help if I said it?"

He was being too nice. It made her nervous. She wanted him to kiss her, and that wasn't going to happen. She didn't even want it to. Yes, she did. No, she didn't. Oh, yeah, she *did*. "Gotta go in," she said hastily, backing up and turning the chair around. "I'm cold."

"Okay." He sounded disappointed. "I've got a family thing with my parents tomorrow night, and a game Friday night, so I guess I won't see you until Saturday night. Seven, remember?"

She would forget her own name before she'd forget that Donovan Ives was picking her up for a date at seven on Saturday night. "Right. See you then."

Lucy sat on the platform for a few minutes after his car, an unglamorous red sedan, disappeared down the street and out of sight. The only time they'd talked about the accident was when she answered his questions for the forms his father had sent. He hadn't asked her how she felt, being in a wheelchair, and she hadn't volunteered the information. So why did she have the feeling that he knew? How could he? How could anyone, unless they'd gone through the same thing?

When she was with Donovan, she almost — but not quite — forgot she couldn't walk. Until moments like the one tonight when she'd thought about being kissed. It had occurred to her then that if she were standing, he wouldn't have to bend over so far to kiss her, and had wished with a sharp pang in her chest that she was up out of the chair and standing on her own two feet.

Was that ever going to happen? She was working so hard. It hurt, and it was exhausting, but she didn't want to need her chair for Liz's wedding, even though Liz herself said, "Why not? You can just roll down the aisle ahead of me. No one will care."

Lucy had argued, "*I'll* care."

Feeling chilled, and not just because of the autumn night, Lucy turned her chair around and went back inside. Her feelings for Donovan weren't the only thing troubling her. It was time to confide in Tia and Kendra about Superguy.

Chapter 33

"I knew it!" Tia shrieked when Lucy told her and Kendra about Superguy. "I knew that accident did something to your brain! That's why it took you so long to get a clue about Dash and Jenny. And now you're telling us you actually gave some Net nut your *phone* number? Lucy, you've totally lost it!"

Kendra asked, "Did he say what he looks like? I wonder if he's cute."

"Ken!" Tia sat on Lucy's bed, her legs folded up underneath her. "Lucy, this guy could be a serial killer. You aren't really going to meet him at the mall, are you?"

"Well, Robin said I should go take a look at him. If he doesn't look like he said he did, or there's anything weird about him, I'll just go back home. Then if he calls again, I'll tell him I lied, that I'm really forty-six years old, and married with seven kids. Married to a *cop*."

Tia looked doubtful. But Lucy could tell she was fighting her natural curiosity. She wanted to get a look at Superguy, too. She just didn't think she *should* want to. "Donovan likes you, Lucy. A lot. Anyone can see that. I thought you liked him, too. You laugh a lot when he's around. If you do like him, why do you care what this other guy looks like?"

Because when Donovan finds out how much trouble I am, Lucy thought, he'll split, like Dash. And then I won't have anyone. Aloud, she said, "He sounded so nice when we met in the chat room. And on the phone. I just don't think I should write him off without at least checking him out." She didn't mention how angry Carl Swenson had sounded on the phone the last time she'd talked to him. Tia wouldn't like that at all.

"We're coming with you." Tia looked at Kendra for confirmation. "You're not going to the mall alone."

Lucy laughed. "Duh. Like I could go alone. How would I get there? It's next Saturday night. You don't have a date, do you?"

"I do," Kendra said. "And it's with Sean Porter. Can't you make it for a different night?"

"I can't do that. He's coming all the way from Ohio, Ken. But you don't have to break your date with Sean. Tia and I can go." Tia might have trouble with the wheelchair. But Lucy didn't want to ask anyone else to help. Bad enough that she'd had to confess to her two best friends how reckless she'd been. She wasn't bringing Tim or Andy in on it, too. She and Tia would just have to manage.

"How tall did he say he was?" Tia asked. Lucy knew then that Tia would show up next Saturday night no matter *who* asked her out between now and then. She was hooked.

As Andy and Nan were leaving later that night, Andy turned to Lucy to say, "I hear you and Donovan are on for Saturday night. Want some company? We could double."

Lucy thought fast. Andy could help with the wheelchair. Maybe Donovan wouldn't mind it so much, then. More important, having two other people along would keep Donovan at a safe distance. Which was where she did — didn't — did want him.

She came very close to saying, Sure, come on along! Two things stopped her. One was the image of herself sitting across a table from Donovan, talking, laughing, having him all to herself. A very enticing picture. The other was the expression she imagined on Donovan's face when Andy and Nan showed up Saturday night. Instinct told her he would be very disappointed. It wouldn't be fair, just because she was too chicken to be alone with him.

"I don't think so," she heard herself saying, and was happy with the words coming out of her mouth. "Maybe another time." If there was another time.

Andy grinned. "Gotcha. Have a great time."

She did. The best. Donovan dealt with the wheelchair and the business of getting her in and out of the car as if he'd been doing it all of his life. Although he could have left the chair in the trunk and easily carried her to and from the restaurant and the movie, she was grateful that he didn't offer. If she ever found herself in Donovan's arms, she didn't want it to be for transportation purposes.

He did ask her, over dinner, if she ever got "really depressed."

Lucy didn't know how to answer. Saying yes would be too much of a downer. They were supposed to be having a good time. But saying no would be a lie. He wasn't someone she wanted to lie to. And if he didn't want the truth, he wouldn't have asked.

She settled for saying, "It's better than it was at first. I think that's probably because of Ted. He just won't let up. He's determined that I'll walk again some day. When I think he's right, I feel better."

"It's not just him." There *was* a candle on the table, in the center. It cast golden shadows over the white tablecloth and warmed Donovan's brown eyes. "You're determined, too, right?"

How would he react if she confessed that she still had many countless nights when she cried herself to sleep because her life wasn't what it used to be? He wouldn't turn and run, leaving her with the check. She was pretty sure that wasn't who he was. But maybe he'd think twice before he ever called her or showed up at the house again. "Yeah, I guess. I wasn't, for a while. When I was at my grandparents, I hardly worked at all." She told him about the bee incident. "I guess that's what woke me up. Feeling so helpless, when Andy was in so much trouble. After that, being back with my family helped a lot, even if the house *was* strange at first."

The movie was funny, a sweet, romantic comedy. Halfway through it, Donovan reached over to Lucy's chair, parked in the center aisle, and took her right hand in his. He held it throughout the movie.

But on the way home, Lucy found herself becomingly increasingly agitated. Her brain was waging a war with her feelings. Her feelings reminded her that she'd been lonely for a long time now; that Donovan was nice and sweet and funny and acted like he cared about her, at least a little; that she ought to shoot down the wall she'd been building against him and just relax. But her brain kept reminding her of

Dash, and how eager he'd been to leave that hospital room and go straight to Jenny Cooper. And how he'd never once showed up at rehab. Her brain then went on relentlessly to remind her that the last thing Donovan Ives needed was a girl who couldn't take care of herself. Couldn't walk into a restaurant or a movie theater, couldn't dance, couldn't even stand up to be kissed. Who needed that? Not Donovan.

By the time he pulled into her driveway and turned off the ignition, Lucy's defenses were solidly in place. Until she could take care of herself again, the way she always had before, she wasn't taking on a new relationship, not even with someone she liked as much as she did Donovan Ives.

Still, she weakened when he turned to her on the front seat, smiled, and said, "I've wanted to do this since the first day I walked into your house," reached out to pull her close to him, and bent his head to kiss her. Lucy kissed him back. She knew she was kissing him back because the kiss lasted a long time, and it couldn't have with only one person doing the kissing. She could feel all of her resolve melting as he held her close to his chest. She felt, for the first time in a long time, safe and warm and content. The way the *old* Lucy had felt most of the time.

In a swift, sudden movement, Lucy pulled away. The old Lucy would have been kissing

Dash — because she hadn't known then that she was about to get her heart broken into tiny little fragments. Why let herself in for that again?

"What's wrong?" Donovan sounded confused. Not that she blamed him. "I thought —"

"I have to go in now." Her words, even to her own ears, sounded stiff and formal. Unfriendly. "We're painting the living room tomorrow, and I want to help. If I'm too tired, I won't be of any use." She wouldn't be of much use, but she intended to try.

"Oh. Sure. Okay. I'll get your chair." He sounded hurt and confused. Had the way she pulled away reminded him again that only four short years ago, he'd been a geek girls weren't interested in kissing? She hadn't meant to do that. He wasn't a geek now, and she'd forgotten that he'd ever gone through that pain, which must have been miserable.

"I'm sorry," she said quietly. But he was already out of the car.

She couldn't let him leave thinking that her rebuff had anything to do with him. On the ramp platform, she tried to explain. "It's just that I don't have time to think about anything but getting well, Donovan. I can't waste time on anything else."

She knew that was a poor choice of words when she saw, in the porch light, the expression on his face. What guy wanted to be told that being with him was a "waste of time"? His eyes had darkened, his mouth was set grimly.

"I didn't mean that," Lucy amended hastily. "But if I'm going to get my old life back, I have to concentrate."

"Your old life?" His voice was cold. "I guess that would include your old boyfriend? The track star?"

Oboy. Her mother must have mentioned Dash during one of those conversations in the law office. "No. That's history. I need to do this for myself, Donovan, not for anyone else."

"Right." He nodded curtly. She could tell he didn't believe her. There was a moment or two of awkward silence. Then he said too politely, "I wish you luck. I hope you get everything you want." He turned to leave, then turned back to say, "I promised Ted and your mom that I'd be here tomorrow to help with the painting. I'm not going to break my promise. But I won't get in your way."

She hadn't *said* she didn't want to see him anymore. "Donovan —" she began.

But he was already down the ramp and getting into his car.

He slammed the door, hard, and drove away too fast.

Chapter 34

Sunday was one of the most miserable days of Lucy's life. Everyone, including Donovan, came to the St. Cloud house to paint the living room a pale, buttery yellow, hang new white drapes at the windows, and rearrange the furniture. Sara had stocked up on food from the grocery deli and Elizabeth's fiancé, Adam, someone Lucy really liked, had driven up from New York City. Andy and Nan, wearing old cutoffs and T-shirts, were in high spirits, eager to get to work. Kendra, fresh from her date with the elusive Sean, was bubbling over with joy. Everyone was in such a good mood, no one seemed to notice that Donovan's face was cold and impassive, Lucy's guilty and anxious. Except Tia. Tia noticed.

"You had a fight with him, didn't you?" They were in the kitchen, collecting cold drinks for everyone. "I can tell. What'd you do, mention Dash?"

"No, I didn't. *He* did. My mother must have told him. But that's not why he's mad."

"Then what?" Tia dumped ice cubes from trays into a plastic ice bucket. "He made a pass at you and you rejected him?" She laughed. "Like that could happen!"

Guilty silence from Lucy, always her response when Tia guessed the truth as she so often did.

Tia clapped a hand to her forehead. The hand was cold from the ice water, and she gasped. Recovering, she cried, "You are so seriously disturbed! Is it Dash? You can't get him out of your head?"

"No. It's *not* Dash himself. It's his treachery that's hard to forget. But it's not just that. I told Donovan the truth . . . I need to concentrate on getting better, on walking again, maybe by December. I don't want to be distracted. He distracts me. Besides, what guy needs a girl in a wheelchair? It'll be different when I'm walking again."

Tia nodded skeptically. "Uh-hum. And you think he's going to hang around until you decide the timing is right? I know he's nice, Lucy, but he's not a lap dog. Look, you were in a wheelchair when he *met* you. That didn't stop him from falling for you . . . fast. People in wheelchairs *do* have romances. Donovan obviously doesn't care if you have two good legs, or if you have any legs at all." Tia glanced over her shoulder into the living room. "I think you really blew it this time. He looks awfully mad."

"I know."

Hoisting the ice bucket in one hand, and placing a tray of plastic glasses on Lucy's lap, Tia grinned and asked, "So tell me, on a scale of one to ten, how was the kiss before you blew him out of the water?"

Remembering, Lucy smiled ruefully. "Eleven. Maybe a twelve."

"Wow! You still going to the mall next Saturday night? To see that computer guy?"

Lucy had forgotten. She didn't want to deal with it now. She was much more interested in getting Donovan to speak to her again, which seemed hopeless at the moment. His face looked like it had been chiseled in stone. "I'm kind of hoping Superguy's figured out that I don't want to meet him. Maybe he'll give up and find some other girl on the Internet. Then he won't call me at all."

But he did call. On Friday night, as promised. Lucy had spent a miserable week. After the painting party, Donovan didn't come to the house once. Determined not to let that spoil her progress, Lucy doubled her therapy hours, to the point where she could finally take a step or two while being supported by the shoulder harness. It felt wonderful, though her legs ached afterwards. Her hard work served two purposes. On Thursday, Ted said in a rare moment of praise, "I wouldn't be surprised if you were in braces by Thanksgiving, after all." The second benefit from working so hard was, Lucy fell into bed at night so thoroughly exhausted she had time for only a few painful moments of wishing Donovan would forgive her.

Kendra, blissfully happy in her new relationship with Sean, suggested, "You could call Donovan, Lucy. He wouldn't hang up on you."

"And say what? That I've changed my mind? I haven't. Donovan should find some other girl who isn't lugging around the same load of baggage that I am."

"I don't think he wants another girl, Lucy. I think he wants you."

Friday night, Lucy was in the dining room alone, exercising. When the phone rang, she thought about ignoring the ring. She guessed who was calling, and wanted to put off the conversation with Superguy as long as possible.

But it kept ringing, and no one else was home. Elizabeth and their mother had gone shopping again, and Tim was at a friend's. Superguy obviously wasn't going to give up. Slipping out of the harness and into her chair, Lucy answered the phone.

"About time. You haven't forgotten our date, have you, Swifty? I can't wait to see you. I'll be sitting at a front table in the food court, and I'll be wearing a red carnation, so you'll know me. You can't miss me."

If she didn't meet him as promised, he'd just come to her house. How was she going to explain *that* to her mother? Or to Ted, who had given both her and Tim a stern warning about the Internet just the other day. "If anyone even *spells* the word s-e-x," he'd said, "you sign off so fast, your keyboard smokes, you got that?"

Lucy was so used to him being around by then, she hadn't been offended that he was telling them what to do. Anyway, she knew he was right to warn them, even if it was a little late for her. Not that Superguy had ever mentioned that word. Hadn't even hinted. But he wanted *something* from her. If it wasn't sex, what was it?

Ted would be furious if he found out she was meeting someone at the mall she'd only talked to on the Net. Well, Ted wasn't her father. Not yet, anyway, though judging by the way her mother looked at him, it was a possibility sometime in the future. And that might be okay.

"I'll be there," she promised Superguy. The important thing was to keep him away from the house. At least until she'd checked him out. "Don't forget, I'm short and thin and blonde. I'll wear..." — she made something up — "...a tan raincoat, okay?" She didn't own a tan raincoat. She looked like death in tan.

When he had hung up, she called Tia. "He didn't change his mind. Superguy. It's still on. Tomorrow night. Pick me up at six-forty-five, okay? We'll sneak in, take a peek. If he looks okay, I'll wheel on over there. The minute he sees my chair, he'll run, right?"

"Donovan didn't. You're the one who ran. Anyway, what if your friend from the Internet is a creep? Then what?"

"Then you and I, we split. Problem is, he's got my address now. But if he does come here looking for me — and he probably won't — when I answer the door, I'll tell him he's got the wrong house. He'll believe me, because I don't look anything like the description I gave him on the Net. Besides, he's definitely not expecting a wheelchair. He'll be sure he's got the wrong house, even if he can't figure out how that happened. So he'll leave."

"You hope."

"Trust me."

Tia sighed. "I'd like to. It's kind of hard when your brain cells seem to have atrophied right along with your legs. At least, *those* are improving."

Lucy didn't get mad. Tia was going with her to the mall. She was too grateful to get mad.

Saturday rushed by far too quickly to suit Lucy. Her mother and Elizabeth had gone into the city for fittings, and Ted had taken Tim fishing. They were staying overnight at the fishing lodge. Andy and Nan were visiting Nan's family in Fishkill for the whole weekend, and Kendra was going out with Sean.

As Lucy got ready to go to the mall, she thought wistfully that this would be a perfect night for Donovan to come over. They'd have the house to themselves, for a change. She'd be able to explain in privacy why she had pushed him away. But she hadn't seen him or talked to him since last Sunday. All he'd said when he left, yellow paint staining his cutoffs and T-shirt, was a curt, "See you, Lucy."

The living room looked great. But every time she wheeled into or past the sunny, buttery-colored room, Lucy thought of Donovan. Which made her feel lonely and sad. How long would it take him to find some other girl, a girl with "no baggage"? Not very long at all, probably.

Lucy had reached the point in her therapy where she could actually stand up and move from the wheelchair to a car seat by herself, as long as the car in question wasn't a van. Those seats were too high. Bear, low to the ground, was no problem. And Tia handled the wheelchair this time like a pro. "It's not so bad when you get the hang of it," she said. "Now let's go check out this Net nut. You ready?"

Lucy nodded grimly. "Maybe he won't be there."

But he was. Lucy laughed nervously when she peered around the corner of a tall, potted plant just outside the food court to take a look. She stared for several minutes before saying with a nervous giggle, "Oh, brother, he's there all right. But he did the same thing I did. Lied through his teeth. Look! He's the one at the front, with the red carnation in that ugly brown jacket he's wearing."

Tia peeked cautiously. "I thought you said he was tall."

"*He* said he was tall." The person they were studying was sitting alone in one of the green booths. He was shorter than Lucy, with a barrel chest and wide shoulders beneath the brown corduroy jacket. He was wearing a gray baseball cap, pulled low over his eyes, which he kept fixed on the wide, open entrance. Lucy was grateful for the enormous potted plant, since she and Tia were hidden just beyond the spot he was watching. His face was square, pale, his jaw thrust forward. He did not look friendly.

Lucy was disappointed. "He's not blond. I can't see his hair very well with that baseball cap on, but it looks brown to me." She kept her voice at a whisper, although he couldn't possibly have heard them over the noise in the food court. "He's *old*! He's gotta be at least twenty-five."

"He's not really ugly," Tia whispered. "I mean, I've seen worse. He just doesn't look anything like you described."

"That's because he doesn't look anything like he said," Lucy retorted. "Okay, come on, let's go. I've seen enough. He's not someone I want to meet. Anyway, he's a liar."

"Oh, and you're not?"

Lucy grinned as she turned her chair around. "Well, yeah, I am. But that's different."

They argued about it on the way home. "If you *had* to get on the Net and talk to someone, and I guess I can understand why you did," Tia said as she drove toward Lucy's house, "why didn't you pick a girl to talk to?"

"Even if I had, maybe it would have been someone just pretending to be a girl, so they could talk to other girls. Could be a guy. Even a really old guy. The thing is, on the Net, you can't tell. You don't really know who you're talking to."

"Then why do it at all? I mean, where's the fun in talking to someone who could be lying through their teeth the whole time?"

"Well, maybe they wouldn't be. Everyone on the Net isn't a liar, Tia. Just some. Like Superguy."

"And like *you*."

"I'm just glad it's over. I will never, *never*, do anything like that again."

Tia pulled Bear into Lucy's driveway. "You don't know it's over. What if he comes here?"

"I already told you that's not a problem. Quit worrying and get my chair."

"Yes, your majesty."

Lucy laughed. "Sorry."

They were in the kitchen, making cinnamon toast, when the doorbell rang. They stopped what they were doing, knives in midair to stare at each other. "Uh-oh," Tia breathed. "Looks like you were wrong about it being over."

Lucy shrugged. "It could be anybody. Maybe Ted and Tim changed their minds about staying overnight at the lodge." But she added, "Come to the door with me. Just in case it's him."

It *was* him. He was standing just beyond the glass door, the baseball cap still low over his eyes. But Lucy could see them, and she thought they looked angry. "Remember," she hissed at Tia as they approached the door, "we don't know any family named St. Cloud, never heard of them, don't know any Lucys or Swiftys, got that?"

Tia nodded.

Lucy opened the door a few inches. She watched without saying hello as he took in her appearance and her wheelchair. Confusion showed on his square, pale face. His eyes were small and set too close together. He glanced down at a small piece of paper in one hand. He looked up again, his eyes studying the black numerals Ted had nailed to the outside wall. Superguy's eyes went back to Lucy. "St. Cloud?" he asked. "Doesn't Lucy St. Cloud live here?"

"Nope." She shook her head. "Not here. You must have the wrong address."

"Really?" He had a thin, high voice. Maybe he was just nervous. "I was sure —"

"Sorry. Our name is . . . Perez." Behind her, Tia cleared her throat as a warning, as if to say, Don't get *my* family involved in this. Too late. "'Bye now. I hope you find whoever you're looking for." A bald-faced lie. Lucy most definitely didn't want him finding the person he was looking for.

Looking more angry now than confused, he turned to leave. Lucy was about to close the door when a small, pink and white truck pulled into the driveway. The logo on the side depicted a huge, pink and white wedding cake, with MITZI'S WEDDINGS sprawled in bright pink paint across the top of the cake. A woman in pink overalls jumped down from the truck, hurried around to the back, and a moment later came up the driveway bearing a large, white box.

Superguy — Carl Swenson — watched with interest as the delivery woman approached Lucy, still sitting at the open door.

Lucy groaned silently. What rotten timing! In one more minute, Superguy would have been gone.

"Another delivery for St. Cloud," the woman said, extending the box. It bore a large, white label that clearly read in fat, black lettering, ELIZABETH ST. CLOUD. Noticing the wheelchair, the woman said in a friendly voice, "You must be the sister. Maid of honor. Lucy, right?" She placed the box in Lucy's lap. "I've got something here for the wedding. Tablecloths, maybe." She handed Lucy a clipboard. "Sign there, okay?"

Stricken silent by this turn of events, Lucy signed, and the woman left, saying she'd "prob'ly be back this way again soon."

When the pink and white truck had pulled out of the driveway, Carl "Superguy" Swenson turned to look at Lucy.

Instead of the fury she'd expected, Lucy saw smug self-satisfaction in the pale eyes staring at her.

Chapter 35

"Thought you could fool me, huh, Swifty?" His voice was cool, smooth. "Guess again. Nothin' gets past Superguy. I knew this was the right place, though I gotta say the wheelchair threw me at first." He shook his head. "You lied a whole lot, Swifty."

"So did you," she answered coldly. Her left hand was on the phone hidden beneath the plaid blanket over her legs. She only had to punch the nine, and a police dispatcher would pick up. "So, now we both know the truth; you can leave. I'm sorry you made the trip for nothing. I guess we both learned a lesson, right?"

He smiled thinly. "Oh, I'm not leaving. I'm not even disappointed." He glanced down at her wheelchair. "In fact, this is great. I mean, I'm sorry you're in that thing, but at least I know you won't get in my way." He glanced around, saw no one on the street, and smiled in satisfaction again. "I know no one else is home, just you two," he said, nodding at Tia, who stood, frozen, behind Lucy's chair. "I've been watching the house all day. Saw them all leave. I guess I can handle the two of you, especially with you like *that*," pointing to Lucy's wheelchair. "Athletic, huh? Sure. And I'm the King of England."

That made her mad. He had lied, too. Big time.

He shoved her chair backward, further inside the house, so suddenly all she could do was gasp. He slammed the door and locked it. To Tia, he said coldly, "You don't belong here." Yanking the closet door open, he grabbed her arm and threw her inside, ignoring Lucy's shouts to stop. Like many old houses, the closets all had keys, which sat in the locks, unused. Until now. Superguy slammed the closet door, ignoring Tia's shouts of rage, and locked it, pocketing the key.

Lucy, taking it all in with disbelieving eyes, pressed the send button on her phone, then pushed down on the nine. She prayed the blanket would muffle the dispatcher's voice so Swenson wouldn't hear it.

"I guess I don't have to worry about *you* going anywhere, Swifty," he said sarcastically. Pulling a small square of black plastic from a jacket pocket, he shook it, opening it into a large trash bag. Then, to Lucy's relief, he darted along the hallway, glancing in doorways as he went, until he came to Elizabeth's room. He rushed inside.

Lucy knew, then, why he was there. Why he had insisted on meeting her, why he had found out her address. "You're a thief!" she shouted after him. "You're just a scuzzball thief!"

He didn't answer.

"You log on to the Internet, talk to people to find out if they own anything of value, then you find out where they live and rob them! Independently wealthy? You forgot to mention that your independence comes from other people's wealth!" She couldn't believe she had brought this horror down upon her family. He was going to take all of Elizabeth's lovely new things. It wasn't bad enough that she'd put a damper on the wedding by being in a wheelchair. Now she was going to be responsible for *this*, too! He was going to steal all of the things that Elizabeth had bought for her new home. And *she* was the one who had told him about the wedding, and how Liz was shopping all the time.

He yelled back from the bedroom, "Oh, and you didn't forget to mention a wheelchair, Swifty? Not that I mind. Makes it a lot easier for me."

A faint, disembodied voice sounded from Lucy's lap. She almost didn't hear it over Tia's shouting, kicking, and pounding. But before she could pull the phone from beneath the blanket, Carl Swenson, the huge bag in his hands half full, ran back down the hallway to grab Lucy's chair and rush her into Elizabeth's room. "I wasn't thinking," he told her when he had parked her in the doorway where he could see her. He returned to the business of emptying the contents of bags and boxes into his own sack. Like Santa Claus, Lucy thought miserably, only in reverse. He's not giving, he's taking. "You could have made a phone call from that chair. You'll have to stay right here where I can keep an eye on you. When I'm done, I'll put you in the closet with your noisy friend."

"Nine-one-one emergency," Lucy heard faintly from her lap. Swenson gave no sign that he had heard over the crackling of paper and the rustle of bubble-wrap as he unfolded item after item and thrust it into his trash bag.

She couldn't very well pick up the phone and answer while he was right there. *"What is your emergency, please?"*

If she didn't do something quickly, the dispatcher would hang up.

"You're a *thief*!" she shouted at the top of her lungs. "You steal from people, and now you're robbing my sister!"

No response from the telephone. Had the dispatcher heard? Did she get it?

"Thief!" she shouted again. "Stop stealing my sister's things!"

Then, *"You're being robbed? Is there a weapon involved? Repeat, does the perpetrator have a weapon?"*

The thief suddenly stood up, frowned, glanced around and asked, "What's that sound? Like someone talking from far away."

"The TV," Lucy answered quickly. "In my brother's room."

"Is there a weapon involved?"

Swenson's frown deepened. "Your brother's not home. I saw him leave. Why would his TV be on?" Dropping the plastic bag, now bulging, he scooted around Lucy into the hall to check out Tim's room. Lucy thrust the phone behind her back. The dispatcher hadn't asked for her address, so it must have shown up on a screen or something, like caller ID. Maybe she'd send help.

The television set in Tim's room was black-screened and silent. Superguy rushed back in to tear the blanket off Lucy's legs. "You got a phone? I heard something . . . where *is* it?" He was about to begin searching for it when the sound of a distant siren froze his hands. His eyes narrowed. "You called the police?"

"No, I . . . maybe the neighbors did." Lucy was afraid he was angry enough to hit her . . . or worse. "They know I'm in a wheelchair. If they saw a strange car in the driveway, they might think something's wrong."

"I'm not going back to jail," he said grimly, his face so close to Lucy's, she could feel warm breath on her cheeks. "No way."

Lucy cringed. *Back* to jail? He'd been there before? She'd been conversing on the Net with a criminal! Everything her mother and Ted had warned her about was true. This was all her fault. "Just go," she urged as the sirens drew closer. "Go out the back way. I promise I won't tell them anything about you. Leave, *now!*"

He drew back from the wheelchair, his upper lip curled in a contemptuous sneer. "And just exactly how do I get away without my car? It's parked out front, not out back." He thought for a minute or two, then said meanly, "You may not be good for much the way you are, Swifty, but you're gonna get me out of this. You're coming with me. The cops won't shoot at a truck that has a hostage in it. Especially a girl."

Lucy's heart stopped at the word "shoot." "I'm not going with you!"

He laughed rudely. "Like you have a choice." Before she could protest again, he reached down and scooped her out of the chair, cradling her awkwardly against his chest. Lucy heard the phone drop to the floor. Not that it would do her any good now.

He smelled of tobacco . . . and something

else . . . fear? Maybe that was *her* fear she smelled. "Like I said," he repeated grimly, "I'm *not* going back to jail!"

There wasn't any point in struggling. Lucy didn't even try. She might be able to claw his face or bite his arm to get him to drop her, but then what? She couldn't very well *run*. He was right. She couldn't even *walk* to get away from him.

Her only satisfaction came from the fact that he couldn't carry her *and* his bag of booty. In his rush to escape, he'd left it behind. Elizabeth's things were safe.

Tia was still kicking and pounding on the closet door as Lucy passed it in Carl Swenson's arms on their way to the front door.

Though the siren was louder now, shrilling through the night, there was no police car in sight when they got outside. The air was chilly. Lucy was wearing only a thin white T-shirt and jeans. Her feet were bare. They were already cold.

Carl Swenson hoisted her into the front seat of his red pickup truck, dropping her unceremoniously before running around to the other side and hopping into the driver's seat. When he pulled out of the driveway and up the road, he was careful not to speed. He drove slightly below the speed limit. Lucy had to admit that was clever. The police would be looking for a car racing away from the scene of the crime, not a truck ambling along as if it had all the time in the world.

Trembling with fear and cold, Lucy glanced in the sideview mirror for some sign of help. There it was . . . the pale-yellow glow of headlights behind them, and above the yellow, a blue, revolving light. Just one police car, not the half dozen she'd hoped for, but better than none at all. Not that close, though. Would they even realize that the thief they sought was in the truck driving leisurely down the avenue, as if some couple was out for a relaxing evening ride? If the cops took the time to stop at the house, to let Tia out and ask what had happened, Superguy — Swenson — could be miles away before they began their pursuit.

He would never take her all the way back to Ohio with him. Once he got away, he'd have no use for a girl who needed a wheelchair just to get around. He'd dump her somewhere. *If* he let her live at all. She knew things about him . . . his name, unless he'd lied about that, too . . . the state he lived in. It wasn't much, but a thief who was desperate to avoid jail might think it was *too* much. Too much to let her live.

He wouldn't even actually have to kill her. All he'd have to do was leave her in the woods somewhere. Without food or water, and no way to go for help, she'd die soon enough.

The headlights behind them stopped at Lucy's house. And went off. Damn! The officers were going inside. They'd have to get Tia out of the closet. How long would that take?

Swenson had seen. Chuckling triumphantly, he turned down a side street that Lucy knew led to the interstate. If they got on that, he'd get away for sure. And what would happen to her?

"Let me out now," she ordered, her voice hardly shaking at all. "You're going to get away, so you don't need me anymore."

"And what, you'll *walk* home? I don't think so. Besides, I still might need you." With no headlights behind them, he relaxed a bit. "What happened to you, anyway? Your legs always been like that?"

Instead of answering, she asked, "Are you going to kill me?"

He laughed. "You'd better lay off the boob tube, Swifty. I'm no killer. Just a thief, like you said. But I've got two strikes against me already." His voice hardened. "Three strikes and you're out."

His words failed to reassure Lucy. She was sick with a terrible sense of helplessness. She'd been doing so well, learning to do so many things from her chair. But they all seemed so trivial now. When it came to something really important — like saving her own life — she was still as helpless as ever.

She glanced in the sideview mirror again. There . . . there, way behind them, the faint glow of yellow. She strained her eyes, searching for a blue light up near the roof . . . blue . . . whirling . . . please, please, let there be a blue light, because if there wasn't, that was just an ordinary car behind them and it would do her no good at all.

There it was then, spinning around like one of the colored globes hanging overhead at Seneca High's formal dances. Swenson's attention was fixed on the road. He hadn't noticed the light yet. Lucy's lips tightened. The minute he saw it, he'd stomp down on the accelerator and a high-speed chase would begin. They'd either crash — and at high speeds, they'd both be killed — or bullets would start flying. She couldn't let that happen. She hadn't lived through this past year to die now . . . not like *this*!

They hadn't reached the interstate yet. He was still driving under forty-five miles an hour. The police car behind them was steadily closing the gap, although she could hear no siren. Whatever happened, they'd be there to help, and they'd be there to make sure Superguy didn't kill her after she'd done what she had to do. Because there was only one way to stop him, and Lucy had to do it.

Memories of the accident in May flooded her

mind. The terrible fear when she'd realized a collision was inevitable. The terror of being trapped inside the wreck for so long. The days ... weeks ... months of pain, still not completely gone. The pills, rehab, her helplessness when Andy desperately needed her. She had to be insane to risk going through all of that again. Why not just let the police catch up to them, let them handle it?

Superguy swore under his breath. He had spotted the blue light. "They're *not* getting their hands on me!" he muttered and sat up, hunching over the wheel.

Lucy knew he was prepared to drive as fast as the truck would go to evade the police. At some point, he could lose control, go careening off the road and into another vehicle, a tree, a cement wall ... and they would both be killed. He had to know that. But he didn't care.

She did. She cared very much. She hadn't survived that terrible accident to die in another one, not after everything she'd been through.

"I didn't live last May to die in this stupid truck with *you!*" she shouted, her voice shrill with both fury and fear. The very last second before his foot slammed down on the gas pedal, Lucy kicked out with her left leg. She nearly fainted from the resulting pain as she hit him, but it worked. There was enough strength in that leg now to knock his foot aside, away from the accelerator. Before he could recover, she reached out with both arms and wrenched the steering wheel to the right with every ounce of her upper-body strength. After all of her hard work in therapy, that strength was considerable. The truck veered wildly off the road, aiming straight for the embankment.

Carl Swenson had made a huge mistake. Because Lucy was in a wheelchair, he had seen her as helpless. He had immediately dismissed her as being no physical threat to him, and hadn't been on guard against her. So her sudden, powerful wrench of the wheel shocked him into paralysis. He didn't even try to correct their wild veer into the side of the embankment.

Lucy heard him gasp, "What the hell?" before she doubled over, her arms shielding her head against the oncoming collision.

They didn't hit that hard. Compared to the accident in May, the noisy jarring they got as they collided with the grassy hill seemed mild to Lucy. But she had been prepared. Swenson wasn't. And he had been in such a hurry to escape that he hadn't bothered with his seat belt. He was thrown forward upon impact. His head slammed into the steering wheel with enough force to knock him unconscious. He slumped forward, limp, making no sound at all as his eyes closed.

Lucy sat up. She rested against the seat,

breathing in short, painful gasps, waiting for the police officers to arrive.

When they did, one officer proceeded to Lucy's side, the other to the driver's side. The passenger's door opened and a policeman shone a flashlight in her face. "Are you Lucy St. Cloud?"

All she could do was nod. She had survived. Again. She hadn't died. She was alive, and the police had come to take her home. Superguy was out of the picture, and she was still in one piece and breathing.

The best part was, she had survived on her own, with no help from anyone.

"You okay?" the officer asked. "Your friend, the one we found in the closet, was worried about you." He moved closer, gesturing to Lucy to slide off the seat and put her arms around his neck. She obeyed, and he lifted her out of the truck. The fresh air felt wonderful. Lucy breathed it in deeply. "She said the guy who snatched you left your wheelchair behind. Said you couldn't manage without it."

Lucy, pale and trembling, managed a shaky smile. "But I did," she said. "And I'm still alive."

Chapter 36

Elizabeth looked beautiful. Lucy had never seen her sister so radiant. She positively glowed as, laughing, she handed Adam a piece of wedding cake.

"It's going very well, don't you think?" Lucy's mother said from behind her. Her hands were resting lightly on the handles of Lucy's wheelchair. "Not a hitch, so far."

Lucy nodded. "It's been great. All your hard work, and Elizabeth's and Adam's, really paid off."

Her mother, looking lovely in a pale-pink suit, came around to kneel beside Lucy's chair. "You've worked harder than anyone else, honey. You walked down the aisle just as you'd promised Elizabeth. You look so beautiful in that dress, and you look older with your hair up like that. I just hope you didn't overdo."

"I feel older." She would be eighteen in three

weeks. "And I didn't overdo, Mom. The only reason I got into the chair after the wedding was, I wanted to save my strength so I'd last through the whole reception. I know I can't dance, the braces won't let me, but I can watch. I want to be here to see Elizabeth and Adam off on their honeymoon, and I don't plan to leave until the band has played the very last song."

Ted came then, to claim her mother for a dance. Lucy sat on the sidelines, watching. Tia was dancing with Andy, Nan guiding an awkward Tim around the floor, his face pursed in concentration. Kendra was at one of the tables, filling a plate. Music and conversation and a feeling of celebration flowed around Lucy, enveloping her, making her feel safe and happy. She wished her march down the aisle ahead of Elizabeth had been smoother. Navigating with braces was tricky. She'd been practicing diligently for long, painful weeks, but she still hadn't quite got the hang of it. And like Jude, she retreated to her wheelchair when exhaustion overtook her. Maybe she would always have to do that. Walk, sit, walk, sit, walk, sit . . . she could live with that. The key word there being "live."

The suit against the trucking company had been settled out of court. She hadn't had to testify. Big relief. And with part of the money, Sara had leased a specially equipped van for

Lucy to drive, allowing her more freedom. She would be returning to Seneca High immediately after midterm break. She'd try it with just the braces, at first. If she got too tired, she'd take the chair with her. Now that she knew she could take care of herself, wheeling through the halls wouldn't be so bad. *She* knew what she could do, even if other people didn't.

Actually, most people knew. Her harrowing adventure in Superguy's truck had been in all the papers. "Heroine" the articles had called her . . . although, just to keep her humble, they had also mentioned that she'd met him on the Internet. Embarrassing. But a lesson for other Net users, her mother had pointed out. To be more careful. She was so right.

She had called Donovan the day after the police brought her safely home. She had called him because if she didn't know anything else by then, she knew she wasn't completely helpless. She could take care of herself. After all, the newspapers *said* so. And she had called him because he *wasn't* like Dash, whom she hadn't seen or spoken to in months and no longer cared to, although she *had* forgiven Jenny, in a long, teary telephone call that same day. Donovan wasn't like Dash, and *she* wasn't helpless. So she called him. "I would like you to come over here," she had told him bluntly, "so I can apologize for being such a jerk."

He was there, breathless, his hair still wet from a hasty shower, within fifteen minutes. She'd seen him every day since then, and wasn't surprised when Elizabeth asked him to be an usher in the wedding.

Now, at the wedding, Donovan crouched beside her chair, smiling at her. "I know you like to do things for yourself, but just this once, considering the importance of the occasion, couldn't you make an exception?"

She saw that smile every night before she fell asleep. "I guess I could, just this once. What did you have in mind?"

"Well, it's like this. We are completely surrounded by romance, flowers, and great music. You are gorgeous in that dress, I am light-years away from geekdom in this handsome tuxedo your sister made me wear, and we would make a stunning couple on the dance floor. So my question is, why aren't we dancing?"

"I can't dance, Donovan."

"Sure, you can. Put yourself in my hands, just this once. I promise it won't become a habit."

Lucy thought about it. The music was slow and sweet and dreamy. And she really wanted to dance. Wasn't there such a thing as being *too* independent? Wasn't that what had kept her away from Donovan for so long?

Tilting her head upward to return Donovan's smile, she said, "Okay, I'm game. What's your plan?"

"Just this." He stood up, bent, and scooped her out of the chair, into his arms. Then, keeping careful time to the music, he danced across the floor with her, her arms around his neck, her head resting on his chest. Other dancers smiled as Donovan danced by with Lucy in his arms.

The wheelchair sat empty on the sidelines.

There were, she knew, long, dark days ahead, days of therapy and pain and tears. One step forward, two steps back, that was the way it would go. What she would have to do was keep going when she didn't want to, when she thought she couldn't, when it seemed impossible. Keep on keeping on, no matter what.

But that was tomorrow and tomorrow and tomorrow. Today, floating above the floor in the safety and warmth of Donovan's arms, she would let herself be carried away by the music and the candlelight and the romance of Elizabeth's wedding.

And so she did.